Silent Witness

Books by Michael Norman

The Commission
Silent Witness

Silent Witness

Michael Norman

Poisoned Pen Press

Poisoned
Pen
Press

Copyright © 2008 by Michael Norman

First Trade Paperback Edition 2008

10 9 8 7 6 5 4 3 2

Library of Congress Catalog Card Number: 2007935735

ISBN: 978-1-59058-576-4 Trade Paperback

Poisoned Pen Press
6962 E. First Ave., Ste. 103
Scottsdale, AZ 85251
www.poisonedpenpress.com
info@poisonedpenpress.com

Printed in the United States of America

This one's for my spouse and best friend,
Diane Brewster-Norman

Praise for *Silent Witness*

"A classic procedural thriller told with a voice of assured authority, *Silent Witness* is a terrific read in the best tradition of Michael Connelly or James O. Born. Sam Kincaid and Kate McConnell make one terrific team, and Michael Norman is a writer to watch."

—Julia Spencer-Fleming, Edgar finalist and author of *I Shall Not Want*

"...[a] solid sequel to his well-received debut, *The Commission*."

—*Publishers Weekly*

"Norman keeps the action moving with numerous plot twists...a fast-paced, suspenseful mystery that will pique interest in the next installment in the series."

—*Booklist*

Praise for *The Commission*
One of *Publishers Weekly's* Best Books of 2007

"This impressive debut from a criminal justice professor and former lawman exudes verisimilitude from start to finish....Norman is off to a fine start with this alternately gripping and repellent crime novel."

—*Publishers Weekly* starred review

"A refreshing throwback to the lean, straight-ahead police procedurals of the Dragnet era. In his fiction debut, Norman's precise, foursquare prose is a perfect match for his story. Bring on the series."

—*Kirkus Reviews*

"A no-frills police procedural, none the worse for its lack of fashionable violence."

—*The London Times*

Acknowledgments

I'd like to thank members of the regular crew: Robert and Sandy Dupont and Eileen Land for their friendship, encouragement, and keen eye when reading drafts of the manuscript. You always make the book better.

Thanks also to friend and Salt Lake City lawyer extraordinaire, Pat Christensen, for patiently answering my questions regarding lawyer/Client privilege and estate matters. I also received valuable help from two former colleagues in the Weber State University Department of Criminal Justice. To Dr. Paul Johnson, for sharing his insights into matters of military protocol; and to Dr. Michelle Heward, for helping me understand child custody legal proceedings—many thanks.

Finally, to everybody at the Poisoned Pen Press who always do so much with so little—Publisher Robert Rosenwald, Associate Publisher Jessica Tribble, and Nan Beams. A special thanks to Marilyn Pizzo for her comments on a draft of the manuscript. And last but certainly not least, a heartfelt thanks to Editor-In-Chief Barbara Peters, without whom I wouldn't have a literary career.

Chapter One

Accountant Arnold Ginsberg glanced at his planner, reviewing his schedule for the remainder of the week. His eyes froze on the nine o'clock entry two days hence. "Shit," he muttered to himself. How had he managed to get himself mixed up in something like this? Talk about being in the wrong place at exactly the wrong time—somehow he'd managed to do it. Now he found himself a reluctant witness against the leader of an ultra conservative band of renegade polygamists with a penchant for robbing armored cars.

He reached in and removed the subpoena from the middle drawer of his desk. It required his appearance as a witness in the courtroom of Judge Homer Wilkinson for a preliminary hearing in the case of Utah versus Walter Anthony Bradshaw. According to the subpoena and what he'd read in the newspapers, Bradshaw and his cohorts had been charged with enough serious felonies to keep them in prison for the rest of their lives, assuming they managed to avoid death sentences, something the local prosecutor seemed intent on securing.

Ginsberg distinctly recalled that autumn morning in September. It had been like watching a violent scene from a Hollywood movie. He had left home early to reach the Super Target store well ahead of the Saturday morning rush of weekend shoppers. As he parked his Passat, he noticed the Wells Fargo armored car parked in front of the store with its engine idling, and he assumed, with a driver inside. Moments later, two uniformed rent-a-cops came out of the store carrying satchels filled with what news accounts would later claim was $85,000 in cash.

The gunmen seemingly materialized out of nowhere. They wore flesh-colored masks made of panty hose, and each carried an automatic weapon. The guards were at the rear of the armored car waiting for the driver to unlock the door when one of the would-be robbers barked a command.

"Everybody freeze. Do not touch your weapon and do not move."

For an instant, everybody froze. Then all hell broke loose. Both guards simultaneously reached for their side-arms—a serious error in judgment. What followed sounded like a fourth of July celebration minus the visual effects of fireworks in the sky. Ginsberg heard the pop, pop, pop sound of gunfire. He dove for cover between two parked cars.

When it was over, both guards were down as well as one of the robbers. He heard the squeal of tires and looked up just in time to see a non-descript-looking white Ford van race across the parking lot with its side door opened. The remaining three gunmen jumped into the moving van, one of them carrying several bags of cash, and sped away. No attempt had been made to pick up their downed comrade. The wounded gunman was later pronounced dead at the scene. One of the guards died later at the hospital. The other survived brain surgery only to lapse into a coma from which he had never regained consciousness.

The police captured the alleged leader of the gang, Walter Bradshaw, in a separate vehicle minutes after the robbery. The rest were still at large. None of the cash had ever been recovered.

In the immediate aftermath, Ginsberg had become an instant media celebrity—something he now regretted. He was interviewed live at the scene, and again later, by both print and television sources. There had been another witness too, a Robin something-or-other. She had managed to maintain a much lower profile, avoiding interviews with the media. They'd met briefly at police headquarters when they were giving statements to the detectives handling the case.

⟨⟩⟨⟩⟨⟩

Ginsberg was tired—tired of the seemingly endless grind of his tax business, tired of the affluent lifestyle to which he, and his young partner, had become accustomed. As the autumn days grew shorter, there wasn't enough Prozac in the world to brighten the otherwise dank mood that hung over him like a constant dark cloud.

He reached into his desk and pulled out a bottle of Wild Turkey and a glass. He poured a shot and sipped the alcohol. He felt its glowing warmth in his throat and stomach as he turned his attention back to the computer screen. "Christ," he muttered. "If I have to look at one more tax form, I think I'll puke." He could hardly wait for the booze to begin taking the edge off.

Ginsberg completed the third quarter tax forms for yet another of his corporate clients, shut down the computer, and leaned back in his leather chair. He gazed out his thirteenth story office window overlooking the Salt Lake City skyline as the last light of day faded below the western horizon, leaving just a touch of orange in a darkening sky. It was so clear that he could see the landing lights and the ghostly shapes of the commercial planes as they descended in orderly fashion into nearby Salt Lake International Airport.

Ginsberg finished the Wild Turkey and reached for his black leather briefcase resting atop the credenza across from his desk. He should have been home an hour ago. He would be late for dinner again, and Rodney would be seriously pissed. But screw Rodney. Much of the reason for putting in such long hours was directly proportional to the amount of Rodney's spending. Rodney was spending it nearly as fast as he could earn it. Lately, Ginsberg was having second thoughts about making a kept man out of the young travel agent. While it was pleasing to his ego and definitely good for his libido, it was killing him financially.

Ginsberg left his State Street office and walked the half-block east on 200 South to the parking garage. He nodded at the attendant and ascended the steel stairs to the third floor. He walked past the elevator door moving silently between rows of parked cars and past several large concrete pillars. As he stepped between a large SUV and a Dodge van, his new Volkswagen Passat came into view. Leaning against the driver's door was a tall, young man wearing a long sleeved flannel shirt, blue jeans, and brown work boots. To Ginsberg, the man looked like a blue collar worker, a construction type maybe.

Ginsberg felt fearful but spoke with as much bravado as he could muster. "Excuse me, but what are you doing next to my car?"

The man pushed away from the Passat, rose to his full height, and smiled at Ginsberg, revealing a large, silver capped front tooth. For a moment, the stranger said nothing but then the grin disappeared, and the man said, "Just waitin' on you. Had to work late tonight, huh?"

Ginsberg looked puzzled. "I don't think I know you. What is it that you want?"

He never saw the second individual who stepped from behind a concrete pillar carrying a three-foot steel tire iron. The man swung the tire iron like a baseball bat, struck the back of Ginsberg's head, and crushed his skull. The force of the blow propelled him forward into the arms of the first man who plunged a double-edged serrated knife deep into his sternum then yanked it upward toward the heart. They left him on the cold concrete floor, his life's blood pooling under his head and torso.

◇◇◇

Rodney Plow waited. The carefully prepared dinner of garlic mashed potatoes, fresh halibut, asparagus spears, and Caesar salad had long since grown cold. It was now after seven. Arnold was supposed to have been home by five. During the intervening hours, Rodney had managed to finish the bottle of Napa Valley chardonnay.

By eight, he contemplated calling the police. Ginsberg hadn't responded to his phone calls placed to Arnold's office and cell phone. Instead, he opened a second bottle of wine. Another hour passed. Just before nine, Rodney called the Salt Lake City police and reported Arnold missing. Within half-an-hour, patrol officers Wendy Ring and Jeremy Steel discovered Ginsberg's lifeless body in the parking garage next to his office. He was rushed by ambulance to the LDS hospital where he was pronounced DOA.

◇◇◇

On the same evening, twenty-four year old University of Utah graduate student Robin Joiner had just finished a meeting with members of her social work study group at the Marriott Library. She loaded her book bag for the long trek across campus to her car. After perfunctory goodbyes, Joiner left the library. She normally tried to get away from the university before dark, but today the study group worked longer than anticipated.

Joiner moved quickly despite the heavy book bag hanging from one shoulder. She felt slightly uneasy walking on the narrow sidewalks between monolithic buildings as dusk dissolved into shadowy darkness. Soon she emerged into a sparsely lit parking lot just south of the social work building. On this night, there were few cars and not a single person in sight.

Joiner heard the sound before she saw it—an engine idling, a noisy engine with a bad muffler. She glanced to her left and saw the dark colored van and the vague shape of someone sitting behind the wheel. She was now on full alert.

Joiner hadn't taken more than a few steps when she sensed movement behind her. Someone grabbed her from behind and a hand covered her mouth. She reacted instantly, biting into the assailant's index finger until she tasted blood, and stomped on the top of his foot. He howled and cursed. She spun around and swung the twenty pound pack like a sledge hammer, striking a glancing blow off her attacker's shoulder and then into the side of his face. He staggered to one side and released his grip long enough for her to drop the book bag and begin running—

running as fast and as far as the legs of the former high school sprinter would carry her. She didn't look back and she didn't stop—not until she reached Kingsbury Hall on the northwest side of the campus where she got lost in a crowd shuffling into the building for a concert.

Joiner left the campus, circled west a block, and then turned south until she reached 400 South. There she boarded the westbound Trax train and rode it into downtown Salt Lake City. She wasted no time transferring to the southbound Trax, which took her several miles, finally dumping her within eye shot of a twenty-four hour IHOP.

She sat at the counter. It wasn't until the server placed the coffee in front of her that her nerves began to relax and she stopped shaking. For the first time since leaving the library, she had a calm moment where she could think. What the hell had just happened? Was this a random attack or could it have something to do with her impending appearance in court as a witness in the aborted armored car robbery and murder?

Joiner decided the only prudent course of action was to assume that the attack had been planned and was not a random event. So what should she do? The book bag contained her wallet, driver's license, credit cards, car keys, and most of her cash. Fortunately, she had her Visa debit card and a small amount of cash in her pocket. Her Honda Civic sat in the university parking lot, but did she dare go get it? Probably not. And what about her apartment? Should she go home and try to retrieve some of her things? She didn't think so.

For the first time in a very long while, Robin Joiner felt vulnerable, afraid, and isolated. Once again in her troubled life, she was on her own and she would have to make do.

Chapter Two

Detective Lieutenant Kate McConnell of the Salt Lake City Police Department Homicide unit was attending a retirement party for one of her colleagues in a Park City restaurant when the call came. She had planned to spend the rest of the evening at the home of her boyfriend, Sam Kincaid. So much for the best laid plans.

She and Sam had become involved after having been thrown together in a high visibility murder investigation six months earlier. Like her, he was a cop and a damned good one. Kincaid managed a unit within the Utah Department of Corrections called the Special Investigations Branch (SIB).

The SIB was a small, covert organization that operated out of offices at the state prison. They were responsible for gathering intelligence information about the activities of inmates inside the prison as well as parolees in the community. The unit also investigated allegations of employee misconduct and served as an important liaison to state and local law enforcement agencies. Sam reported directly to the executive director of the department and was required to maintain offices at both the state prison and at department headquarters in Salt Lake City.

The dispatcher gave her only the basics. "DL1, see the officers at the parking garage, 220 East, 300 South. Unknown white male reported down at that location."

"Ten-four." A parking garage in downtown Salt Lake—probably a mugging gone bad, she thought.

By the time she arrived, the area had been cordoned off and the forensics team was busy at work. The victim, a middle-aged male, had been stabbed and bludgeoned to death.

"What have you got, Rob?"

"Not a hell of a lot so far, Lieutenant," replied Sergeant Rob Porter, supervisor of the CSI team. "The vic never made it home from work. Somebody at his house reported him missing. The uniforms started looking for him at his accounting office in the Towers. When they couldn't locate him, they backtracked here where they found him lying next to his car. The EMTs hustled him to the hospital, but I'm afraid it was too late."

There was blood everywhere. Almost to herself, Kate said, "God, what a mess."

"You're right about that, Lieutenant," said Porter, glancing around the concrete floor. "Stab wounds and blunt force trauma always seem to produce the biggest bleeders."

"For sure. Did anybody report seeing anything?"

"Not that we know of. The garage attendant saw the victim enter but doesn't recall seeing him leave. Of course, that's because he didn't leave. The attendant is a college kid who, I'm guessing, doesn't pay much attention to the comings and goings of this place. Nobody's taken a formal statement from him—figured you'd probably want to do that."

"Yeah, I'll talk to him. Any evidence left lying around—like maybe the perp's wallet with a picture ID and a current address?"

Porter smiled, "Afraid not, Kate. One of the EMT's mentioned blunt force trauma to the back of the victim's head and a jagged stab wound in the chest area. We haven't found any physical evidence here consistent with those types of wounds. We did find the victim's wallet dumped on the next aisle over, minus credit cards and cash. We'll process the wallet for latent prints as well as his Passat."

"Okay. Have your people conduct a thorough search of every floor of the garage. Also have them canvass a two block area in every direction. There's an alley immediately east of us with a couple of dumpsters. Search those as well. If you need more help, call in the uniforms."

"Will do."

"By the way, who is our victim?"

Porter reached for his clip board. "Driver's license identified him as Arnold Ginsberg, white male, age forty-four."

Kate looked puzzled. "That name sounds familiar to me, but I can't place it. Has anybody run him through records?"

"Not as far as I know," said Porter.

McConnell radioed the dispatch-records office and ran Ginsberg's name through the system. Before dispatch could respond, it came to her. Why hadn't she remembered? Arnold Ginsberg was a witness in the upcoming trial of rogue, polygamist leader Walter Bradshaw. In fact, Bradshaw was scheduled for a preliminary hearing in the next few days. She'd heard that from members of the homicide team who'd handled the original investigation. Ginsberg's murder might have been a coincidence, but McConnell didn't much believe in coincidences.

A chilling thought entered her mind. There had been another witness in this case, a female college student from the University of Utah. When records came back confirming Ginsberg's status as a witness in the case, Kate also asked for the name of the second witness and her home address.

A patrol sergeant, Dennis Martinez, met Kate at Robin Joiner's home. It was an older apartment complex about a mile south and west of the university campus. Joiner occupied a ground floor unit that had a covered patio and a sliding door at the rear. Kate sent Martinez behind the apartment to cover the patio exit while she approached the front door. She saw it immediately. The door had fresh pry marks dug into the wood around the lock. Somebody had used a screwdriver or pry bar to jimmy the lock. Kate drew her nine millimeter, quietly turned the door knob, and pushed open the front door. She paused momentarily. The apartment was dark and quiet.

"Hello, Salt Lake City Police."

Silence.

She slipped into the apartment and turned on the light in the hallway. She moved quickly through the living room, opened the drapes, and unlocked the sliding patio door. A cursory search of the apartment failed to turn up any sign of Robin Joiner. Equally disturbing, it was clear that the apartment had been tossed. Drawers in the kitchen, bathroom, and bedroom had been pulled open, and the contents dumped on the floor. Somebody was obviously looking for something.

"What do you make of this, Lieutenant?"

Martinez was standing in the small kitchen looking into a round fruit bowl on the dining room table containing two overly ripe bananas in it. On top of the bananas was a hand-printed note. It read: I'M LOOKING FOR YOU AND I WILL FIND YOU.

"I haven't a clue, Sergeant, but let's not touch it. I'd like you to sit tight for a few minutes. I'm going to request a forensics team and see if I can locate an on-site apartment manager. Maybe the manager will be able to tell us something about the whereabouts of Ms. Joiner."

"Okay."

Outside McConnell found an 'apartment manager' sign stuck in the front lawn with an arrow pointing south to an adjacent building. She located a woman who was just putting the finishing touches on a lease agreement with a new tenant. When she finished, Kate introduced herself and flashed credentials.

"Sorry to bother you, but I'm looking for the tenant in apartment number 106. Robin Joiner is her name."

"I haven't seen Robin for the past couple of days but that's not unusual. Is everything okay?"

"I hope so, but we're not sure. Does Robin rent the unit by herself or does she have a roommate?"

"The lease is in Robin's name only, no roommate as far as I know."

"How about friends? Do you have any idea who she hangs out with?"

"That's almost impossible to keep track of. Most of our tenants are students attending Westminster College or the

University of Utah. We've got people coming and going at all hours of the day and night all the time."

"Do you recall ever seeing her with anyone?"

She paused. "Come to think of it, I guess I have seen Robin a time or two, mostly with young women I assumed were her friends, probably students. But I don't have any names for you. Sorry. Can I ask what this is about?"

"Robin is a witness in a case of ours. I just need to ask her a few questions. How about boyfriends? Anybody come to mind?"

Another pause. "Yeah, one guy a few times. Never met him though. I'm sorry that I'm not being more helpful."

"That's okay. You're doing the best you can. Do you think you could describe the boyfriend for me?"

"Sure. He was a cute guy, tall, maybe six-two, six-three, slim build, sandy hair, fair complexion."

"About how old?"

"I'd say early twenties."

"Thanks. Would you happen to know what kind of vehicle she drives?"

She smiled. "I can help you with that one. It's an older, red, subcompact, a Honda, I think, but let me check her lease application." It turned out to be a 98 Honda Civic with Nevada plates. On her way back to the apartment, Kate checked the parking lot. No sign of the car.

McConnell didn't like the feel of any of this. Could Robin Joiner have suffered the same fate as Arnold Ginsberg? The note left in her apartment gave Kate hope that the intruders hadn't found Joiner, at least not yet. But where could she be? It had Walter Bradshaw's name written all over it, yet he was sitting in a cell at the Utah State Prison.

Kate reached for her cell phone and made two calls. The first brought a crime scene unit to Robin Joiner's apartment. The second call went to the home of Sam Kincaid.

Chapter Three

It was nearly eleven o'clock when I heard the phone ring. I couldn't get it, but I knew Aunt June would. It was the third consecutive night that I hadn't been able to get my nine-year-old daughter, Sara, settled down in bed. Since the traumatic events surrounding members of the Commission five months earlier, things in our home had not been the same. The incident traumatized Sara beyond anything I could have imagined. Most nights she wanted to sleep with either me or Aunt June. Putting her to bed alone required leaving the bedroom light on and was usually accompanied by stalling and lots of tears. I had her back in weekly counseling sessions with a child psychologist.

Aunt June handed me the phone. "It's Kate."

"We missed you tonight. Is everything okay?"

She sighed. "Sorry I couldn't make it. Homicides never seem to happen at convenient times anymore."

"Ain't that the truth. Is there anything I can help you with?"

"Be careful what you wish for, but, as a matter of fact, there is. I've got a disturbing murder, maybe two, and I think they might be connected to Walter Bradshaw."

"Hmm. In what way?"

"I don't know whether you remember the witnesses from the armored car robbery and murder—there were two. Tonight we found one of them murdered. We can't find the other one, and it looks like her apartment has been tossed."

"That's not good, but I can't say I'm surprised. With the other family members still at large, and the old man in prison, it stands to reason that they might try something."

"That's exactly what I've been thinking. Maybe we should have anticipated that something like this might happen and taken steps to protect those witnesses."

"Don't be so hard on yourself, Kate. Nobody could have predicted this. Let's just hope the second witness is still alive and you can find her before they do."

Kate paused. "You mean I better hope the second witness is still alive and WE can find her before they do."

"Now I get it. You'll have to pardon me. I can be a little slow on the uptake sometimes."

"I've noticed."

I laughed. "Don't be a smart ass, particularly when you've got your hand out asking for help."

Her turn to laugh. "Good point. Walter's preliminary hearing is scheduled for the day after tomorrow."

"I'm aware of that. We've been asked to lean on every snitch in the joint to see if anybody has heard any scuttlebutt about the whereabouts or intentions of the rest of the Bradshaw clan. Prisoner transportation and courtroom security are top priorities right now."

"Learn anything from your snitches?"

"Lot's of rumors, but so far, nothing reliable. The most consistent story we're hearing is that the family split and has gone into hiding somewhere in southern Utah, along the Arizona strip. But I don't put much credence in that."

"Because?"

"First, consider the source. The inmate rumor mill is rife with misinformation. Besides, I just don't believe that the Bradshaw family is willing to abandon the prophet to whatever fate awaits him, which might well be a date with the executioner."

"Makes sense," said Kate. "You think they're unwilling to put Bradshaw's fate in the hands of the Lord?"

"Doubt it. What kind of help do you need?"

"Why don't you start with Walter Bradshaw. Why don't you pay him a visit and see what he has to say. And I know you're going to love this one, but how much will it cost me to get you to attend the autopsy?"

"It's going to be very expensive but everything's negotiable. In the meantime, what will you be doing?"

"I'll start scheduling interviews. There's going to be a boatload of people to talk to. I'll also find out what the CSI unit has come up with, although it might be too soon on that score. After then we can hook up and see where things stand."

"Sounds like a plan."

"What about your new boss? Should you touch base with him before you commit to work on this one?"

"Thanks for asking. The rules of the game have definitely changed, but I think he'll go along."

The new boss Kate referred to was Benjamin Cates. Cates had recently been appointed executive director of the Utah Department of Corrections.

In the aftermath of the massive scandal that had rocked the corrections department, the governor, with the encouragement of the state legislature, had moved quickly to make changes. His first step was to fire my former boss, Norm Sloan, and replace him with a reform-minded, retired sheriff from the King County Sheriff's Department in Seattle, Washington.

From what I had learned, Benjamin Cates was a highly regarded sheriff who also had the responsibility of running one of the largest jails in the country. He purportedly ran a tight ship and had a zero tolerance policy for staff who tried to operate outside the rules. That was a good thing.

Cates had wasted no time cleaning house. He left probation and parole largely intact, but came down with a vengeance on the prison. He demoted several prison managers, reassigned others, and fired two, including the second highest ranking member of the department, the Director of Institutional Operations. Several other supervisors with enough years in the system simply opted to retire.

As for me, I had somehow managed to survive what the newspapers had dubbed the "weekend massacre." My unit, the Special Investigations Branch (SIB), had emerged from the scandal relatively unscathed. The closet thing to criticism we received came from a couple of state legislators who made vague public statements that the scandal should have been discovered and squashed before it ever became one.

Yet my relationship with Cates felt like a tentative one. I was under the microscope. He knew it, and so did I.

Chapter Four

I left my Park City home early the next morning and headed for my office at the state prison. Juggling a cell phone, a cup of hot coffee, and a cinnamon roll, while rocketing down I-80 with the other Nascar commuters, was a serious challenge.

I phoned Patti Wheeler, my secretary, and asked her to pull the inmate file on Walter Bradshaw. I had been worried about Bradshaw and his impending, preliminary hearing even before the call from Kate the previous night. The prospect of transporting a high-risk inmate, like Bradshaw, was daunting knowing that the other fugitive members of his family were still at large. Add to that the murder of one of the witnesses and the apparent disappearance of another. Mere coincidence seemed an unlikely explanation for this chain of events.

My immediate challenge was how to approach Bradshaw for the interview. It wasn't like I could play the old carrot-and-stick game. He was already being held without bail in the maximum security unit at the prison. That's living about as deprived as one can get. In addition, he was facing a plethora of new criminal charges sufficient to keep him breathing stale prison air for the remainder of his days. His record as an inmate wasn't particularly good either. The prison staff viewed him as an agitator and a trouble-maker. Even among the inmate population, Bradshaw was perceived to be at the far end of the nut-meter.

About the only carrot I had at my disposal might be the opportunity to have him reclassified and moved into a medium security housing unit where life would be easier. The difficulty with that option was that I would have to convince the prison classification committee that moving Bradshaw to a less secure housing unit was in the best interest of the prison and something he deserved—both difficult sells. From experience I knew that convincing the classification committee to transfer an inmate based solely on providing snitch information, while difficult, wasn't impossible. I'd done it before. But it required me to expend political capital, something I didn't relish doing.

Bradshaw had been captured minutes after the stick-up and had been held initially at the Salt Lake County Jail. The state parole board immediately dispatched a hearing officer to the jail who determined there was probable cause to believe that he was in violation of several conditions of his parole agreement. That triggered his transfer back to the prison, a fact that undoubtedly made the sheriff's office happy. It made us responsible for not only holding him, but also for his transportation to and from court.

When I got to the office, I called Patti in. "I need you to do a couple of other things for me when you get a minute."

"That 'when you get a minute' usually means you want it done yesterday. Which is it?"

"Yesterday."

"That's what I thought. What do you need?"

"Get me a copy of Walter Bradshaw's visitor and correspondence log. I need to know who is on his approved visitor list and with whom he corresponds. Also, get me a list of his outgoing telephone calls for the past month." Tracking inmate mail and phone calls, while laborious, wasn't difficult. They weren't allowed to receive incoming telephone calls, and we selectively monitored calls they made to the outside world.

"Anything else?"

"Yeah, three things, actually. Call the executive director's office. See if I can get in to see him later this morning. Then call the court clerk for Judge Homer Wilkinson. He's the judge scheduled to hear Bradshaw's preliminary hearing tomorrow.

Try to get me an appointment to see him this afternoon. And as much as I hate it, find out when the state medical examiner's office has scheduled the autopsy for Arnold Ginsberg."

She giggled. "What?" I asked.

"Oh, I just wondered," she said loudly, "since you're going to an autopsy, do I need to order some fresh pipe tobacco or would you just like smelling salts?" In the background, I could hear somebody laughing.

"I suppose I'll be hearing about this for the next month."

"Count on it," she said.

<>‹›‹>

The morning wake-up bell sounded promptly as it always did at six-thirty in Uintah I, the Utah state prison's maximum security housing unit. Walter Bradshaw woke with a start to the sound of the high-pitched whistle and sighed. He rolled stiffly from his side onto his back and then continued the roll until he sat upright with his bare feet touching the cold, concrete floor. He dropped quickly to the floor where he performed a daily routine of fifty pushups followed by two-hundred sit-ups and a couple of stretching exercises for his forty-five year old limbs.

Life inside max was austere at best. That suited Bradshaw because it gave him ample time to read the scriptures and study the words of the first prophet, Joseph Smith. His trials were all a part of God's plan, of that he was certain. The eight by twelve foot cell was encased in concrete and steel. The bed, if you could call it that, was a single concrete slab attached to a concrete wall with a too-thin mattress tossed on top. Anchored to the floor in one corner was a toilet with a small steel sink mounted on the wall next to it.

His routine consisted of twenty-three hours a day spent in his house with one hour out for exercise and a five minute shower. He was required to stand four times a day for scheduled counts. Meals were served in his cell. He couldn't have a job, and he was not allowed to attend prison programs or school. Excluding his lawyer, he was allowed two non-contact visits a week. All of this because prison administrators had decided that he was the leader of a so-called Security Threat Group, or STG. As far as Bradshaw was concerned, the prison administration was a gang.

Bradshaw was the founder and self-proclaimed leader of the Reformed Church of the Divine Christ. He had founded the Church in late 2002 after being expelled by Warren Jeffs from the Fundamentalist Church of Jesus Christ of Latter Day Saints. Bradshaw was determined to establish a polygamist religious sanctuary in the desert of southern Utah. There, he and his small band of followers would be free to practice their religious beliefs without interference from the government while at the same time insulated from the evils of the secular world.

Just thinking about Warren Jeffs made Bradshaw angry—the kind of anger that sits in your belly, unrelenting, like hot acid. It had been excruciating watching Warren manipulate his way to head of the church, systematically eliminating anyone he perceived to be a threat. Any who dared question his judgment or authority were unceremoniously banished. Even some who hadn't questioned, teenage boys like his sons, were tossed from the community like used garbage. How could people have been so naïve?

He detested Warren Jeffs. He recalled the shock when a group of men—his friends—came to his home to take his first wife, Janine, and her sister wives, Dora, and Emma to their new husbands. He could still see the self-righteous looks on the faces of the brethren.

The humiliation of not being able to fight back, to defend his family, haunted him every day. Seeing fear on the faces of his younger children was excruciating. Some were crying. Others just withdrew. All of them learned a harsh lesson that day about obedience under Warren Jeffs. And when Janine refused to go, she had been forced to leave their precious daughters behind. There was simply no way to take them. Did the children understand? Did they feel betrayed? He promised that he'd come back for them, but now he knew he'd never get them back. The oldest two had already been married off.

Bradshaw remembered with pleasure the crimes of retribution, the Lord calling out to him in righteous indignation, to punish the Jeffs' empire. And punish they did. At every turn and in every way possible, the Bradshaws had exacted revenge on Warren Jeffs and the FLDS church. What started out as acts of vandalism against church-owned property became crimes of theft, burglary, even arson.

His thoughts were interrupted by the voice of one of the prison guards. "Bradshaw, you got a visitor. Step over to the cell door and turn around, hands behind your back—you know the drill." The cuff port door opened. He stood and turned around, extending his hands until he felt the cold steel of the handcuffs bite into his wrists. His cell door opened and two burly correctional officers attached a leash to his handcuffs. An ankle chain was secured to each ankle requiring him to walk taking baby steps.

⟨⟩⟨⟩⟨⟩

I went to see Bradshaw with the rudiments of a plan. I was certain that going to him in a conventional way, reciting the Miranda warnings with the expectation of hearing some startling confession, stood little chance of success. Instead, I intended to set a trap and see if he walked into it. We met in a small office in the Uintah I housing unit used mostly by staff for writing reports and conducting inmate disciplinary hearings. I carried a concealed voice-activated tape recorder in my shirt pocket.

Walter Bradshaw looked remarkably undistinguished. He was a slight man, maybe six feet, slim, with short black hair and a full salt and pepper beard. The beard aged him beyond his forty-five years I thought. His only feature that I would describe as striking were his eyes—eyes like Paul Newman, only these were a bright emerald green and they seemed to look right through you. He stared at me intently as I entered the room and sat down, wondering, I'm sure, who I was and what I wanted.

After perfunctory introductions and a minute or so of idle chit-chat designed to establish rapport or some such nonsense from Interrogation 101 training, I got down to business.

"Mr. Bradshaw, Salt Lake P.D. homicide contacted me last night with some disturbing information. It seems that one of the witnesses in the pending case against you was found murdered last evening, and a second witness in the case is also missing. What can you tell me about that?"

The non-verbal expression on his face was one of surprise. For a moment he said nothing, probably trying to process what I'd just told him. "I wouldn't know a thing about it. Why are you talking to me anyway, Mr. Kincaid? I've been in prison for the past several weeks, and while I believe in the power of holy miracles, I think we'd both agree that the likelihood of my being in two places at the same time is highly remote."

"I'm talking to you, Walter, because the crime lab team discovered physical evidence at the scene linking members of your family to the killing," I lied.

"I don't believe that any member of the Reformed Church would have anything to do with such a crime. And even if I did, I wouldn't be talking to you about it now would I?"

"Probably not, but maybe you should. You're facing enough new charges to keep you locked up for a long time. And that doesn't count the parole violations. I can assure you that the state parole board is eager to meet with you just as soon as the court disposes of the new charges. A good word from me to the prosecutor and the parole board wouldn't hurt and just might help."

"The Lord will take care of my needs, Mr. Kincaid. I am not seeking, nor am I interested in, receiving help from anyone who is employed by the State of Utah. Government is the oppressor, and you, sir, are an instrument of that oppression."

He paused for a moment, looking pensive, and then he continued. "Tell me something Mr. Kincaid, which witness was killed—the man or the young girl?"

"Why do you ask?"

"Curiosity, I suppose, although I'd hate to see that beautiful, young woman hurt. No harm at all if it was the queer sinner. God's justice, you know."

"How did you even know there was a male and female witness?"

"TV and newspapers for starters. And my attorney knows. We know the names of all the witnesses because the government is required to provide that information."

He was right about that.

I tried a different tactic. "You know, Walter, life in max is pretty damned hard. I guess I don't have to tell you that. If you change your mind and decide to cooperate, I might be able to get you transferred into a medium security housing unit where you aren't locked down twenty-three hours a day. Think about it." I slid my business card across the table toward him.

He looked at it for a moment and then slid it back. "This conversation is over, sir."

Chapter Five

On one level, my interview with Walter Bradshaw appeared to have been a bust. I hadn't expected a confession and he didn't offer one. On the other hand, my assertion that physical evidence found at the crime scene had linked his gang to the murder of Arnold Ginsberg seemed to have caught him off-guard. If he'd ordered the murder the only surprise should have been my lie about the existence of physical evidence. If he didn't, the entire episode should have shocked him.

On my way out of Uintah I, I stopped at the office of Captain Jerry Branch. "Jerry, I need your help with something. If Bradshaw makes any phone calls in the next day or two, I'd like you to record them and notify my office immediately. Same thing if he receives visitors."

"Sure. Anything in particular you'd like us to be listening for?" I explained the possible connection to the Ginsberg murder.

Back in my office, I reviewed Bradshaw's visitation history. Since his return to prison, he had received at least one family visitor per week and sometimes two. The approved visitors were his wife, Janine, and his daughter-in-law, Amanda. Amanda was married to Walter's eldest son, twenty-six year old Albert. Albert was a fugitive and wanted in the armored car robbery and murder.

The other visitor was Bradshaw's lawyer, a man named Gordon Dixon. I'd never heard of him. Dixon wasn't an employee in the public defenders office, that much I knew. That meant that he was in private practice and was either hired by the family or appointed by the court to represent Walter. In his past legal scrapes, Bradshaw had always claimed poverty and was represented by court appointed counsel, usually a public defender. Dixon had been in to see Bradshaw on three occasions in the past several weeks, ostensibly to discuss legal strategy for his impending trial. Absent suspicious circumstances, the attorney-client privilege prevented the prison from reading mail or eavesdropping on conversations between a convict and his lawyer. I decided to find out more about Gordon Dixon and the nature of his law practice.

Patti stuck her head in my office. "You'd better get moving. You've got a busy day in front of you. Director Cates is expecting you at eleven and Judge Wilkinson agreed to see you at noon. His afternoon court docket was full, but he offered to see you briefly during his lunch hour—didn't sound too happy about it though."

"Dandy." I stood up and reached for my coat when it struck me. "What's that smell? Have you started wearing peppermint perfume these days?" Then I saw them lying on top of my file cabinet—automobile air fresheners, several of them in fragrances ranging from peppermint, to sage, vanilla, and orange spice. "What the hell am I supposed to do with these?"

She was laughing now. "Terry bought those for you. He thought you could wear them around your neck at Ginsberg's autopsy this afternoon. It's scheduled for one-thirty."

"Very funny. That boy obviously doesn't have enough to do. I'll have to fix that."

<>‹›‹›

I was ushered into Director Cates' office promptly at eleven. He was known, among other things, for his punctuality. Unfortunately, I was not, but I was attempting to mend my ways, if for no other reason than to get off on the right foot with my new boss.

For a moment I thought Cates was going to remain behind a large, walnut desk, but he stood and pointed me in the general direction of a round conference table in one corner of his office. We sat. There was no idle chit-chat.

"I understand that you wanted to see me about the murder last night of the Salt Lake City businessman, Ginsberg, I think his name was. Frankly, I wondered what that had to do with us, but I'm sure you'll fill me in."

I explained the possible connection of Walter Bradshaw to the murder of Arnold Ginsberg and the request from Salt Lake City P.D. for our help with the investigation.

"It strikes me that we should help with the case, but I'm going to leave that to your discretion. What I do expect is that you keep me in the loop and always exercise good judgment before committing us to these kinds of investigations. Tell me this. Has the press connected Ginsberg's murder to the Bradshaw case?"

"Not yet, but I think it's only a matter of time. It's possible that Salt Lake P.D. might release that information in the normal course of business. But even if they don't, it's only a matter of time before some good investigative reporter will uncover the fact that Ginsberg was a witness in the case and that Bradshaw was on parole at the time of the robbery/murder."

Cates was a note-taker. As we talked, he busily scribbled notes to himself in a planner. "Okay," he said. "I'll pass this information along to our public information officer in case the media starts asking questions. Anything else?"

"Only that Bradshaw's preliminary hearing is scheduled for tomorrow, and the prison's Special Operations Tactical Team will shuttle him back-and-forth between the courthouse and prison. With the other members of his gang still at large, security is tight."

"Appreciate the information, Sam. I'll consider it. Before you leave there's something I'd like to discuss with you."

That put me on full alert.

"I'm sorry that until now I haven't had time to sit down with you and go over some things. My first few weeks on the job have been a little hectic. And I want you to understand that while I don't hold you or the Special Investigations Branch responsible for the recent scandal, there are some people, both in and out of the department, who have pointed the finger of blame in your direction."

"I'm sure that's true."

"I considered reassigning you but decided against it, in part, because of a conversation I had with my predecessor, Norm Sloan. Sloan gave you high marks for not only your professional skills but also your loyalty to him, and your dedication to the department. You'll soon discover that I will demand the same level of personal loyalty and dedication."

"I appreciate Director Sloan's kind words of support. And of course I'll try to provide you with the same level of dedication and support that I gave him. And if it turns out that that's not good enough, we'll both know that it's time for me to move on."

"Fair enough," Cates said. "The issue I wanted to discuss with you today is how to keep the department operating on sound ethical principles and the role you and the SIB will have to play in that endeavor. I ran a tight ship for twenty-eight years in the King County Sheriff's Department and I intend to run a tight ship here. People in this department are going to quickly learn that I have a zero tolerance policy for rogue employees who think they can operate outside the rules. Tell me something, Sam, how do you think we can prevent future scandals like that recent business with the so-called Commission?"

"Like a lot of people, I've had plenty of time to think about it. And I've concluded that, as a department, we should have been doing some things differently."

"Such as?"

"Hiring for starters. In the name of saving money, the department gutted the budget for conducting full-field background investigations on prospective employees. Also, we eliminated psychological screening completely from the personnel selection process. That was a mistake."

"I couldn't agree more," said Cates. "And that's why I've shifted background investigations from the personnel department back to your office. And from now on, nobody gets hired without a psychological evaluation. We've already put that service out for bid.

"What else?"

I started to wonder if this was a test. "Scheduling of line staff and supervisors probably should have been done differently."

"How so?"

"The prison allowed, even encouraged, the same line staff and supervisors to work together for too long a period of time in the same area. It would have been better to rotate and mix line staff and managers more often. That would have prevented the formation of tight cliques of staff and supervisors, making it harder to organize and control illicit activities."

I don't know whether he liked this idea but he was back scribbling notes in his planner. Maybe he was writing that I was a flaming nut-case and had begun the paper trail that would lead to my ultimate removal from the department. Or maybe I was just being paranoid.

He looked up from his planner. "Here's my plan and how the SIB has an integral role its success. It starts with my office. Employees have to know that illegal and unethical behavior won't be tolerated. I have to set the tone for that right from the get-go with stronger written policies and procedures, improved training, increased emphasis on ethics, and, of course, vigorous enforcement. In part, that's where your office comes in. Every allegation of employee misconduct must be investigated quickly and thoroughly, and appropriate corrective action taken immediately.

I interrupted. "That's all well and good. I assume we'll get the resources to pay for it because, at the moment, I don't have the budget or staff to carry out the mandate, or to conduct full-field background investigations on all applicants. I don't have a problem with the SIB having the responsibility as long as we have the necessary resources."

"Tell me what you think you need."

"Right now, the SIB functions with six investigators counting myself, and one overworked secretary. I need, as a minimum, one additional full-time investigator, two would be better, and an additional clerical support person."

Cates thought about it for a moment. "Here's what I can do for you now. I'll find the money in the current budget to get you another secretary. When the new fiscal year begins, I'll get you another investigator. Until then, you'll have to make do."

Our meeting ended. I'd been blunt. I wasn't sure whether he appreciated my candor. His demeanor didn't give much away. But I knew that I'd been set up to fail if I couldn't command sufficient resources to implement his plan for greater staff accountability. In the meantime, I had a murder investigation to work.

Chapter Six

Robin Joiner slept until almost noon. She had spent nearly two hours drinking coffee and eating a late night dinner of eggs, hash browns, and toast at the IHOP, several miles south and west of the University of Utah campus. The attempted kidnapping had frightened her beyond anything she had ever experienced.

After dinner, she walked several blocks on Main Street until she found a motel that looked clean enough to pass the smell test. Joiner debated about whether to use her remaining cash to register for the room using a false name but ultimately decided against it. It seemed prudent to hoard her cash for emergencies and use her debit card for the room, knowing that using the card would create a paper trail. After a restless hour in which she couldn't get to sleep, she got up and walked a block to a twenty-four hour convenience store where she purchased some Tylenol PM. The sleep medication had done its job, but it had also left her with a major hangover.

Joiner got up, showered, and wandered over to the motel's lobby. The dump had advertised a continental breakfast. She needed to sit down and figure out what to do. As she poured a cup of coffee, Joiner glanced down at the front page headlines of the *Salt Lake Tribune*. Something caught her attention, something familiar. And then it hit her like punch in the gut. There had been a murder in Salt Lake City last night. The victim was Arnold Ginsberg, the same Arnold Ginsberg whom she'd met at police headquarters the day of the armored car robbery. She collapsed in a chair and read the story with a sinking feeling in the pit of her stomach.

This changed everything. Over watered-down coffee, juice, and a stale Danish, Joiner carefully considered her options. In time a plan began to take shape in her head, a plan that gave her a glimmer of hope.

<>‹>‹>

I was irritated as I sat outside the chambers of district court judge Homer Wilkinson. I was supposed to see him at noon. His secretary had left for lunch shortly after twelve having assured me that the judge would be out momentarily. It was now after twelve-thirty and he still hadn't made an appearance. Finally, the office door opened and an apologetic judge beckoned me inside.

I had testified in front of Wilkinson on a couple of old prison cases, but I could tell that he didn't remember me. I introduced myself, and we chatted briefly about nothing of significance. Finally, he asked, "So, Mr. Kincaid, what brings you to see me today?"

I asked him if he'd heard anything about the murder of Arnold Ginsberg. He had. What he didn't know, only because it hadn't yet come to the attention of the press, was Ginsberg's status as a witness in the Bradshaw case.

"Judge, the victim in this homicide was scheduled to appear in your courtroom tomorrow as a prosecution witness in the preliminary hearing of Walter Bradshaw. As you probably know, the rest of the Bradshaw gang remains at-large. Salt Lake City P.D. believes that Ginsberg's murder may not be random and may, in fact, be connected to his status as a witness in the case." Now I had his complete attention.

"What kind of evidence do the police have that leads them to conclude that Mr. Ginsberg's murder is connected to this case?" A good question I thought, one I had anticipated.

"It just so happens that a second witness, a young woman named Robin Joiner, is also missing. When the police became concerned, they immediately went to Ms. Joiner's apartment to check on her welfare. When they arrived, they found her missing and the apartment ransacked."

"Dear God," muttered Wilkinson. He sat in silence for a moment then asked, "Is there something you want me to do about this, or are you merely providing information?"

"Actually, Judge, I do have a request, one that I think you should seriously consider."

"Go on."

"We're holding Mr. Bradshaw at the prison as a parole violator. We have a room on the prison grounds that the state parole board uses to conduct hearings. It's a room that could easily be adapted for you to conduct Bradshaw's preliminary hearing. The setting is more secure than the courthouse, and we don't have to risk transporting him."

"If I understand you correctly, Mr. Kincaid, you'd like me to move the hearing from my courtroom down to the state prison. Is that it?"

"Yes, Judge. That's what I'm suggesting."

"I'm sorry, but I can't do that. In the first place, the hearing is scheduled in less than twenty-four hours. I'm certain that the logistics necessary to move the hearing couldn't be completed in such a short time. Besides court employees, we've got lawyers involved, the victim's family, and even the press. Moreover, as a jurist, I'm philosophically opposed to the notion of moving judicial hearings out of the courthouse to the safe confines of the local jail or prison. It denies the public access and it just doesn't seem right."

The judge had a good point, at least about the logistics associated with moving the hearing on such short notice. I thanked him and got up to leave. As I got to the door, he stopped me. "You know, Mr. Kincaid, in light of the current circumstances, I'm somewhat surprised that I haven't received a motion for a continuance from the district attorney's office. If I were to receive such a motion, I can tell you that I would likely grant it."

◇◇◇

I left the Scott Matheson courthouse and drove the short distance to police headquarters. I found McConnell cloistered in her office with materials from the Ginsberg file spread across her desk including some colored glossies from the crime scene that made me grimace. Looking over her shoulder, I said, "Hope you didn't have a large biscuits and gravy breakfast this morning."

"You know, Kincaid, for a veteran cop who has seen some really nasty stuff at the state prison, you sure have a delicate stomach." I couldn't deny it.

"How'd it go with Bradshaw this morning?"

"About like I thought it would—complete denial of any involvement in the killing. He kept his cool, didn't give much away—hard to get a read on the guy. He surprised me with one thing he said, and that was that the death of the 'queer sinner,' referring to Mr. Ginsberg, was preferable to the loss of the beautiful, young woman."

"Hmm. Interesting that he knew something about the witnesses."

"Exactly what I thought. He explained it away by saying that his lawyer got the witness information from the DA through pretrial discovery."

"Probably true."

"I lied and told him that evidence discovered at the crime scene linked the members of his gang to the murder. That seemed to shock him a bit. Now we'll monitor his communication carefully and see who he talks to and exactly what he says."

"Good idea. And by the way, you may not have lied to him about the evidence. A patrolman discovered a bloody knife and a tire iron tossed in a dumpster about a block from the scene. Those items are being processed now for prints and other trace evidence."

"That's good. So what you've been up to?"

"I've been on the phone with the crime lab, and setting up interviews with people we need to talk to—friends, family, business associates.

"I did have an interesting interview with the victim's partner, a guy named Rodney Plow. He was very emotional, broke down several times and just sobbed. At the risk of seeming insensitive, it almost felt contrived, like I was witnessing a performance—theater if you will. I think Mr. Plow was a kept man."

"Nothing particularly unusual about that."

"Maybe." She abruptly changed the subject. "I'm starving. Want to grab a quick sandwich?"

I looked at her. "I'll pass. In case you've forgotten, I've got a date with the M.E. in about twenty minutes for the vic's autopsy. I think I'll wait until after."

She was smiling, making fun of me actually. "Queasy stomach, huh."

I got up to leave. When I reached her office door, I turned. "Hey, you need any auto air fresheners?"

Chapter Seven

I arrived at the Utah State Medical Examiner's Office on Salt Lake City's east bench about ten minutes ahead of the scheduled autopsy. The office was located in University Park only a short distance south of the University of Utah campus.

When I entered the building, I was surprised, and slightly amused, to discover that the state had opened a small gift shop in the lobby. Maybe the state budget was in worse shape than I thought. Two black cotton tees were displayed on a rack near the store's entrance with lettering across the top that read, "Utah State Medical Examiner." Additional print on one of the shirts said, "Any day above ground is a good day" and on the other, "Our day begins when yours ends." That was enough for me.

I was ushered into the autopsy suite promptly at one-thirty. I was greeted by Dr. Francis Chandler-Soames, forensic pathologist and the Chief Medical Examiner for the State of Utah. "Well, well, if it isn't Sam Kincaid. Don't see you often at these parties."

"A favor to Lt. McConnell," I said. "We're assisting her office on this investigation."

Chandler-Soames introduced me to her assistant, a young intern from the University of Utah medical school, training in forensic pathology. She offered me a mask laced with some kind of peppermint concoction. I declined. "Thanks, but I came prepared." I smeared my upper lip with Vicks Vaporub and we went to work.

The guest of honor was zipped in a black, plastic body bag and had been placed on a metal table. The autopsy suite was outfitted with all the latest technological gadgets—a pair of overhead microphones dangled from the ceiling connected to a voice recorder activated by a foot pedal. A Sony camcorder mounted on a tripod sat next to the table to videotape the festivities.

Chandler-Soames and her assistant deftly removed the deceased from the body bag. A trickle of dried blood was visible from the nose and both ears. The assistant began snapping photographs while Chandler-Soames made her initial observations. The blunt force trauma to the back of Ginsberg's head was the most obvious injury. That changed as soon as the forensics team began removing the vic's clothing. I couldn't miss the elongated stab wound that began just under the sternum and continued its jagged path upward toward the heart.

Stab wounds were familiar to me, much more than firearms, since cutting instruments were the most common form of weapon available to prison inmates. Stab wounds were always difficult to analyze but it was a safe bet that the weapon used in this attack was a bit more substantial than a pocket knife.

Fingernail scrapings were taken as well as blood, urine, and hair samples. Mouth and rectal swabs were obtained for subsequent use in toxicological studies. Chandler-Soames used a laser light to examine the body carefully for trace evidence not easily seen by the naked eye. Next, the body was washed, measured, and weighed.

The internal examination began with a large and deep Y incision from shoulder-to-shoulder and down to the pubic bone. Skin, muscle, and soft tissue were then peeled back to expose the internal organs. The internal organs were systematically removed, weighed, and carefully examined. The stomach was also removed and the contents weighed and examined in order to determine what was eaten and when.

Mercifully, the entire procedure took just a little over three hours. I've attended autopsies that lasted double that. Chandler-Soames met me for a debriefing in a conference room near the autopsy suite.

"Sam, do you want us to turn Mr. Ginsberg's clothing and personal effects over to you?"

"I don't think so. That would put me square in the middle of the chain-of-custody. Kate's going to want to have a look at everything anyway. Just hold the evidence and let her assume custody of it."

"That's fine. Let me begin by giving you a brief summary of our findings. Mr. Ginsberg died, and probably very quickly, as the direct result of severe blunt force trauma to the back of his skull sufficient to cause significant epidural intracranial bleeding. An epidural bleed like this one occurs in the space between the brain and the skull."

I interrupted. "Doc, could you drop that down a decimal or two and put it into layman's language for me."

"Sure. Mr. Ginsberg suffered a serious brain concussion probably sufficient to cause immediate unconsciousness. The force of the blow caused a severe skull fracture which tore epidural arteries producing internal bleeding around the brain. If you remember seeing the small amount of dried blood around both ears and the nose, that's often a symptom of a skull fracture. Arterial bleeding is usually brisk and will cause a coma and death quite rapidly."

"And what about the knife wound?"

In this case either of the wounds was sufficient to cause death. With the combined wounds, he had little chance of survival. If my theory is correct, this is what probably happened to Mr. Ginsberg: He was struck from behind by a male using some type of pipe or tire iron about three inches in diameter. At about the same time, a second assailant inflicted the fatal stab wound to the chest area."

"What makes you think the attacker was male?"

"Aside from the fact that women don't often kill by bludgeoning somebody to death, the amount of blunt trauma to the back of the victim's head was extreme. It would take an awfully strong woman to inflict that kind of damage—possible, yes, but not likely. Second, the angle of the head wound tells me that you are probably looking for a suspect who is two or three inches taller than your victim. We measured him at six-foot-two."

"You mean the attacker swung the murder weapon in a downward arc across the back of the vic's head."

"Exactly."

"So, we're probably looking for a tall, male perp, maybe six-four or five."

"I think so, yes."

"And the stab wound. You don't think it could have been inflicted while the victim was lying prone?"

"I don't believe so," said Chandler-Soames. "Whoever inflicted the stab wound went in deep and hard just under the sternum. The perp yanked the blade upward with a hell of a lot of force, inflicting a great deal of internal damage on the way to the heart. The victim would have suffered significant bleeding both internally and externally from the knife wound. Death would have come more slowly, and, of course, if it hadn't been for the head wound, he might have been able to call out for help."

"What kind of knife?"

"I'll have to get back to you on that one after I've had time to do more analysis. I can tell you that you're looking for a large knife with approximately a seven to eight inch blade, serrated on at least one edge." I remembered Kate telling me that somebody had found what she thought were the murder weapons in a dumpster near the crime scene. I couldn't recall the specifics on the type of knife.

"Fair enough. I'll pass this information along to Lt. McConnell, and I'm sure if she has questions, she'll be in touch. How long before we have a report?"

"Two days minimum, three at the outside. And I'll see if I can have the tox studies ready as well."

Chapter Eight

I left the medical examiner's office and made a mad dash for Park City. I figured that if I drove like Michael Andretti at the Indianapolis 500, I might make Sara's four-thirty soccer game. This was her second year playing soccer, and she was turning into a first rate little goalie. If I miss one of her games, my most favored Dad rating takes a nose dive, not only on Sara's scale, but on Aunt June's as well. That's real pressure. Sometimes circumstances make it impossible for me to attend a game, but I've managed to make most of them.

On my way up the mountain, I tried to call Kate on her cell. This was high speed multi-tasking at its very best, and I'm happy to report that I didn't kill anyone in the process. Kate didn't answer so I left a message promising to call her first thing in the morning. I also found a message on my cell from Patti telling me to contact Captain Jerry Branch, day shift commander of the Uintah I prison housing unit. Perhaps my interview with Walter Bradshaw resulted in a flurry of communication with his contacts on the outside. I would soon find out.

The game was being played at the middle school near Kimball Junction. I made it just as the game began. I took over from Aunt June who had driven Sara and two of her teammates to the game. Sara managed fourteen saves but her team lost two to one. In order to lift team spirits, yours truly sprang for Pizza Hut pizza for what seemed like half the team.

When we got home, I observed an unmarked Summit County Sheriff's Department car parked across the street from my house. Because of the nature of my work, I pay particular attention to unfamiliar vehicles parked anywhere near my home. I sent Sara on into the house. An older, plain-clothes suit got out of the sheriff's vehicle and walked toward me carrying what looked like a legal file. I didn't recognize him.

"Excuse me," he said. "Would you be Sam Kincaid?"

"I am. And you are?"

"Jerry Grover." He reached out and shook my hand. "I'm a retired deputy with the sheriff's department. I still work part-time serving legal process."

I was puzzled. "And what brings you to see me, Jerry?"

He broke eye contact and looked slightly embarrassed. "I'm sorry, but I have the unpleasant task of having to serve you with court papers."

I had a sinking feeling. "What kind of court papers?"

"Family court documents—appears to be a child custody law suit." I accepted service of the documents and Grover departed. I should have seen this coming.

My former spouse, Nicole Bingham-Kincaid, had gone ballistic when she heard about the violent incident that occurred in our home several months earlier. In the confusion of the moment, it never occurred to me that I'd better call her in Atlanta and explain what happened before somebody else did. Well, somebody else did, and Nicole was furious that she got the news from someone else, and furious that my work had placed our daughter in imminent danger.

She arrived in Salt Lake City the next morning on the first available flight from Atlanta. Because Nicole is an Atlanta-based flight attendant for Delta Airlines, she was able to arrange her schedule over the next several weeks so that she was routed through Salt Lake City. This allowed her to spend more time with Sara. During the ensuing summer months, Sara spent several weeks in Atlanta with Nicole. When Nicole had to fly, Sara stayed with her grandparents who reside about thirty minutes outside Atlanta.

Standing in my driveway, I quickly perused the legal paperwork. The documents notified me of Nicole's intent to seek primary custody of Sara and move her to Atlanta. A hearing had been scheduled in three weeks. Nicole had made noises to me about this during the summer, but I had chosen to ignore her, believing that things would calm down and it would all blow over. Not so.

I felt sick to my stomach. What would I say to Aunt June and Sara? Should I even tell Sara at this point? Since the divorce, with a lot of help from Aunt June, we had managed to become a loving, cohesive family. Surely, no family court judge would choose to turn Sara's and our lives upside down.

And what was Nicole thinking? Her life, the life that she had chosen ahead of marriage and family, was a life flying to destinations all over the globe. She could only make this arrangement work with the help of her parents or a live-in nanny. I slipped the documents into my briefcase and went in the house.

Aunt June was waiting for me in the kitchen wearing a concerned look on her face. "Who was that man and what did he want?"

"We need to talk. Where's Sara?"

"Downstairs playing computer games. What's this all about? He came to the door looking for you. When I told him that you weren't home from work, he thanked me and then just sat in his car. He's been out there for almost an hour."

I showed her the paperwork and explained what I thought it meant. In my entire life, Aunt June had always been calm and stoic in the face of difficulty. I had seen tears only once, and that was at the funeral of my parents, both killed in a light plane crash while vacationing. On this occasion, I could see tears welling in the corners of both eyes. She dabbed them with a tissue. What came next surprised me. The emotion had quickly given way to something between anger and outright defiance.

"We're going to fight this, aren't we?" she asked. "We'll hire the best damn attorney money can buy. And we'll fight her. What in heavens name could Nicole be thinking—to tear this little girl from a loving and stable environment and move her clear across the country?" A fair question I thought.

"Yes, I suspect we will," I said. "But we've got to think it through very carefully. This would be a poor time for a knee-jerk response. In the meantime, we say nothing to Sara. There'll probably come a time when we will have to tell her, but not now." I knew myself well enough to understand that I'm not particularly good at figuring things out on the fly—thinking quickly on my feet had never been my forte. Given a little time, things would come into focus, and I would know what to do.

Sleep did not come easy. I read, tossed and turned, read some more, and tossed and turned some more. I did what I often do in situations like this. I got up and went to work. I tip-toed down the hall, looked in on Sara, and then slipped into my office.

I began by reviewing the SIB's intelligence file on the Reformed Church of the Divine Christ. Intelligence information, sketchy as it was, had determined that the church was established sometime in late 2002 after Bradshaw and several members of his family had been evicted from the Fundamentalist Church of Jesus Christ of Latter Day Saints (FLDS) compound on the Arizona-Utah border.

Scuttlebutt was that the church intended to purchase land in the desert red rock country of southern Utah large enough to support a growing band of polygamist church members, and remain independent from other Mormon fundamentalist groups. That plan, of course, required money, and the brethren seemed to have little compunction about stealing and robbing to get it.

In the beginning, burglary and theft seemed to be their crimes of choice. There was a long string of unsolved property crimes committed against FLDS property all along the Utah-Arizona border. More recently, Bradshaw and his followers escalated their lawbreaking behavior to include armed robberies.

Since his arrest and return to the Utah State Prison, Walter had received no fewer than two visits from detectives from the Las Vegas Metropolitan Police and the Denver Police Department. In both instances, he was questioned about unsolved armored car robberies occurring in Vegas and Denver where the perps followed the same MO as the Salt Lake City heist. So far, no charges had been filed in either case because of insufficient evidence.

As far I could tell, the church's core membership consisted of patriarch Walter, his two sons, Albert and Joseph, their wives and children, a nephew of Walter, and two cousins. The nephew had been killed in the armored car robbery. The cousins, Randy and Robert Allred, both had extensive criminal records. Like Walter, Randy Allred was a parole violator wanted by authorities in Arizona.

The Allred brothers and both of Walter's sons were wanted for murder and aggravated robbery in the armored car mess. And it certainly wasn't a big stretch to believe that the gang might be involved in Ginsberg's murder as well as the disappearance of the other witness, Robin Joiner.

I spent the better part of the next hour listening to my tape recorded interview with Walter Bradshaw hoping that I missed some small but important detail or subtlety in our conversation. When I reached the part where Bradshaw talked about Ginsberg and Joiner, something he said stopped me cold. I rewound the tape and played it again, and then once more. Maybe I'd found something. It was a small thing and it would take some digging.

Eventually sheer exhaustion overtook my ability to listen or think. I spent the next two hours dozing on an old leather couch in the corner of my office until the first rays of sunshine touched the wood blinds and woke me.

Chapter Nine

I found my way into the kitchen intent on fixing a pot of coffee, then banana waffles for Sara and me. Raisin Bran with berries or a banana was Aunt June's daily fare, and, unless we were all going out for breakfast, she seldom varied it.

I decided not to say anything to Sara about the child custody issue until I had more information. That meant finding an attorney to represent us in Atlanta, no small feat in itself, and talking to my ex, Nicole. At the moment, I was angry at Nicole and wasn't sure whether I could have a civil conversation with her. I guess I felt that she should have given me a heads-up about what she planned to do. But maybe she had, and I'd just missed the signals.

Anger aside, I had to admit that Nicole was only doing what she believed was in Sara's best interest. Yet I couldn't reconcile how Nicole had arrived at the conclusion that moving Sara across the country, away from all her friends and everything familiar to her, was preferable to a stable home with a full-time dad and the loving presence of Aunt June. It just didn't make sense. Unless Nicole planned to hire a live-in nanny, Sara would have to be shuffled to the home of her grandparents every time Nicole flew. And because of her seniority with the airline and her desire to visit far off places, Nicole frequently traveled abroad.

After breakfast and a quick review of the words on her spelling test scheduled for later in the day, I dropped Sara at school and headed to my office at the state prison.

<>< ><>

I made it into the office before Terry Burnham arrived. I had devised a get-even scheme for the assortment of auto air fresheners Burnham had planted in my office prior to Ginsberg's autopsy. He was late, and this gave me the perfect opportunity to implement my plan.

I grabbed the master key that would unlock his desk and a bottle of glue. At the risk of ending up charged with the destruction of state property, I resisted the temptation to use Super Glue and stuck to the ordinary kind. With the deft touch of Van Gogh, who was only slightly crazier than I am, I slapped a coat of the stuff along the lip of the middle drawer of Burnham's desk. I did the same to each of his side drawers.

Patti, my secretary, and Marcy Everest, one of my investigators, hardly glanced in my direction as they hovered over the office coffee maker like a pair of addicts waiting in line at the local crack house. Finally, Marcy looked over and said, "What the hell kind of mischief are you up to now?"

I smiled. "Wait and see."

When I finished, I relocked his desk and hustled back to my office to await his arrival and the show that would surely follow.

A few minutes later, Burnham rolled in looking haggard and thoroughly hung over. He avoided eye contact with everyone and barely grumbled a hello at Marcy who had spoken to him. Keys in hand, he plopped down at his desk, and unlocked it. He gave the middle drawer a tug—nothing happened. He pulled again, still nothing.

In a half whisper, he muttered, "What the fuck?" Then he gave the drawer a major pull and still nothing happened. The laughter around him started with a soft chuckle and quickly built to a crescendo.

"Okay, I get it. Who fucked with my desk?"

At that moment, I walked past him on my way out of the office to attend a nine o'clock budget meeting. When I got next to him, I whispered, "Pay-back's a bitch, isn't it?"

As I closed the office door, the last thing I heard him mutter was, "You dirty dog."

‹›‹›‹›

When I returned from my management meeting, I called Patti in. "I've got a little research job for you. It could be a wild goose chase, but I want you to go back several months and pull every newspaper article about the armored car robbery and murder that appeared in the *Deseret News*, the *Salt Lake Tribune*, and even the *City Weekly*. Then I want you to contact the local TV stations and find out if they did on-camera interviews with any of the witnesses."

"Mind telling me what this is about?"

"Something Walter Bradshaw said during my interview with him. It's probably nothing but when I told him about Ginsberg's murder, he said that he was pleased that it wasn't that beautiful, young woman."

"So what?"

"How would Bradshaw have known that she was beautiful and young?"

Patti paused. "Maybe he saw her picture in the newspaper."

"Bingo. Or maybe she was interviewed by one of the TV stations and he saw that from his jail cell. That's what I want you to find out."

"I'll get right on it."

There were two voice messages on my office phone. The first was from Kate and the other was from Captain Jerry Branch. The call from Branch probably had something to do with Walter Bradshaw having received visitors after my interview with him. Maybe now we'd find out whether Walter was conducting gang business from the confines of his house at the state prison.

I called Branch first. "Hi, Jerry, what's up?"

"Walter's wife, Janine, came to see him yesterday afternoon at two-thirty. You weren't out of the unit for more than ten minutes, and he was on the phone with her."

"Anything interesting come up in their conversation?"

"Not really. Just run-of-the-mill bullshit stuff about family, future plans, and which bodily orifices of hers he intends to violate once he gets out. He didn't say anything about the current case or the murder of Ginsberg, and nothing was spoken in code."

Knowing that their phone calls were often monitored, gang leaders sometimes spoke on prison phones using code as a way of issuing orders to subordinates on the outside. Prison intelligence units like the SIB invariably had someone skilled at breaking those codes. Discussion in code was a sure sign of criminal gang activity in the community. The conversations usually related to drug trafficking or hits on rival gang members. There was nothing in the Reformed Church file to indicate that the Bradshaw family had ever used code when conversing on prison phones.

Branch continued. "Bradshaw asked Janine to call his lawyer—a guy named Gordon Dixon. His office called this morning and said he'd be here between nine and nine-thirty—no sign of him yet, though. Want me to listen in?"

I glanced at my watch. It was nearly nine-thirty. "Naw, I don't want to put you in a bad spot, Jerry. I'm afraid that's a privileged conversation between lawyer and client. I'll come right over and take care of it myself." He snorted a laugh and hung up.

I'm not normally prone to violating the rules in order to further an investigation, but on occasion, I've been known to bend a rule to the breaking point. Normally, eavesdropping on a privileged conversation in prison between a lawyer and an inmate client was definitely a no-no unless reasonable grounds existed to believe that something illegal was going on. In this instance, it was a hell of a stretch, and I knew it.

If Bradshaw was directing church activities from inside the prison, and those activities were criminal in nature, as I suspected, he had to be communicating with someone on the outside. He could only be doing that through letters, phone calls, or during non-contact visits. Besides his attorney, Bradshaw's only visitors were members of his immediate family. Surveillance carried out by prison staff hadn't turned up anything suspicious regarding family members. If the illegal communication wasn't occurring through family contact then the only person left was his lawyer, Gordon Dixon. And by law, Dixon's access had been completely unmonitored—at least until now.

I was cloistered in a closet-like office in the prison's administration building wearing a head-set and listening to a lot of line static. I was surrounded by telephone company equipment and sophisticated hi-tech gadgetry designed to eavesdrop on telephone calls and monitor conversations between inmates and their visitors.

When Dixon and Bradshaw picked up their respective phones, the static gave way to absolute clarity. The first thing one of them said in a barely audible whisper was, "Not here." They exchanged greetings and made small talk until Dixon turned the conversation to a strategy discussion for the preliminary hearing scheduled for later in the day.

After Dixon left Uintah 1, I caught up with Jerry Branch in his office. Branch had observed the visit through one-way glass and saw something that confirmed my suspicions. As the two men stared at each other through the glass partition and reached for the phones, Dixon made a sweeping motion with his left hand, brushing his index finger across his lips in a gesture meant to say, keep quiet. That must have occurred just before I heard somebody whisper, "not here."

The entire conversation took less than fifteen minutes, and yet I'd learned something important. There was something Dixon didn't want to discuss with Walter Bradshaw over the prison phones, but what was it?

Chapter Ten

The other message had been from Kate. She wanted me to meet her at the home of Arnold Ginsberg for what would be a follow-up interview with the victim's live-in partner, Rodney Plow. She didn't come right out and say it, but I think she wanted me along to provide my impressions of the bereaved partner. Clearly, something about Plow's demeanor during his first interview had made Kate uncomfortable.

Ginsberg lived in an older, but exclusive neighborhood, high on Salt Lake City's east bench off Wasatch Boulevard, between Big and Little Cottonwood Canyons. The directions Kate had provided carried me up the side of the mountain along roads that snaked back-and-forth like switch-back trails. Eventually, I topped out on Ridge View Drive and realized that I could climb no higher. Ginsberg's home had been carved out of the side of the mountain. It was located on the eastside of Ridge View and commanded striking views of the entire Salt Lake valley and the Oquirrh Mountains to the west.

Kate was parked in front of the house when I arrived. According to Kate, Plow had been so emotionally distraught upon learning of Ginsberg's death that she hadn't been able to conduct a particularly thorough interview. She hoped to finish the interview today. From the street, we walked up a steep, narrow asphalt driveway that lead to a triple car garage. Looking back, I said, "Gorgeous views up here, but how would you like to try to get down that driveway in a blizzard?"

"It looks a bit intimidating. If you didn't have a four-wheel drive vehicle, you'd be screwed."

"You might be screwed even with four-wheel drive. If you slid down the driveway and couldn't get control when you hit the street, you might end up in the living room of that house across the street."

Rodney Plow wasn't what I expected. He was tall, tanned, slim, and looked twenty years younger than Ginsberg. He walked us through the foyer into the living room where we were introduced to a friend, a guy named Chad Emery, who seemed to be there for moral support. Rodney and Emery sat across from us on a sun flower print couch huddled together holding hands. Each had a partially consumed cup of java sitting on the glass coffee table. A box of tissues sat on the seat cushion next to Plow.

After condolences, Kate began. "Mr. Plow, when we spoke yesterday, I didn't have the opportunity to ask you whether Arnold ever gave you any indication that he might be having problems or be in conflict with someone? Could anyone in your social circle or among his business associates have been threatening him?"

He pondered the question for a moment before answering. "Nothing comes to mind. Arnie never had an enemy in the world. Everybody who knew him loved him. That certainly included our friends as well as his business clients. You probably don't know this but many of Arnie's business clients were also our friends."

"Tell me about that."

"Well, several of Arnie's corporate clients are travel agencies. If you know anything about the travel industry, you know that many people who own and work in the travel business come from the gay community. I'll bet Arnie prepared most of the individual tax returns for gay travel agents in Salt Lake City."

"Interesting," said Kate. "And aren't you a travel agent? Is that how the two of you met?"

He gave Kate a big toothy grin. "Yes and yes. I was employed at Rocky Mountain Travel, and Arnie handled their corporate taxes. Like a lot of other travel agents, I started having him prepare my individual tax returns, and well, one thing led to another, and pretty soon we were an item."

"And how long ago was that?" replied Kate, returning the big friendly smile.

Tears welled in the corners of his eyes. He reached for a tissue. "I was just thinking about that this morning. It was exactly three years ago this month," he said, choking back a sob.

Kate gave him a moment to compose himself and then continued. "I know this is difficult for you, Mr. Plow, but just a few more questions and we'll be finished. Back to my previous question, you aren't aware of anyone who might have been a threat to Mr. Ginsberg?"

For the moment, he seemed to have regained control of his emotions. "The one thing Arnie worried about was having to be a witness against that awful man, you know, the guy who robbed and killed those people outside the Target store."

"And you know this because......"

Plow interrupted before Kate could finish the question. "He told me so, several times in fact."

"Told you what?"

"That he was afraid of having to testify in court against that man, Bradshaw, I think his name is. He said this Bradshaw was a member of a violent group of Mormon fundamentalists who probably hated gays. And I don't think it was much comfort to Arnie that Bradshaw was in jail."

"And why was that?"

"Because the police never caught the rest of them," said Plow, a touch of anger and accusation in his voice.

"Then you believe Mr. Ginsberg was killed by members of Bradshaw's gang?"

Plow hesitated. "Well, of course, I don't know who killed him for sure, but yeah, the church freaks would seem like a pretty good bet, don't you think?"

Kate nodded.

"How would you describe your relationship with the victim?"

More tears. Out came another tissue. "It was extremely close and loving. We were committed to each other for life."

"Did you ever have fights?"

"Almost never. Oh, we'd have the occasional quarrel, but it never amounted to much."

"One last question," said Kate, "and please don't be offended. It's a routine question that we have to ask in these kinds of cases. We need to know your whereabouts around the time of the murder?"

Plow momentarily looked shocked but answered without hesitation. "We had planned a quiet dinner at home, just the two of us. He was supposed to be home at five. I stayed around the house that morning but left a little after noon."

"Where did you go?"

"First, I went to the Cottonwood Athletic Club where I swam and tanned. My tanning appointment was at one so I would have left there at around one-thirty. After that I dropped by the Wild Oats Market on Ft. Union Boulevard for a few groceries, and then I stopped at the Market Street Grill in Cottonwood where I bought the fresh halibut we were supposed to have for dinner."

"And what time did you arrive home?"

"Three-thirty, maybe three-forty-five."

"Did you remain at home for the remainder of the day?"

"I never left home after that. I was busy fixing dinner. When Arnie didn't show, I called the police."

"Would you happen to have the receipts from the purchases you made at Wild Oats and Market Street?"

"Sure do." He was off the couch and back momentarily with the receipts.

We thanked him and left. Back at our cars, Kate asked, "Well, what do you think?"

"He seemed sincere to me. His responses to your questions didn't sound canned or rehearsed. He's obviously a very emotional guy—seemed like he was turning those tears on-and-off like a faucet. On balance, I didn't see any major red flags. You've got some leg-work to do to confirm his alibi, but nothing seemed out of the ordinary there either."

"He didn't seem so flaky to me today either. Thanks for coming along and giving me your read on the guy," said Kate.

"Anytime. Now let's go have some lunch. I'm starving and you're buying. Consider that the price for my having to attend that miserable autopsy for you."

She laughed. "Where should we go?"

"How about the Lonestar on Ft. Union?—best fish tacos in town."

"See you there."

Chapter Eleven

Over grilled halibut fish tacos I gave Kate the low-down on my impending child custody battle with Sara's mother. She listened attentively until I finished before weighing in. While Kate had developed a fondness for Sara, something nurtured over the past several months of our relationship, I knew that she would bring a level-headed approach to a problem that I was buried in emotionally.

When I finished venting, she said, "Aunt June must be beside herself over this. Have you spoken to Sara about it yet?"

"Aunt June is about as upset as I've ever seen her. And no, I haven't said anything to Sara, but I know I'm going to have to do that soon. I'm worried about how to present it to her. She loves us and she loves her mom. I don't want her caught in the middle feeling like she has to make a choice between living with me or her mother. I'm so pissed at Nicole right now that I can't bring myself to call her, but I know we need to talk, and soon."

"Look, Sam, as far as Nicole goes, get over it. You do need to talk with her and right away. Maybe there's a chance this can be stopped short of a showdown in court. Everybody involved needs to keep their eye on the ball, and that means looking out for what's best for Sara."

I knew what Kate said was true. "I can hardly bring myself to say anything to Sara. That little girl has gone through a lot over the past couple of years, first the divorce, and then that nightmare at our home last spring."

"She's been through a lot for an eight year old, I'll give you that. But she's a smart little girl and I know she'll bounce back. She just needs some time," said Kate. She reached into her planner and pulled out one of her business cards. She wrote a name and phone number on the back and handed it to me. "I want you to call this guy. His name is Jim Reilly. He's a good friend of Tom's. He used to work at the DA's office in the juvenile court. He went private about a year-and-a-half ago. He specializes in the practice of family law, adoption, child custody, that sort of thing."

The Tom she referred to was Tom Stoddard, her former boyfriend who worked in the Salt Lake County DA's office. "Thanks for the lead. I'll give him a call right away. Do you really think he can help?"

"You're going to need a lawyer in Atlanta that's for sure. But Jim can certainly answer questions and give us a clear picture of the legal procedures involved."

I liked hearing the 'us' part. It felt like we were in this thing together—like I had a partner.

⟨⟩⟨⟩⟨⟩

We finished lunch and turned our attention back to the murder investigation. Besides the interviews with Rodney Plow, McConnell had also spoken at length with Ginsberg's secretary and the other two CPA's with whom he shared office space.

"Have you found any inconsistencies between what Plow told you and what his business associates had to say?" I asked.

"Only one thing and I'm not sure how much credence to give it."

"What was it?"

"It has to do with the domestic tranquility bit Plow laid on us this morning. According to the secretary, all was not as rosy on the home front as Rodney would have us believe."

"Hmm. What do you make of that?" I asked.

"I'm not sure. It's not unusual in murder investigations for the grieving partner to paint a rosier picture of the relationship than really existed. And most of the time, it doesn't mean anything.

It's certainly not a valid indication of spousal involvement in the murder, that's for sure."

"What exactly did the secretary say?"

She glanced down at her notes. "The secretary, her name was Linda Beggs, said that over the past several months the victim had confided to her several times that he was growing increasingly unhappy with the relationship."

"Yeah, but why?"

"What do couples usually fight over? Fidelity and money. It seems that Ginsberg came to believe that a much younger Rodney might be sowing his oats, so to speak, with someone else."

"You'd better find out if that's true."

"I plan to," said Kate.

"Add to that concern Ginsberg's worry that Plow liked nice things and rarely bothered to look at price tags."

"So, Ginsberg might have been under some financial strain. Have you had time to figure out who stood to gain from Ginsberg's death?"

"Not yet, but I'm working on it. I'll keep you posted. Tell me about the autopsy."

I spent the next few minutes updating her on the preliminary findings from the delightful afternoon I'd spent at the medical examiner's office. "You're probably still a day or two out before Chandler-Soames gets you the final report as well as the tox results. I didn't want to get into your chain so you'll need to stop and pick up the physical evidence as well as the vic's personal effects."

"More work for the lab crew," said Kate. "That reminds me, I need to call them later today and see how close they are to completing the forensics work."

I told Kate what I'd overheard during Gordon Dixon's visit with his client earlier in the day. "I think Bradshaw may be directing things through his lawyer."

"Really. Are you sure you heard one of them whisper, 'not here'?"

"I'm not sure who said it, but I definitely heard it. And Jerry Branch actually observed Dixon give Walter the signal to keep quiet."

"What do we know about Gordon Dixon?" asked Kate.

"Not much, but I'm about to find out more. You ever run across him?"

"Never heard of him. If he did much criminal defense work, you'd think one of us would have. Keep me posted on this."

I shifted gears. "What's your take on the missing witness, this Robin Joiner?"

"Hard to say. At the time of the armored car robbery, she gave us a local address and then another one for her mother someplace in Nevada. I think the parents might be divorced, but I'm not sure. It's another detail I just haven't had time to follow up on."

I told Kate about the comment Bradshaw made during our interview and the project I had Patti working on. "Assuming that she isn't dead or that she hasn't been snatched by the family, it's hard to understand why she hasn't contacted us."

"Maybe she will. She's young and probably scared half to death. The truth is we don't even know for sure that her disappearance is in any way connected to the Bradshaw clan. And if it is, we can at least take some comfort in knowing that when they broke in and tossed her apartment, they didn't find her."

"You could be right. Maybe she just decided to take a break from her classes and get away for a few days. Have you had time to look for her at the university?"

Kate looked discouraged. "Not yet," she sighed.

"Look, Kate, since I'm already snooping into her background, I'll go ahead and follow up with the university and her family. That's one less thing you'll have to do."

"You're my hero," said Kate. "I'll e-mail a copy of the information I have on her family to your office. It's not much, but it'll get you started. In the meantime, I'll continue contacting family, friends, and Ginsberg's business associates, and we'll see where that takes us."

⟨⟩⟨⟩⟨⟩

After lunch, I had just enough time to make it to the Matheson courthouse before the start of Bradshaw's preliminary hearing.

Transporting dangerous felons to court presented several points of vulnerability. In this case the greatest danger existed with the actual drive from the prison to the courthouse. If the Bradshaw gang had hatched an escape plan for Walter, their best chance for success would be to try to intercept the transportation vehicle while it was traveling to or from court. By the time I got there, the special ops team had already arrived and Walter was sequestered in a holding cell near Judge Wilkinson's court room.

Security in the courtroom was tight. Uniformed sheriff's deputies swarmed the place like flies on a fresh cow pie. Nobody got in without a thorough search. Besides a walk through the metal detector, visitors in significant numbers were being pulled off to one side and treated to a more invasive search.

Walter Bradshaw was led into the courtroom flanked by two burly sheriff's deputies. He sat at the defense table next to his lawyer, Gordon Dixon, and an unknown female who was probably a legal assistant. The low murmur in the court room turned to silence as the assembled guests got their first look at the accused. There wasn't an empty seat in the room.

The ankle and waist chains had been removed. He was out of his orange prison jump suit and dressed in gray slacks and an open-collared blue dress shirt with no tie. The civilian clothes made him look significantly less menacing I thought—no doubt a good thing from a defense point of view. He nodded and gave a weak smile to his wife and daughter-in-law who were seated in the audience. Glancing around the room, Walter looked almost amused by the spectacle.

I found two of my investigators, Terry Burnham and Marcy Everest, assisting sheriff's deputies at a checkpoint which allowed news media personnel through security and into the courtroom. Bradshaw's impending trial would have drawn media attention anyway, but the disclosure by Salt Lake P.D. that Arnold

Ginsberg's murder might be connected to the case had created a feeding frenzy. It hadn't helped that Rodney Plow was talking to the press and making similar assertions. The judge had wisely decided to ban cameras, but reporters and sketch artists still occupied the entire first two rows of the courtroom.

Burnham glanced up, spotted me, and walked over. "You seem to be enjoying tormenting those media people. I thought you were going to make that last guy drop trou before you let him pass," I said.

He laughed. "I almost did. I'd forgotten how much fun it is to hassle these self-important SOBs."

"How was the trip in?" I asked.

"In a word, uneventful. Those special ops guys are about as anal a group as I've ever seen. They wouldn't even tell Everest and me the route until we showed up at their little briefing. And that was ten minutes before we left the prison."

"And you won't be told the route they plan to take back to the prison until right before you leave. How many personnel did they assign?"

"Try Bradshaw in the backseat of a Suburban surrounded by four special ops guys. I led the procession and Marcy brought up the rear."

At a preliminary hearing, the prosecutor's job was to put on just enough evidence to convince the judge that probable cause existed to hold the defendant for trial. The trick was not to put on more of the case than was necessary to get a favorable ruling from the judge. In this instance I wasn't sure who the DA intended to call as witnesses. But I knew the names of two witnesses who wouldn't be testifying: Arnold Ginsberg because he was dead, and Robin Joiner because she was hiding, kidnapped, or possibly dead herself.

As much as I wanted to stay and watch the preliminary hearing, I was focused on a more important priority—becoming better acquainted with lawyer Gordon Dixon.

Chapter Twelve

Have you ever tried looking up the name of a lawyer in the yellow pages of the phone book? In a small community, that's probably exactly what you should do. But in a big city, like Salt Lake City, it's an exercise in futility. Gordon Dixon wasn't in the yellow pages. I know because I spent the better part of half-an-hour standing at a public counter in the district court clerk's office scouring the pages trying to find him, growing more and more frustrated by the minute. I used my cell phone and called the Salt Lake County Lawyer Referral service. Nothing there either.

In the end I was left with two less than magnanimous thoughts. The first was that in any large city the yellow pages were a living testimonial to the excessive number of graduates being produced by American law schools. The second was that there was more than one way to locate a missing lawyer.

I left the court house and drove a few short blocks to the Utah Secretary of State's Office. In the business licensing division I discovered an LLC registered to Gordon Dixon & Associates, 5140 South Main Street, Murray, Utah. The only other member of the LLC was an individual identified as Joan Dixon. Maybe Joan Dixon was Mrs. Gordon Dixon. Maybe Joan Dixon was the same woman I saw seated at the defense table next to the defendant and Gordon Dixon. I drove to the Murray office for a look-see.

Dixon's office was located in an older one-story brick building that, at one time, must have been a bank. One side of the building had a covered canopy with a drive-through window.

The bank had obviously moved on to fancier digs. Dixon shared the building with a title insurance company. The outside sign simply read Law Office.

When I entered the lobby it became clear that the title company occupied most of the building. Dixon's law practice leased space only slightly larger than a broom closet. The lights were off and the curtains drawn. I peeked in through the glass door. The space consisted of a small secretarial area and an equally small private office behind that. If Dixon had any associates they weren't working here. This place had the feeling of a small mom-and-pop store front kind of law practice.

I approached the receptionist at the title company. Her work station looked across the lobby into Dixon's office. She looked up from her computer screen and smiled. "Good morning, sir. How can I help you?"

Not wanting to arouse suspicion, I introduced myself as someone needing legal assistance. "Good morning. I'm looking for Mr. Dixon. Have you seen him today?"

"They were in early this morning but the office has been closed since around noon. I don't know where they are."

"Maybe you can help me," I said. I gave her my most embarrassed look. "I was arrested a couple of nights ago for DUI. A friend recommended that I ask Mr. Dixon to represent me. It's just that I don't know much about him."

The friendly smile disappeared. Suddenly she was looking at me like I was the local pedophile who had just moved into her zip code. "I really don't know anything about Mr. Dixon's law practice." Her tone had grown markedly cooler.

"Does his office seem busy—that's usually a sign of a good lawyer?"

"It never seems busy to me. In fact, some days I never see anybody go in. I wonder how they make the rent."

I wondered that, too.

"I take it Mr. Dixon doesn't own the building," I said.

"No. My boss, the man who owns the title company also owns the building. Mr. Dixon leases space from him." I thanked her and left.

◇◇◇

From Dixon's office, I drove to the University of Utah campus. I wanted to find out as much about Robin Joiner as I could and figured that university records would be a good place to start. If Joiner was alive, she was either being held by the Bradshaw's or she was hiding somewhere. The nagging question I kept asking myself was why Joiner hadn't contacted authorities. Family members would be a good starting place although if she was frightened, she probably wouldn't go home—too obvious a place for somebody to find her.

My first stop was the Registrar's Office in the administration building. I tried to convince the associate registrar that I was doing routine follow up on a missing person's case. She didn't buy it. I got the answer I expected—no subpoena, no academic records, no matter how routine the investigation sounded. That sent me immediately to Plan B.

I headed off to the social and behavioral sciences building where I contacted one of my former criminology professors. Dr. Richard Bond was an academic mentor from whom I had taken classes twenty years ago. He was now the chairman of the Sociology Department, a position he had held for the past half dozen years. It was late in the afternoon when I caught up with him. Bond was working alone in his office, the department secretary apparently gone for the day. When I tapped on his office door, he glanced up from his computer screen and looked at me over the top of wire-rimmed glasses perched precariously on the end of his nose.

"Well, if it isn't Sam Kincaid," he said, smiling. He stood and extended a hand. "Come in and sit down." We chatted about careers and family for a few minutes before he brought the conversation back to the business at hand. "It's awfully nice to see you, Sam, but I suspect your visit today is a bit more than a social call. Am I correct?"

"It is, Doc. I need your help tracking down a student." I explained what I needed and why.

"I take it you're on my door step because you don't have a subpoena and the Registrar's Office turned you away."

"You haven't lost a step, Doc." That brought a smile.

"Okay, let's see what we can find." He closed the file he was working on, opened another, plugged in Joiner's name, and the records appeared. "It's amazing the amount of information that's available with a couple of key strokes. I've been here long enough to remember the old days when everything was a paper file. Not anymore. Like a lot of other businesses, higher ed has gone paperless," he said. "I'm not sure what you're looking for, Sam, and I'm not going to make you hard copies, so why don't you just write down what you need."

The records search produced what Joiner had listed as a home address in Mesquite, Nevada, a small gaming town an hour north of Las Vegas. She'd listed her mother, Betty Joiner, at the Mesquite address, as the person to contact in case of an emergency. Joiner already held a bachelor's degree in social work from the university and was currently enrolled in the Graduate School of Social Work in pursuit of a master's degree. The local address was the same apartment near the university that had been broken into and trashed. I wondered what brought Joiner to Utah. I didn't see a local connection.

"Can you pull up her current class schedule and maybe the name of her academic advisor?"

In seconds I had her class schedule—three grad courses, all in social work. "I can't help you on the academic advisor. We don't put that information into the records system. You'll need to get that directly from somebody in social work."

"Fair enough. You've been a great help."

"Glad to do it. And remember, Sam, always protect your sources. You didn't get those records from me." With that admonishment he ushered me out the door.

As I left the campus I drove past the social work building and into the adjacent parking lot where social work students would probably park. Kate had mentioned that Joiner drove an older Honda Civic. I found one with Nevada plates. It was registered to Joiner.

I walked around the car being careful not to touch anything. I was sure that Kate would want a forensics team to process the car for prints. She might even opt to leave the car in the parking lot and establish surveillance on it. The car had been broken into and searched. The front passenger window had been smashed and glass was scattered all over the front seat and on the ground next to the door. The glove box was open, and the visors above the windshield were pulled down. Whoever broke in was looking for something, but what?

<>‹›‹>

Kincaid wasn't the only person watching the Honda. Albert Bradshaw watched the gray Chevrolet Impala move slowly through the parking lot until it stopped a couple of stalls away from the Civic. The Impala had cop written all over it, and so did the guy who got out of it.

Bradshaw slid lower into the bucket seat of the stolen Dodge Neon and removed the nine millimeter Glock from the waste band of his pants. He reached under a towel on the passenger side floor board and placed the short barreled shotgun on the seat next to him. The cop didn't touch anything on the Honda but he looked it over carefully. When he finished, he looked around the parking lot, and for just an instant, Bradshaw was certain that their eyes locked. Bradshaw looked away and held his breath. In the next instant the guy was back in his car and talking on his police radio.

Bradshaw choked down a growing sense of panic. Had the cop made him? He couldn't afford to sit still and wait. What if the pig was on his radio calling for back up? He started the Neon and eased it out of the parking stall in the direction of the nearest exit. He drove slowly, watching through the rearview mirror to see if the Impala followed. Albert had made one decision: If the cop tried to follow him, the cop was a dead man. At first, the Impala didn't move and Albert started to relax. When he looked a second time, the Impala was moving.

<><><>

Ever have that feeling that someone or something is watching you? That's how I felt standing outside the Honda. I glanced around, and, at first, I didn't see anything. Then, for just a second, my eyes locked on somebody who was looking in my direction. The guy was sitting alone in what looked like a late model Dodge or Plymouth Neon.

I walked casually back to my car and reached for the radio. I'd decided to call for backup. I no sooner had the radio in-hand, when the white Neon began to move. It was too far for my middle-aged eyes to make out the plate number or to get much of a look at the driver.

At first, the Neon moved slowly, but as soon as I began to follow, the driver punched it. He raced through the lot, narrowly missing a group of students who had just unloaded from a university bus and were scattering to their respective cars. By the time I dodged the pedestrian traffic, the Neon had opened a good sized lead. The driver burst through a red light on Foothill Boulevard, causing a big SUV to lock its brakes and spin sideways in the intersection. The Neon almost struck a city bus as it sped southbound on Foothill.

Foothill Boulevard is a busy, four-lane road that runs through a neighborhood with a mix of residential and light business. Most of the retail stores are confined to strip malls. It quickly became apparent that my only hope of catching this guy was to drive him into other units that had been dispatched as backup. Within minutes, I had hooked up with two Salt Lake P.D. patrol cars and one from the sheriff's department. Unfortunately, the mystery man had done a vanishing act.

In no time, the area was crawling with cops. Kate showed, and so did her partner, Detective Vince Turner. It took almost a half hour before one of the patrol cars discovered the abandoned

Neon on a residential street two blocks west of Foothill behind a large strip mall.

I got to the Neon a couple of minutes ahead of Kate. This was definitely the vehicle I'd seen in the U parking lot. Up close, it looked like it had recently been repainted by one of those companies that advertises paint jobs on the cheap.

The patrolman who found the Neon told me that the license plates were registered to a 2003 Ford Taurus belonging to a couple in Provo. The plates hadn't been reported stolen. When I looked inside, I saw a sawed off shotgun lying on the passenger front seat. I suggested that he run the Neon's VIN number through NCIC. The car came back stolen from a West Valley City shopping mall nearly a month ago.

When Kate arrived, she immediately organized a thorough search of the area around where the car was discovered. As I stood visiting with Vince Turner, Kate came up beside me and gave my arm a squeeze. "I hope you realize that you cause a lot of work for my department," she said, smiling.

"Well, at least for the crime lab guys," I said.

"I've got a team responding here right now, and when they're finished, they'll head over to the U and process Joiner's car. In the meantime, the University of Utah Police agreed to have somebody watch her car until we can get back there. You think we ought to tow the Honda or leave it out as bait?"

"That depends on whether you want to commit the time and resources to put the car under surveillance. Whoever I just ran off sure as hell won't be back."

"If I was a betting woman, and I'm not, I'd give you odds that the prints we're going to find on this car and on Joiner's will match somebody from the Bradshaw family."

"I suspect you're right. They might have taken the time to wipe down Joiner's car after breaking in, but not this guy. You can bet that he bailed out of here in a hurry."

A search of the area failed to turn up a suspect. It didn't help that I couldn't provide much of a description. All I could say for sure was that the guy was a white, male, with dark hair, and probably under forty. Not much to go on.

With some personnel from my unit, Kate and I agreed to place Joiner's Honda under surveillance for the next several nights. It was a gamble, and one that might prove a waste of time. If it was someone from the Bradshaw family I had just encountered, he wouldn't return. On the other hand, maybe Robin Joiner would.

Chapter Thirteen

It was after seven when Kate and I got home. Baxter Shaw's Lincoln Town Car was parked in the driveway. Aunt June had invited Baxter for dinner, and Kate and I were late as usual.

We found them in the great room sipping a glass of Merlot in front of a roaring fire. Fall in Utah is my favorite time of year. At seven thousand feet above sea level, the nights, while chilly, are more than offset by warm daytime temperatures, and the autumn colors are spectacular especially the aspens that change from green to bright golden hues. The magnificent colors are, of course, a harbinger of the cold, snowy months to follow.

It was too early to tell if their relationship had legs. They were taking things slow and easy, probably a generational thing. I thought they made a cute couple. Every time I mentioned that to Aunt June, she turned a shade of crimson and tried to kick me in the shins.

Kate leaned over the couch and gave Baxter a peck on the cheek. "Sorry we're late. I hope you went ahead and ate."

"We figured you might be late. It's hardly the first time. Baxter and I decided to enjoy our wine and wait for you kids," said Aunt June.

"If we could just get the bad guys to cooperate, we'd be home every night by five," I countered.

"I'm not going to hold my breath on that one," said Aunt June. "We went ahead and fed Sara. She was starving. I tell you that girl has a hollow leg."

I could tell they were enjoying the wine. The bottle was almost empty and Aunt June was acting giddy. Baxter was being his polite, reserved, southern self. We settled in the dining room to a good old-fashioned dinner of Aunt June's meatloaf, mashed potatoes and gravy, a pear salad, and green beans. We Kincaids come from a long line of basic meat and potatoes eaters—no fancy continental cuisine or French soufflé, thank you very much. I did have to admit that since Kate and I began seeing each other, she'd pushed my culinary boundaries to new levels.

Kate opened a second bottle of Merlot for the wine drinkers, and I grabbed a cold Corona from the refrigerator. Before long I could tell that the second bottle of wine was well on its way to extinction. "Kate," I said, "you should be ashamed of yourself—contributing to the delinquency of seniors like this." That brought a smile from Kate and a giggle from Aunt June.

Baxter grunted. "Perhaps someone should remind this young man to drink his beer and mind his own business." More tittering from Aunt June.

Sara joined us for dessert. I swear the kid can smell dessert a mile away. She has her Dad's sweet tooth. It was rewarded with hot French apple pie topped with, what else, French vanilla ice cream.

After dinner, Kate and I cleaned up while Aunt June and Baxter retired to the great room to cap the evening with a glass of port. I cleared the table while Kate rinsed and loaded the dishwasher. When I brought the last load of dishes into the kitchen, Kate was standing with her back to me rinsing the sink. I walked up behind her and wrapped my arms around her waist burying my face in the side of her neck. As I kissed her neck and cheek, she straightened and leaned back against me resting the back of her head on my shoulder. My hands caressed her breasts. She sighed. "I need a hug," I whispered.

"Oh, yeah. Judging from that thing that's poking me, I'd say that you need a little more than a hug."

"I think you're right."

She turned, put her arms around my neck, and we began a deep, slow kiss, one that might have lasted for a long time had

Sara not popped into the kitchen at that exact moment. "Daddy, you're kissing," she teased.

"And you're nosy," I said. "What do you need, baby?"

"Would you help me with my home-work?" I spent the next few minutes helping Sara with her math assignment. It wasn't going to be long before my limited math literacy would render me useless in helping her—math tutor here we come. Tonight Sara settled into bed, without a fuss, and fell asleep quickly.

Kate had joined Baxter and Aunt June in the great room. The discussion quickly turned to my impending child custody hearing in Atlanta.

Baxter said, "Sam, your Aunt June was telling me earlier today about the problem with Sara. While I don't want to pry into your affairs, I think I can help you with this."

"Any help would be greatly appreciated," I replied.

"Before I moved to Utah, I had business interests all over the southeast including Georgia. When I heard about your problem, I took the liberty of calling the law firm in Atlanta that handled my business affairs." He paused and reached into the pocket of his sports coat and produced a piece of paper with a name and phone number on it.

"Go on," I said.

He handed me the slip of paper. "My old law firm put me in touch with this lady. They assured me that her reputation as a family law attorney in the Atlanta area is second to none. In fact, and pardon my language, they described Ms. Kittridge as a real ball-buster. She called me back late this afternoon and we had a delightful conversation. I think you should call her."

I thanked Baxter and promised to call Allison Kittridge the next day. "And don't forget to call Jim Reilly tomorrow, too. He's expecting your call," said Kate.

It was getting late and everybody was tired. We offered Baxter the guest bedroom but he declined. After he left, Aunt June bid us good night and toddled down the hall to her bedroom.

I checked on Sara and then Kate and I retired to my bedroom. We made love for a long time and then fell asleep tangled in each others arms. I woke early. It was a little after five. Kate was gone. She left a note on her pillow thanking me for a nice evening and promising to catch up later in the day. Until now, we had been cautious about sleep-overs. While Kate and Sara had grown close, I wasn't sure whether Sara was ready to find a woman in bed with her dad.

I got up quietly, dressed, left a note for Aunt June on the kitchen chalkboard, and headed to my office at the prison. Since the new executive director had arrived, I'd been spending less and less time in my office at department headquarters and more time in my office at the prison. I'm not sure why—out of sight, out of mind perhaps.

Chapter Fourteen

As soon as I arrived at the office, I called Patti in. "I want you to dig around and find anything you can about Walter Bradshaw's lawyer. The guy's name is Gordon Dixon. And while you're at it, also run the name Joan Dixon." I gave her the LLC information I'd received the previous day at the Secretary of State's office.

"What kind of information are you looking for?"

"I'm fishing. Anything you can find. Why don't you start by doing a Google search? Then run them through the public record sites. See if they own property in Utah."

"I'll get right on it. You want me to run them through NCIC and UBCI?"

"Absolutely."

"By the way, what did you find out about Robin Joiner?" I asked.

"It's exactly what you suspected. None of the newspapers knew about her, same for the television stations."

"You mean they didn't even know that she was a witness," I said, sounding incredulous.

"That's exactly what I mean. None of them talked to her because they didn't know anything about her. I pulled as many newspaper articles as I could find, and Robin Joiner isn't mentioned anywhere. That's not true of Arnold Ginsberg. He was interviewed on television and his name was mentioned by nearly every print source—something of an instant media celebrity, I'd say."

That gave me pause for reflection. If Joiner wasn't on the radar screen of any media sources, why would Walter Bradshaw have described her as "that beautiful, young woman." How would he have known?

I gave Patti a copy of the information I'd received from Dr. Richard Bond at the university the previous day. "The mother's name is Betty Joiner. See if you can find a home phone number for her. And then run a criminal history check on Robin. Assuming she grew up in Nevada, there could be a juvenile history. I know the juvie record might be hard to get, but see what you can do. If necessary, I'll call a friend in the Nevada Department of Corrections who can help us."

<>< ><>

Robin Joiner woke early, feeling decidedly anxious. This had been her second night in the motel and it no longer felt safe. She knew it was time to move before somebody figured out where she was.

She dialed the number again, and for the umpteenth time, she got no answer. She had been trying to reach Tracy Sanders, a member of her study group at school, and her closest friend. But Tracy wasn't answering, and she was hesitant to leave a message. Tracy had a boyfriend and often spent nights at his house, but she didn't have that number. She'd even called the Outback Steakhouse where Tracy worked as a hostess, only to discover that she wasn't scheduled to work that night.

Her next best option was to call another member of the study group. His name was Michael Baker. Michael clearly had the hots for her. He would help her, she was sure of it. Unfortunately, she didn't have the same feelings for him. And she didn't understand why. He was cute, smart, and a really nice guy. Maybe that was the problem. Sadly, she had never been attracted to nice guys who treated her well. Instead, she had always been attracted to the bad boys, several of whom had left her with bruises to prove it.

Baker answered on the second ring. "Michael, this is Robin. I'm in trouble, and I need your help."

He didn't hesitate. "Anything, Rob, what do you need?"

"I need you to do me a big favor and not ask me any questions about it."

He paused. "Okay. What's the favor?"

"I need you to pick up my car in the U parking lot, and then meet me someplace so that I can get it from you."

"What about the key?"

"You'll find a spare in one of those magnetic key holders above the driver's side front tire. How soon do you think you can get it for me?"

"How about right now?" he said. "Where do you want me to meet you?"

"You're really sweet. Why don't I call your cell, in say, two hours? That should give you time to pick it up, and then we can arrange a place to meet."

"Sounds kind of mysterious to me. You sure you're okay?"

"I'm okay. I'll call you in two hours."

◇◇◇

A few minutes after nine, I was headed back to the University of Utah. If we were going to find Robin Joiner, one approach was to contact teachers and as many of her student friends as possible. I started at the Graduate School of Social Work. Joiner's class schedule showed three social work courses, two of them taught by the same professor. I found Dr. Joyce Barrows working on her computer in an office filled with enough clutter to make my clutter insignificant by comparison.

Her mild curiosity changed to concern when I explained that Joiner was missing. Barrows was helpful. As Joiner's academic advisor, she was able to supply me with the names of several grad students who were part of a study group Joiner belonged to. "All of those students, Detective Kincaid, are enrolled in my class this evening. You're welcome to stop by when the class starts at four-thirty and talk to them."

I told her I would do that. "Dr. Barrows, has Robin contacted you in the last day or so?"

"As a matter of fact, I found a voice message from her when I came into the office this morning. Would you like to listen to it?"

The message from Joiner explained that she would miss her classes this week as the result of what she described as a family problem in Nevada. The implication was that she'd already departed for Nevada and might be gone for a few days. That I suspected was a ruse.

I thanked Dr. Barrows for her help and headed across campus to the Sociology Department in the hope that I might catch Richard Bond in his office. While Dr. Barrows had provided me with the names of Robin Joiner's study group, she hadn't offered to dig into student records and provide me with home addresses and telephone numbers. Bond, I was certain, would. Time mattered, and I saw no point in waiting until four-thirty in the afternoon to interview Joiner's friends. When I arrived, Bond's secretary informed me that he was teaching a class and would not be available until late in the morning. I left her my cell number and asked that he call me.

Once in a great while, a purely fortuitous event helps to break a case. For reasons I can't explain, I decided to leave the campus by driving past Robin Joiner's Honda. When I got within eyeshot of the car, I observed a young man kneeling next to the front tire. He didn't look familiar to me. I couldn't place him as a member of the Bradshaw family, but I wasn't about to take any chances. In seconds, I had him spread-eagled over the hood of Joiner's car.

He was scared and it showed. "What the hell is this all about, man? I haven't done anything," he said, his legs splayed out behind him, and his cheek resting uncomfortably on the hood of the Honda.

"Maybe not," I replied, "but what are you doing messing around this car? It doesn't belong to you." After I completed the frisk, I stood him up and demanded to see identification. His name was Michael Baker, the same Michael Baker whose name I had just been given by Dr. Barrows. He was a member of Robin Joiner's study group.

Frightened as he was, Baker summoned the courage to look me in the eye and state, "I don't have to tell you anything. I know my rights."

"You might know your rights, but you've just managed to put yourself in the middle of a murder investigation, and unless you answer my questions right now, you may find yourself with a one-way ticket to the Salt Lake County Jail on an Obstruction beef."

That seemed to get his attention. The bravado disappeared. He took a more conciliatory tone, and so did I. "Look, Michael, if you're really concerned about Robin's welfare, the best thing you can do is to help us find her. She's missing, and we believe that her life is in danger. Did she ask you to come and get the car?"

He paused and looked away, probably trying to decide whether or not to cooperate. "What kind of trouble is she in?"

"You may not know this, but Robin was a witness in a murder, armed robbery case that went down a couple of months ago. She's gone missing, and somebody's broken into her apartment and, as you can see, her car. We don't know where she is or why she hasn't contacted us. We just hope the bad guys don't know either."

He was still unconvinced.

"The night before last, a guy named Arnold Ginsberg was murdered in downtown Salt Lake City. Did you hear about it on the news?" He nodded.

"Besides Robin, Mr. Ginsberg was the only other witness in the case. Now, he's dead, and Robin is missing. We're afraid she's next, and I think you can help us find her. Do that for her sake so that she doesn't end up like Ginsberg."

He relented. "Okay. Robin called me a little while ago and asked me to get the car for her." He glanced at his watch. "She's supposed to call me back in about an hour and fifteen minutes, and then we're supposed to meet someplace."

"Did she tell you where?"

He shook his head. "She acted pretty paranoid about the whole thing. Now I guess I understand why. She said we'd figure out a place to meet when she called back."

"Where did she call from, do you know?"

He shook his head again. "She didn't say and the number was blocked."

"This is what I need you to do, Michael. When she calls, tell her you've got the car and set up the meeting. I'll go with you, and we'll bring her in together."

He considered this but only for a moment. "I won't do it. I won't deceive her like that, I just can't."

"Christ, Michael, how are you going to feel if you don't help us find her, and she ends up dead like Arnold Ginsberg? Can you live with that?"

He thought some more and then proposed a compromise. "What if, when she calls, I try to talk her into coming in? I'll even let you talk to her."

It wasn't what I wanted, but it was the best deal I was going to get, so I agreed.

Chapter Fifteen

An hour later, Michael Baker, Kate, and I were sequestered in McConnell's office when Baker's cell phone rang. We could only hear one side of the conversation, but he looked decidedly uncomfortable, and his voice sounded strained.

"Hello. Hi, Rob. I need you to listen to me. I got stopped by the cops trying to get your car. I know what's going on, and I'm worried about you. The cops are too. No, I'm not under arrest. I'm okay. But I think you need to let us come and get you. It's the only way you'll be safe." He talked in a whisper, and we could barely hear him.

There was a long pause during which Baker listened. "Hold on, don't hang up. I want you to talk to this detective. I think you can trust him."

He handed me the phone. "Hi, Robin, my name is Sam Kincaid, and I'm a police officer. We've been trying to find you for a couple of days. We have good reason to believe that your life is in danger, and we can't protect you if you don't come in."

Silence. "Like you protected Arnold Ginsberg," she finally said.

She had a point. "Listen to me for a moment. We didn't know you or Ginsberg were in danger until after he was killed. We've been looking for you ever since."

"What makes you so sure that I am in danger?"

"Besides Ginsberg's murder, your apartment has been broken into and tossed—same for your car. Somebody was sitting in the U parking lot yesterday watching your Honda. I know that because I ran him off, but the guy got away. He was driving a stolen car and left a sawed off shotgun on the front seat as a calling card. I think you're in real danger, Robin, and I think these guys play for keeps."

When she didn't respond, I continued.

"We have to assume that Walter Bradshaw's gang of crackpots is behind this, unless you can tell us something different. Is there anyone you can think of who might be stalking you—angry boyfriend, ex-husband, anything like that?"

"No, and I want you to leave me the hell alone. I want you to stop meddling in my life. I haven't asked for your help, and I don't want it. Am I making myself clear?"

She sounded rational and relatively unemotional. "Perfectly, but I'm afraid we can't do that, Robin. You're a material witness in a murder and armed robbery case. You've got to come in, or we have to keep looking for you. It's that simple."

"It's never that simple."

"Tell me something, Robin. What are these guys looking for? They've searched your apartment and your car—they're looking for something. And I think you know what that something is."

That pissed her off. "Up yours, you son of a bitch. Leave me alone, and I mean it," she shouted into the phone. And then she hung up. So much for rational and unemotional behavior I thought.

"What did she have to say?" asked Kate.

"Other than an unflattering reference to my family lineage, very little, I'm afraid."

We sent Michael Baker on his merry way with a promise that he would contact Kate or me if he heard from Joiner again, something I thought highly unlikely. She probably felt betrayed by his cooperation with us. I didn't bother to tell him that I'd be waiting for him at the start of his class later in the afternoon. I wanted to interview the rest of Joiner's study group. And, I thought, why spoil a nice surprise?

After he left, I gave Kate my impressions of the abbreviated telephone conversation I'd had with Joiner. "Two things stood out. The first was how freaked out she became when I asked her if she knew what these guys were looking for when they broke into her apartment and her car."

"What do you make of that?" said Kate.

"I can't be sure, but I think she's hiding something. I just don't know what it is or why she's doing it. What I can tell you is that she didn't want to talk about it. The other thing is that it seemed that when she asked if I really thought she was in danger, she was fishing for information."

"You mean she was trying to get you to provide her with information that she didn't already know."

"Yeah, it seemed like that."

"Well," said Kate, "nothing's changed. All we can do is continue to try to find her and hope, in the meantime, that she changes her mind and comes in on her own. Now, let me bring you up to speed on a couple of things you don't know."

"Good news, I hope."

"Absolutely. I just heard from the crime lab on the suspected murder weapons. We came up empty on the tire iron, but on the knife, we've got a partial thumb print. They found it on the handle. It's not complete, but they tell me it is sufficient for comparison. I've asked them to run the partial against Bradshaw's fugitive family members."

"And that would include…"

"Both of Walter's sons, Albert and Joseph, as well as the two cousins, Randy and Robby Allred."

"That is good news. Has the lab confirmed the tire iron and knife as the actual murder weapons?"

"Blood samples from both weapons match the vic's blood type. The DNA test results won't be available to confirm it for at least another week, but we're ninety-nine percent sure we've got the murder weapons. They're a close match to what the medical examiner told us to be looking for."

"What about the vic's car and wallet?"

"Nothing yet, but guess what? Joseph Bradshaw and Randy Allred left their fingerprints all over Joiner's apartment. Joseph's were also found on the handwritten note left in the apartment."

"No big surprise, I guess. Just what these guys need—more new criminal charges," I said. "That certainly removes any doubt about who's trying to find her."

◇◇◇

"Come on," I said to Kate. "We've got a lunch date downtown and we're supposed to be there in ten minutes."

That was news to her. As it turned out, the lunch date I'd arranged was with Jim Reilly, the family practice lawyer who had agreed to advise me on my pending child custody battle. Reilly had agreed to meet us between court appearances for lunch at Lamb's Café in downtown Salt Lake City. Lamb's was believed to be the oldest operating restaurant in Utah. It served consistently good food without having to take out a second mortgage on your home.

Reilly was a rotund, late thirties guy, sporting a mostly bald dome with a very bad comb-over. He wore a pair of khaki pants, a corduroy sport coat over a blue dress shirt with a red striped tie—professional looking but not expensive.

I thanked him for agreeing to meet us, and I offered to pay him his hourly rate.

"Not necessary," he said. "I'm happy to do it. But I'll tell you what. You can buy my lunch, how's that?"

"You're a cheap date," I said.

He laughed. "You don't know the half of it. Here's what I think you should expect. And please understand that procedurally, things can vary from state to state. First thing I would advise is to retain a reputable family practice attorney in Atlanta."

"I think we got a handle on that one," said Kate.

"Good. Next, you'll need to be prepared for a court-ordered evaluation of your home and that of your ex-wife. I can assure you that the judge will insist on that. It goes directly to the issue the court is going to be most concerned about, and that is, which family can best provide for the needs of your daughter."

"Tell me how this home evaluation works," I said. "Does the judge assign a social worker to visit both homes?"

"The court can order its own evaluation, but that's not typically how it works. What usually happens is that each side hires its own person to conduct the evaluation unless the two sides can agree on a single individual."

"I would think that a judge would prefer a single person to do the home studies," said Kate.

"You're right about that. Courts generally prefer one qualified therapist to evaluate both homes. In this case, it's probably best to follow the advice of your Atlanta lawyer. If we had jurisdiction here, I'm reasonably confident that I'd be able to find one person to evaluate both homes. But often it depends upon factors such as the level of acrimony between the parents, who the lawyers are, those sorts of things."

"What about jurisdiction?" I asked. "Is there any chance we could get the case transferred to Utah?"

"None. Jurisdiction is determined by where the divorce occurred. Kate told me that your ex filed in Georgia, so that's where the jurisdiction remains—nothing you can do about that."

"Any land mines I need to be watching for, Jim?"

"There's one, and it's important. In child custody cases, a sure fire way of alienating the judge is for either parent to get caught trying to pressure or manipulate the child into saying that he wants to live with one parent over the other. Remember, we're not talking about a jury decision here. The judge makes the call, and if the judge is pissed at you, you might end up with an outcome you don't like."

"That's a sobering thought," I said.

"It is. Even if you discover that your ex is engaged in that kind behavior, don't you do it. Just make sure the judge hears about what she's doing. It won't help her case, I can assure you of that.

"Well, I'm due in court in exactly fifteen minutes." He stood and extended his hand. "Nice meeting you, Sam. If you think of any other questions, and you probably will, don't hesitate to call." As he walked past Kate, Reilly leaned down and gave her a smile and a peck on the cheek.

I resisted the growing sense of panic I felt deep in the pit of my stomach. I wanted Reilly to reassure me that everything would be alright—that I wouldn't lose custody of my daughter, but I knew he couldn't do that. Nobody could. The mere thought of seeing Sara torn from our lives by a juvenile court judge halfway across the country who didn't know our family and who didn't know Sara, was almost to painful to contemplate. It made me feel vulnerable, it made me feel powerless, and it made me feel angry.

Chapter Sixteen

When we left Lamb's Café, Kate and I parted company. We planned to meet later for dinner at a new place somebody in her office recommended. When it comes to restaurants, I have to admit to being a creature of habit. Once I find one I like, I'll eat there over and over again. Kate, on the other hand, is always on the look-out for a new and different dining experience. Slowly, and by sheer force of will, she has been expanding my culinary experiences.

I had a late afternoon date at the university with the rest of Robin Joiner's study group although they didn't know it. That left me with just enough time for a stop at the Utah State Bar Association office near downtown. The Bar's Office of Professional Conduct was responsible for investigating allegations of lawyer misconduct and meeting out disciplinary action when appropriate.

I checked my cell and noticed that I had a new voicemail message. It was Patti, asking me to call her. She answered on the first ring.

"Hi, Patti. What's up?"

"Regarding Robin Joiner—no adult record whatsoever. She was arrested twice in Las Vegas as a juvenile, both misdemeanors, one for minor in possession of alcohol; the other was a marijuana possession charge. She received fines and community service in both cases. She was never formally supervised by Nevada youth corrections."

"Nothing very unusual about any of that," I said.

"There's more. The juvenile court referred me to a caseworker in the child welfare department. It seems that all was not well in the Joiner home. Her father has never been in the picture. The mother, Betty, is a recovering drug addict, apparently in and out of treatment programs multiple times over the years. Anyway, she's supposed to be clean now and working as a Black Jack dealer in a Mesquite casino. Robin has a long history of foster home placements. The records show that she was a reported runaway on three different occasions."

"Sounds like a difficult childhood," I said. "Have you been able to locate the mother?"

"The address you got from the university records seems to be the current one. I found a phone number at that address listed under the name, B. Joiner. I called. It's a working number. I didn't leave a message—figured you'd want to do that."

"Thanks, Patti. I'll follow up with a phone call when I get back to the office. Anything yet on Bradshaw's lawyer, Gordon Dixon?"

"I'm workin on it. I should have something for you shortly."

"Call me when you do."

〈〉〈〉〈〉

I parked in the Bar Association's underground parking terrace and took the elevator up one floor to the public reception area. I suspected that the Utah Bar Association would be about as accessible as CIA headquarters or perhaps Fort Knox. Trying to get information about misbehaving lawyers was always a challenge. Fortunately, I had a contact but not one I called on often.

I signed in, received a visitor's badge, and was ushered into the office of Melissa Miller. I had known Miller for nearly fifteen years. She came into the Salt Lake County District Attorney's Office a short time after I began my career in the corrections department. After several years of prosecuting bad guys, she accepted a position with the Bar Association prosecuting naughty lawyers whose behaviors ranged from ethics violations to outright criminal conduct.

Miller had been my only misadventure in the weeks after the breakup of my marriage to Nicole. She was between boyfriends, and I was trying to adjust to the notion of being single again after eleven years of marriage. Our encounter was a disaster. We ran into each other in a downtown Salt Lake City nightclub frequented by cops and lawyers. Long story short, after too many drinks, we ended up at her place in the sack. I couldn't get it up. She took it personally and was seriously pissed. After that, we avoided each other for months.

In time, things became more comfortable. She remarried, and I adjusted to life as a single parent, avoiding the dating scene almost completely. That finally changed when fate brought Kate and me together.

Miller came around her desk and gave me a smile and a polite hug. She invited me to sit while she closed her office door. "Gosh, Sam, what's it been, almost a year?"

"All of that, Melissa. How's the newlywed?"

"Couldn't be happier. He's a real sweetheart—works in the public defender's office. Thanks for asking. What brings you to see me today, Sam?"

"Business, I'm afraid."

"God, not another lawyer trying to smuggle dope into the prison for one of his clients, I hope."

"Not this time," I said. "No dope or guns, but I might have one who's passing gang information into and out of the prison. What can you tell me about a lawyer by the name of Gordon Dixon?"

"Is this the guy I read about in the newspaper who represents the Mormon fundamentalist, Walter Bradshaw?"

"One and the same," I said.

She turned to her computer screen and inputted his name. "Okay. Well, our records show that he graduated from the University of Arizona Law School ten years ago, passed the Arizona State Bar exam one year later, and ran a solo practice in Flagstaff for the next five years. He passed the Utah Bar three and a half years ago and opened another solo practice with an office in Murray. This shows that his license is still active in Arizona."

"Any disciplinary record or complaints about the guy?"

She paused. "There is something." She made a couple of additional key strokes and switched to a different screen. "Our records show that Mr. Dixon was arrested for Disorderly Conduct in Tucson while an undergraduate student at the University of Arizona. It seems he was forcibly removed from a lecture hall after continually interrupting a speaker who had been invited to campus to discuss the sexual abuse of young girls living in polygamist communities along the Arizona Strip."

"That might explain his interest in providing legal representation to the leader of a Mormon fundamentalist group that just happens to practice polygamy," I said.

Miller was still reading something from her computer screen. "We've had two minor complaints about him since he came to Utah. In one, a client complained that Dixon failed to return a small amount of money from a retainer. He eventually did. We gave him a letter of reprimand on that one. In the other case, a client claimed that he failed to complete legal work after she'd paid him. He denied the allegation, kissed and made up with her, and she subsequently withdrew the complaint. That's all we've got."

"You've been more than helpful, Melissa. I can't thank you enough." At that moment, my cell phone rang. It was Patti calling with information about Gordon Dixon.

"Yeah, Patti. What have you got for me?"

"Something I think you're going to find most interesting, two things, actually. Joan Dixon is actually Mrs. Gordon Dixon, but that's not the interesting part. The interesting part is that Joan Dixon's maiden name was Bradshaw. She's Walter Bradshaw's younger sister."

"Wow," I said. "That helps put some pieces of the puzzle into perspective."

"And that's not all," said Patti. "Gordon, through his LLC, holds the deed of trust to nearly two hundred acres of land in the desert of southern Utah off Highway 89, somewhere between Kanab and a little town called Big Water. I guess I'm not familiar with Big Water."

"It's a small town just north of Lake Powell that used to be the stronghold of another polygamist sect that was headed by Alex Joseph. He's been dead a while."

I left the Utah Bar Association feeling that I now had a better understanding of exactly how Gordon Dixon fit into the picture. Dixon was the front guy, the legal mouthpiece who handled the church's legal and business affairs. I decided it was time to pay him a visit.

‹›‹›‹›

Robin Joiner had begun to feel a growing sense of desperation. The phone conversation with the cop, Kincaid was his name, had been disturbing. From him, she had learned that they had broken in to her apartment and her car. They were hunting for her, of that she was certain.

She was also concerned about the fact that the cops had apprehended Michael Baker while he was trying to retrieve her car. If she couldn't recover her car or go back to her apartment, what was she to do? Calling home to her dear mother wasn't a good option. Not only was her mother unreliable, but maybe she was being watched. Since the cops had identified Michael, did they also know about Tracy Sanders and her other friends from the university study group? Even worse, if the cops had gotten this close to her, how far behind could the Bradshaws be?

Limited options or not, Joiner needed to make a move. And move she did. First, she checked out of the motel and caught the city bus, which took her closer to downtown. There she checked into another motel that turned out to be as big a dive as the one she'd just left. The new motel was located three blocks from the Outback Steakhouse where her best friend, Tracy Sanders, worked. Joiner called the restaurant and learned that Sanders was scheduled to work the lunch shift the following day from eleven until three-thirty. She would contact Sanders when she got off work the next day. In the meantime, she'd lay low in her new digs.

Chapter Seventeen

At four-thirty in the afternoon, I found myself wandering the halls of the Graduate School of Social Work looking for a third floor classroom. I'd spent enough time on the University of Utah campus over the past couple of days to begin feeling like I was back in school again.

I poked my head into room 322 at the same time Dr. Joyce Barrows looked up from her lecture notes and saw me standing in the doorway. She interrupted the class, and marched me and four students—Michael Baker and three females—to an empty classroom across the hall. Baker didn't seem overly pleased to see me again, especially so soon.

"Would you like me to join you, Detective Kincaid?" asked Barrows.

"Please do." She closed the door behind her. I didn't see any harm in her remaining, and perhaps her presence would engender a bit more cooperation from the members of Joiner's study group.

I explained briefly who I was and the purpose of my visit. I wondered if Baker had already done that for me.

I started with the obvious question: "Other than Michael, who received a phone call from Robin, have any of you heard from her during the past three days?"

Nobody had.

"Do any of you know where I might find her?"

Nobody did.

"Does Robin have any friends or relatives living locally who she might go to for help?"

Tracy Sanders spoke. "I don't think Rob has any family in Salt Lake. She doesn't have any brothers or sisters. Her Mother lives somewhere in Nevada. As for friends, I'm probably Rob's closest friend, and I haven't spoken with her since our study group meeting in the library three nights ago. I called her apartment a couple of times and left messages, but she never returned my calls."

Dr. Barrows interjected herself into the discussion. "Can any of you think of anything that might help Detective Kincaid locate Robin? It seems perfectly clear to me that she's in trouble, and we need to do everything we can to help the police find her."

"Wait a minute," said Sanders. "One time Robin stopped by my apartment to let me borrow her lecture notes from a class that I'd missed. She had a cute guy with her. I assumed he was her boyfriend."

"Do you recall his name?"

She paused. "Yeah, I think she introduced him as Joey, but I'm not positive."

"Is he a student here at the U?"

"I don't know. He didn't talk much, and Rob didn't say."

"Any idea about how I might be able to find him?"

"Sorry," said Sanders. "Rob never talked much about the guys in her life. The subject rarely came up, and when it did, she usually didn't have much to say."

Nobody else in the study group had ever met the guy.

I gave business cards to everybody and tried to convince them to contact me immediately if they heard from Joiner. I left the meeting with the distinct feeling that nobody would.

I hadn't learned much about Robin Joiner from the members of her study group. I sensed that she was a very private, young woman, even to the exclusion of close friends like Tracy Sanders. I wasn't sure what to do next, but contacting her mother in Mesquite, Nevada, seemed like a good next step.

⟨⟩⟨⟩⟨⟩

I left the university and hooked up with Kate at a restaurant on the edge of the Avenues District near downtown Salt Lake City. The place was called the East India Star, billed as the finest in traditional Indian cuisine. We had never tried it. Someone in the D.A.'s office had recommended it to Kate. I'd suggested the Black Angus Steakhouse, but, in the tug-of-war that followed, ended up agreeing to try the East India Star. The closest thing to Indian food I had ever eaten was fry bread and mutton stew on the Navaho reservation.

Dinner out actually served multiple purposes. It gave us a chance to decompress, enjoy some private time together, and in this instance, it gave us the opportunity to exchange theories about the case and organize the next steps. So far, we'd been following leads largely independent of each another, and I was beginning to feel disorganized, never a good thing in a homicide case. My old mentor who had run the SIB for years prior to my taking over had an old saying mounted on his office wall that read, "If you don't know where you're going, any road will take you there." He was adamant that being disorganized was exactly how not to run any kind of an investigation.

Kate was already seated when I arrived. She was sipping a class of red wine, probably a Cab, and perusing the restaurant menu. It was early, and the place hadn't begun to fill.

"You look a little pensive," I said. It was then that I noticed the empty wine glass sitting next to her on the table. The glass she was sipping from now was her second.

"I'm a little perplexed, actually."

"And why is that?"

"Just before I left the office, I got a call from the crime lab. It seems that our partial thumb print doesn't match any of the suspects. Go figure."

"You mean that among the Allred cousins and Joseph and Albert Bradshaw, you didn't get a print match."

"That's what I'm telling you. I thought it was a slam dunk. We've got one dead witness and a second on the run. In Joiner's apartment, we've got prints from Randy Allred and Joseph Bradshaw plastered everywhere. Albert Bradshaw's prints were all over the shotgun and the stolen Neon. How could one of them not be the killer?"

"Yeah. I'd have given odds that the print would have matched one of them. But here's something to think about. Nobody knows for sure how many members belong to the Reformed Church of the Divine Christ."

"True," said Kate.

"We know that Walter is the self-proclaimed prophet along with his two sons and the Allred cousins. That leaves Walter's wife and Albert's two wives. As far as we know, the other son, Joseph, and Robby and Randy Allred, don't have wives. But there could be other members of the church that law enforcement intelligence hasn't identified."

"You're saying that maybe the killers belong to the church but just haven't showed up on anybody's radar screen."

"Exactly."

"Possible, I guess. Frankly, I'm not sure what to think," said Kate.

"Are you having the print run through the Automated Fingerprint Identification System?"

"Yeah, they're checking AFIS locally and statewide. If we don't get a hit on that, we'll submit to the FBI in Virginia and run the print through the national database."

"What else have you found?"

"I canvassed the neighborhood. Nothing unusual from the neighbors concerning the vic's relationship with Rodney Plow. No fights, disturbances, rumors, nothing."

"And his alibi."

"It checked out. I back-tracked his movements, and he went everyplace he said he did—his timeline was accurate, too."

"What other leads have you got?"

"I found a message late this afternoon from Ginsberg's secretary. She said she's got something important to tell me, but she didn't want to go into it on the phone. She was gone by the time

I called her back. I plan to go see her first thing in the morning. Want to come along?"

"Probably, but let me see what I've got going in the morning. Is there anything else?"

"Yeah, there's the adultery angle. I've got an appointment tomorrow with the attorney handling Ginsberg's estate. We need to figure out who stood to gain financially from Arnold's death. In particular, I want to know if Rodney has been provided for, and if so, for how much."

"You're going to need a warrant."

"Maybe. The attorney is a guy. I'll try to charm the information out of him. It saves time and it's worked before. I can always go get a warrant."

I was grinning.

"What?" she said.

"You could charm that information off of me, right along with my jockeys, without a warrant." I quipped.

"Pervert."

I sighed. "I know."

I let Kate order dinner for both of us. The menu at the East India Star might as well have been printed in Greek. My only request was that she order something with meat, lamb excluded, something that wouldn't require me to wash it down with a bottle of Tums. Fortunately, I was able to comprehend the imported beer list. Two Coronas later, dinner was served.

We ate in silence, which was fine with both of us. My chicken was okay. It had been prepared in some kind of yellowish sauce that tasted mildly like ginger. The flavor seemed foreign to me (no pun intended) but all-in-all I judged it a passable meal. For desert, we opted for two skinny vanilla lattes.

Over the lattes, Kate said, "You've just experienced a first, Sam. How did you like the Indian food?"

I looked at her for a moment. "Well, Kate, I'd say the meal was average, but at least it was expensive. What did you think?"

She blinked. "What?" Slowly her face broke into a smile, and she delivered a sharp elbow to my ribcage.

"Actually, I didn't think the food was too great either. We'll scratch this place off our preferred dining list."

"What did you learn this afternoon from Joiner's study group?"

"Not a hell of a lot. She's got no siblings, few close friends, no contact with her father, and a mother with a long drug history who works for one of the casinos in Mesquite. Oh, and a possible boyfriend named Joey that nobody knows anything about."

"God, that's helpful," said Kate. A moment passed. "What was the boyfriend's name again?"

"Joey." Then it hit me. "Joey, as in Joseph."

We looked at each other without speaking before Kate said, "Are you thinking what I'm thinking?"

"Yeah, seems like a helleva long shot though, don't you think?"

"Absolutely, but let's check it out?"

"No question. One of the study group members, a Tracy Sanders, met this Joey. I'll pull Joseph Bradshaw's mug shot and show it to her. We'll see if she can identify him."

"While you're at it," said Kate, "drop by Joiner's apartment complex and show Bradshaw's photo to the apartment manager. She met a boyfriend, too. Wouldn't it be interesting if it turns out to be yours truly, Joseph Bradshaw? Think of the possible implications of that."

Chapter Eighteen

By the time I made it home, Aunt June had finally managed to get Sara to go to sleep, but it had been another trying evening.

Aunt June had an idea. "Let's get Sara a dog. I think it would help with the current problem and be good for her in other ways, too."

I raised my eyebrows. "At this point, I'd be willing to consider just about anything if it would help make her less afraid."

Aunt June continued. "I think it would go a long way toward calming her down and getting her to go to sleep. She'd have a friend who could sleep right on the bed with her."

"And it would probably teach her some lessons about responsibility," I added.

"There are lots of dogs that need a good home. Should we contact some of the area shelters and see if we can find a dachshund that needs to be rescued?" As a child, I'd grown up with dachshunds. They were the only breed I'd ever had.

"We could do that," said Aunt June. "But I might already have a line on a nice little dog that really needs a good home."

I smiled. "You didn't just think of this idea, did you? It's been simmering in that head of yours for awhile."

She smiled back. "Yes, I guess it has."

"So what have you found?"

"Well, it just so happens that one of the women in my reading group has a son here in Park City whose company just transferred him to South America, and he can't take his dog."

"What kind of dog is it?"

"He's a real cutie. His name is Bob and he's a four-year-old male Basset Hound."

"Bob," I laughed. "You've already seen the dog I take it."

"I sure have, and I think Sara would love him."

"Okay. Let's talk to Sara about it at breakfast in the morning and see when we can all go over and introduce ourselves to Bob." You don't see many Basset Hounds in the mountain town of Park City. What you do see by the boatload are Labs and Golden Retrievers. So a Basset Hound named Bob sounded like a nice addition to our family.

The other news of the day was that my ex-wife called from Atlanta asking that I call her back. While my initial anger had receded, I still wasn't sure if I could have a civil conversation with her. What was there to talk about? Short of my asking her to reconsider her decision to initiate the child custody action, it didn't seem like there was much to say. And the likelihood that she would do a one-eighty on the lawsuit seemed extremely remote. Nicole was not the type of person to second guess previously made decisions. It just wasn't in her nature. Besides, her parents had never liked the idea of leaving Sara in Utah, and they would probably be delighted to bankroll the entire fiasco. I decided to call my soon-to-be Atlanta lawyer, Allison Kittridge first.

At six-thirty in the morning, eight-thirty Atlanta time, I was on the phone with Allison Kittridge. Her style was no nonsense and she didn't mince words. I liked that about her right away. She would be an aggressive advocate, of that I felt certain. I mentioned the call the previous evening from Nicole.

"I don't have any problem with your talking to Nicole. In fact, if you can convince her to withdraw the lawsuit, it will save you both a lot of grief, time, and money. There are two things I want you to be cautious of. First, don't get angry with her and lose your temper—just keep it civil. Anger might make you feel better, but it won't help your case. Second, if she asks how Sara is doing, don't go into a lot of detail. Just tell her she's fine."

"But she's not fine," I said, "and Nicole knows it." I explained the problems Sara was experiencing and the fact that she was attending weekly counseling sessions.

"That's all going to come out, and there's nothing we can do about it. It's also all explainable. Don't spend a lot of time worrying about it. I understand from my conversation with your family friend, Baxter Shaw, that Sara suffered another traumatic loss—the death of her grandparents."

"That's true. Both my parents were killed in an accident nearly three years ago."

"None of these things, Mr. Kincaid, can be blamed on you. They are not a reflection of your parenting skills, your home, or your love for your daughter. Just as importantly, these tragic events do not represent a pattern in your or Sara's life, nor were they predictable. All of that works in our favor."

"Do you know the lawyer representing my ex?"

"Not personally. I do know the firm, Baker, Henley, and Wyatt. They're an old law firm that's been in business twenty-five, thirty years. Your former spouse is represented by one of the partners, Bill Wyatt. I haven't called him. I wanted to speak with you first."

"Okay, what happens next?"

"I'd like to fax you a retainer agreement, have you sign it, and fax it back to me. I'll also need a $10,000 retainer. I charge $250.00 an hour. Is that going to be alright?"

"Sure," I gulped. What the hell was I supposed to say? 'Sorry, I can't afford you.' "I'll sign the agreement and get it right back to you. I'll put the retainer in the mail later today."

"Very well," said Kittridge. "Unless this case goes away quietly, I think you should expect that I may need you here in Atlanta several times. I'll give you plenty of notice so that you can plan your schedule accordingly."

"Will Sara have to appear?"

"If this goes to trial, yes. Also, if we do go to trial, I, or one of my associates, will have to fly to Salt Lake City to depose a number of witnesses."

"Anything else?"

"There is the matter of a home evaluation. We will have to retain a licensed clinical social worker to undertake an evaluation of your home and that of your ex wife. But I'm getting ahead of myself. We don't have to worry about any of that today."

Overwhelmed would best describe how I felt when I got off the phone. I needed time to process everything I had just heard. My savings account was about to become $10,000 lighter, but that was the least of my concerns. I didn't bother calling Nicole. Call it procrastination, but, at the moment, I just didn't feel like it.

I had breakfast with Sara and Aunt June. We discussed Bob the Basset hound, and agreed to go see him. I dropped Sara at her school on my way into the office.

It felt like the beginning of a very long day.

Chapter Nineteen

I spent most of the morning at the state prison returning phone calls and putting out fires on several SIB cases. I made repeated calls to the home of Robin Joiner's mother, Betty, in Mesquite, Nevada. She didn't answer. On the last call I left her a message asking that she call me back as soon as possible.

That done, I collected a mug shot of Joseph Bradshaw and drove to Joiner's apartment complex in Salt Lake City. I located the apartment manager and showed her Bradshaw's picture.

She looked at it and then looked at it some more. Finally, she shook her head and said, "This sure looks a lot like the boy I've seen Robin with, but I'm not absolutely certain. I saw them together a couple of times but he was always wearing a baseball cap. And I never actually met him."

I left the apartment manager and tried to reach Tracy Sanders at home. She didn't answer, so I left her a message and then tried her cell number. She picked up and we agreed to meet at an Einstein's Bagel shop near downtown. I was starting to get a bad feeling about a possible connection between Robin Joiner and Joseph Bradshaw. Perhaps Tracy would be able to help clear things up.

Sanders was seated at a table near the back of the bagel shop when I arrived. She was drinking a cup of tea and seemed to be completely immersed in something on her laptop. She glanced up and flashed a tentative smile as I sat down.

"No coffee," she said. "I thought all cops lived on caffeine."

"Contrary to popular belief, some of us don't. I try to limit myself to a couple of cups in the morning. For me it isn't the caffeine so much as the fact that I turn the coffee into a liquid candy bar—too much cream and sugar.

"But what about you? Unless that tea is decaf, I'm going to assume that you're not a member of the dominant religion. Otherwise, you'd be standing in the hot cocoa line."

She smiled. "I grew up in the church, but I haven't been active in years."

We chatted like that for a few minutes, mostly small talk. Finally, I showed her the mug shot of Joseph Bradshaw. She heaved a sigh and said, "For Robin's sake, I hoped that it wouldn't be him. But it is. I'm sure of it."

"And you only met him that one time, at your apartment, I think you said."

"Only once, and that was the time that Rob let me borrow her lecture notes from a class I'd missed. I hadn't met him before, and I've never seen him since."

"But you're sure it's him?"

"Absolutely."

"Can you remember anything else about him?"

"Hmm. Not really. Like I said, he didn't say much. They were only in my apartment for a couple of minutes—just time to give me the notes and say a quick hello."

"When did you meet him, do you recall?"

"Last spring semester."

"Any idea how they met?"

"Sorry."

I left the coffee shop after extracting a promise from Sanders to contact me if she thought of anything else.

⟨⟩⟨⟩⟨⟩

I spotted Kate's department-issued Dodge parked illegally in front of the law firm of Smith, Samuelson, and Wood. I met her in the lobby of the building. She had just come out of a meeting with one of the partners, Greg Samuelson. Samuelson was

Arnold Ginsberg's personal attorney, and Kate had gone to see him in the hope of learning the details of the victim's estate.

"Well, did you manage to charm the information out of him?"

"No, but he wanted to meet me after work for drinks, dinner, and who knows what else. It's going to take a warrant to get the estate information from Mr. Samuelson, I'm afraid."

"And that takes probable cause, something we don't have at the moment," I countered.

She agreed. "We can work around this issue for the time being and come back to it if we have to. How did you make out with the photo identification of Bradshaw?"

"I got a positive ID from Tracy Sanders and a probable one from the apartment manager. The apartment manager never met him and isn't one hundred percent sure."

"So what do you make of the connection between Joiner and Joseph Bradshaw?"

"I'm not entirely sure, but whatever it is, it can't be good. We probably ought to go back over the reports of the armored car heist. The million dollar question, of course, is how exactly did Robin Joiner happen to end up at the scene of a violent crime that her friend, Joey Bradshaw, took part in?"

"Coincidence," said Kate and then smiled. "You figure she's involved, right?"

"Right, unless it's one hell of a coincidence, which seems highly unlikely."

"I'll go over the reports with the detectives who handled the investigation and find out how Joiner surfaced as a witness in the case. Maybe we can jog somebody's memory," said Kate.

"It doesn't track for me," she said. "Think about it: A university student pulling a masters degree in a do-gooder field like social work. She's had a difficult childhood but no significant criminal history—nothing in her background to suggest that she might become a part of something like this. As far as we know, she's never been involved in polygamy or with polygamist groups."

"I agree, Kate, but unless you want to go back to the coincidence theory, I don't know how you arrive at any other conclusion."

"It makes her failure to come in more understandable. And don't forget that the Bradshaw boys are breaking their backs trying to find her? If she was involved, what was her role in the heist and why would she choose to run from Joey?"

"She could have acted as a lookout," I said. "Maybe she was an unwilling participant. Do you remember the Patty Hearst case?"

"Vaguely. I think we studied it in the police academy."

"So you think she was coerced in some way. Maybe you're right. But there's got to be something else."

"I don't know, Kate. How about true love? Sometimes love makes people do some crazy things."

◇◇◇

We hopped into her car and drove four blocks to State Street. She parked illegally again, this time in front of the State Street Office Plaza where Arnold Ginsberg had run his accounting business. The complex provided space for assorted law firms, accountants, and a large, commercial real estate business.

Ginsberg's office suite occupied the top floor, which he shared with two other accountants. They also shared a secretary, the same secretary who had left Kate a message the previous day that she possessed additional information pertinent to Arnold Ginsberg's murder.

We sat with Linda Beggs at a conference table in Ginsberg's spacious office. The digs were first rate, great views of the Oquirrh Mountains to the west.

"Thanks for getting back with me so promptly. The information I'm about to share with you is information I withheld during our discussion several days ago."

"And why did you do that?" asked Kate.

"Arnold's privacy, I guess. Arnold was such a good man, a really sweet spirit. I'm going to miss him terribly. But he was also a very private man. He would have hated for this information to be revealed. I'd hoped the crime would have been solved quickly, so that this information need never have surfaced. But the case hasn't been resolved quickly, and maybe it will turn out to be important."

"Go on."

"Well, about three months ago Arnold confided in me that he was concerned that his partner, Rodney Plow, had become unfaithful, and might be seeing someone else."

"I remember your telling me that. What made him believe Rodney was being unfaithful?"

"I think he felt that the relationship was changing. Rodney was less affectionate and seemed to be distant and distracted. And, on several occasions, Rodney wasn't where he said he was going to be. When Arnold pressed him about it, Rodney became evasive and angry."

"Arnold told you all of this?"

"Yes, he did. He also said that he tried following Rodney on several occasions hoping that it might lead to this mysterious other man. Apparently it never did because about five, maybe six weeks ago, Arnold asked me to find him a private investigator."

"Ostensibly to track the whereabouts of Rodney and determine whether he was being unfaithful?" said Kate.

"Exactly. He insisted on a female PI from one of those companies that claims they will discreetly determine whether somebody's spouse is cheating on them. He didn't want to meet here. He had me set up the appointment away from the office."

"Sounds downright mysterious," I said. "Why a female PI, and why not meet right here in the privacy of his own office?"

"To your first question, I think he was just more comfortable discussing the problem with a woman. Arnold could be a painfully shy man. To some degree, I think he found this entire incident embarrassing and humiliating. Meeting away from the office provided more anonymity, something I'm certain he wanted."

"We're going to need the contact information on the PI," said Kate.

"I've got that right here." She reached across the table and handed me a slip of paper. On it, she'd written, Susan Fleming & Associates, 590 South, 600 East, Salt Lake City, and a phone number. I didn't recognize the firm.

"Did Arnold ever tell you what he learned from Susan Fleming & Associates?" I asked.

"That's the funny part, and oh, so very Arnold. Not only did he not tell me what he learned, he didn't even bother to tell me whether he hired Ms. Fleming. Never said another word about it."

"And you asked him?"

"I did, twice actually. He changed the subject both times."

I turned to Kate. "Did your search of his office turn up anything from a PI firm?"

She shook her head.

I looked around the office. "It looks like you've been packing some of Arnold's things."

She nodded.

"Have you seen any correspondence from Susan Fleming & Associates or any other PI firm?"

"Not a thing and trust me, I've been looking."

Kate wasn't quite finished. "Did Mr. Ginsberg ever tell you whether he had provided financially for Mr. Plow in the event something happened to him?"

"If you mean an inheritance, I wouldn't be surprised, but I don't know for sure. Arnold and I never spoke about it."

"What makes you think he did?"

"Because Arnold was a very generous man. He donated significant dollars to a variety of charitable groups. I know that because I wrote many of the checks."

"So you think because Arnold donated money to various charities that he wouldn't have overlooked Rodney, is that what you're saying?"

"Something like that, yes. Arnold had a lot of friends in the travel industry. I wouldn't be at all surprised if he left small, cash gifts to many of them in his will. He was just that kind of man. If I'm right about that, it would hardly be surprising if he left some part of his estate to Rodney."

"Given his suspicions about Rodney, do you think in the last weeks of his life he might have been considering changes to his estate?"

"I don't know about that. You'd better speak to Greg Samuelson. I did give you his number, didn't I?"

"Yes, you did."

<>‹›<>

On our way down the elevator, Kate said, "What do you make of the PI thing?"

"I think we've got a PI firm that ought to be our next stop."

"I agree. And depending on what we learn, it might be time to serve a court order on Smith, Samuelson, and Wood."

Chapter Twenty

The office of Susan Fleming & Associates was located a short distance from downtown in an old house that had probably been built in the boom shortly after World War II. It was a red brick, two story affair with a make-shift wooden sign over the front door that read: Fleming & Associates – Investigative Services.

We pulled into the driveway and parked behind a late model Lexus. Kate and I glanced at each other. "PI business must be pretty good," I mused.

"Ever hear of Susan Fleming?"

"Can't say that I have, you?"

"Me neither."

"Assuming Ginsberg hired her, I think it's a little odd that she hasn't called you."

"Even if he didn't hire her, you'd think she might have contacted us. Maybe she doesn't read or listen to the news."

"Let's go find out."

A buzzer sounded as we opened the front door announcing our presence. The living room served as the business office. Two oak desks with high-back leather chairs faced each other from opposite corners of the room. A rectangular shaped Persian rug in the center partially covered reconditioned, hardwood floors. A female voice from somewhere in the back of the house said, "Please have a seat, I'll be with you in a minute."

Moments later in walked a woman who, if one were to describe her in a word, stunning would have said it best. Tall, leggy, blond hair that looked natural and a tan that didn't. She had enormous green eyes, and puffy, Angelina Jolie lips. A PI, I didn't think so; a model out of the pages of a Victoria's Secret catalogue, that I could see.

We introduced ourselves. She was Susan Fleming. She offered us coffee or tea. We declined and got down to business. "I think I know why you're here," she said. "It's concerning Arnold Ginsberg, isn't it?"

We nodded.

"And you're probably wondering why I haven't contacted you."

"As a matter of fact, Sam and I were discussing that on our way over here."

"It's a fair question. The answer is that my partner and I just returned from a business trip to Lake Tahoe. We didn't hear about the murder until we got back."

I explained to Fleming that Ginsberg's secretary, Linda Beggs, had given us her name. "Did Arnold retain your services prior to his death?"

"He did."

"And you were retained to do what?"

She hesitated momentarily. "My client is now deceased so I guess that terminates the existing confidentiality agreement he insisted I sign."

I nodded. "The best thing that you can do for Arnold Ginsberg is to help us catch the people who killed him."

She agreed. She reached into a file cabinet behind her desk and removed a file folder with Ginsberg's name on it. "I met Arnold over lunch about three weeks prior to his murder. He expressed concern that his live-in partner, Rodney Plow, might be having an affair with someone behind his back."

"And he wanted you to verify if this was true?"

"That's a lot of what we do in this agency. And yes, he asked us to make that determination."

"What did you learn?"

"Unfortunately, I had to deliver bad news. Our surveillance, conducted over a period of almost a week, revealed that Mr. Plow was indeed involved with another man, intimately, I'm afraid."

"And who was this other man?" Kate asked.

"His personal trainer and massage therapist." Fleming paused while she read the file. "Yeah, here it is. His name is Steven Ambrose. Mr. Ambrose is a personal fitness trainer who works out of the same health club that Rodney and Arnold belonged to. I suspect that's how they met, although I'm not certain of that. He's got an office at 90th South State Street, where he takes his massage appointments."

"How often were they seeing each other?"

"My colleague and I followed Rodney on-and-off for six days. He and Ambrose only met during the day, never at night. Rodney had plenty of opportunity during the day because Arnold worked. At night, he was always home with Ginsberg. They had lunch together twice, and both times went back to Ambrose's Midvale condo afterward for what we assumed was a nooner. The other time they met at the massage studio."

Kate would be sorry that she asked the next question. "How did you determine that Rodney and Mr. Ambrose were intimate?"

"You really want to know....I feigned a mistake and actually walked in on them during a massage at Ambrose's office. They were doing a sixty-nine with Rodney on top and Ambrose underneath. They were giving each other's Johnson a serious workout."

"I hope nobody was injured," I said.

Fleming smiled, Kate didn't. "All in a day's work," Fleming said.

"How did Ginsberg react when you gave him the news?" asked Kate.

"Genuine emotion—he broke down and cried. Whenever I have to deliver this kind of news, emotions tend to run the gamut from feelings of anger, betrayal, sorrow, to self pity, and occasionally, rage. In this instance, shame and sorrow probably best describe Arnold's reaction."

"When did you report the results of your investigation to Arnold?"

That gave her pause. She checked her day planner. "Damn," she finally said. "I guess I didn't write it down. I remember that Arnold asked me to meet him for lunch downtown. I think it was about a week before his murder."

"Did Arnold ever express anything to you that led you to believe that he was in danger? Threats from anybody. Anything like that?"

"He never gave me any indication that his life might be in danger. Just sadness at what I think he believed would be the end of his relationship with Plow."

"Did you ever confront Plow?"

"No. I almost never do that. Clients typically don't ask us to. They want us to bring them evidence, surveillance notes, digital stills, video—that sort of thing. I carry a piece, but why push my luck."

She had a good point.

"Are these the kinds of cases your firm usually handles?" Kate asked.

"Unfortunately, we handle a lot of domestic cases—cheating spouses, child custody, that sort of thing. We do some employment backgrounds, and I occasionally pick up a personal injury or wrongful death case."

"Been in business long?"

"Two years next month. Right after my divorce I bought this place, managed to get the city to give me a zoning variance, got my PI license and opened for business, all in a matter of a few weeks."

Susan Fleming had been helpful. Before we left, she gave us a copy of her report as well as digital photos and a CD Rom with surveillance video clips of Ambrose and Plow.

◇◇◇

We had worked through the lunch hour and both of us were starving. We stopped at a Crown Royal burger joint on Fourth

South, ordered sandwiches at the drive up window, and ate them in the car.

"Now what do you think of the bereaved partner?"

"Makes me think that my original instincts about him were on the mark all along," replied Kate.

"You mean the Oscar performance as the distraught, grieving partner?"

"Yup."

"Might be a motive for murder," I said, "but only if we can establish that the victim was about to disinherit Rodney over the infidelity, and Rodney found out about it."

"It wouldn't be the first murder case to come down the pike with infidelity and greed as the motive." She paused. "You ever wonder why guys spend so much time thinking with their dicks?"

"Can't say that I have. Which reminds me, did I ever tell you about the guy who named his own penis?"

Kate looked at me warily. "Can't say that you have, but I think you're about to."

"Yeah, he named it Earl. The reason he did it is because he didn't like the idea of a total stranger making ninety percent of his decisions for him."

Kate laughed. "Jesus, you're hopeless."

Chapter Twenty-one

Robin Joiner slept until after eleven in the morning, hung over from the effects of another night of sleep meds. She got up, showered, dressed, and checked out of the dingy motel. Another memorable night in the lap of luxury, she thought.

Joiner walked three blocks to a nearby Applebee's Restaurant where she took a seat at the bar in the lounge. A big screen television mounted overhead was broadcasting some kind of celebrity pro-am tennis match. Any other time, she would have found the tennis match an entertaining distraction while she waited for her food. Today it annoyed her. She bummed a copy of the morning *Deseret News* from a guy seated two stools away, and read through it while she waited for her cheeseburger, fries, and cup of clam chowder. She had eaten little the previous day, and she was famished.

Joiner discovered a short article about the Ginsberg murder case in which a police spokesperson refused to talk about physical evidence purportedly found at the crime scene. The article was largely devoid of specifics and full of the usual vaguely worded bullshit about all leads being actively pursued. Her name wasn't mentioned at all.

Joiner knew she was taking a chance. She was dangerously close to being out of money. She decided to hang out at Applebee's until three and then walk the short distance to the Outback Steakhouse about the time Tracy Sanders would be ending her lunch shift. Tracy would help her, she was sure of it. It was a risk, but one she felt she had to take.

Shortly after three, Joiner approached the Outback. Her senses were on full alert. Her otherwise carefree spirit had given way to an almost paranoid sense of caution. She scanned the parking lot looking for anything that appeared suspicious, and for Sander's blue Toyota Corolla. Nothing seemed out of the ordinary. Sander's car was parked behind the restaurant near two large garbage dumpsters.

When she entered the restaurant, Joiner spotted Sanders almost immediately, nodded at her, and walked directly into the women's restroom. Sanders followed.

They were alone in the restroom. "God, Rob, what are you doing here? Everybody is looking for you."

"I'm sorry, Tracy. You've got to help me, please."

Sanders hesitated as if she were about to decline. Then she shook her head and said, "Okay, wait here until I get off shift. It'll just be a few minutes. Lock yourself in a stall and don't come out until I come back for you."

"I can trust you, can't I," pleaded Joiner.

Tracy nodded.

A little after three-thirty, Sanders exited through the back door of the restaurant, looked around, and then motioned for Joiner to follow. They left the restaurant parking lot and headed east on Sixth South toward the university and Sander's apartment complex.

"You don't know how risky this is," said Sanders. "The cops have been all over our study group. They even came to the campus."

Looking out the passenger side window, Joiner said, "I'm so sorry to have gotten all of you involved in this."

"Forget it. Nobody feels that way about it, well, on second thought, maybe Michael. He hadn't planned on ending up spread-eagled over the hood of your car and then hauled down to the police department."

"God, I'm so embarrassed about that. He must hate me."

"Nobody hates you, Rob. We're your friends, and we're concerned about your welfare, that's all."

"What questions did they ask?"

"Questions about how they might be able to find you. They think you're in real danger. Surely you know by now that the guy who was murdered the other night was the other witness in the armored car robbery."

Joiner nodded. "Have the cops been to your apartment looking for me?"

"No. Like I said, this cop, Kincaid, came to school and pulled the entire study group out of class and was asking us all kinds of questions about you. But he never came to the apartment. That doesn't mean he won't or that they're not watching."

"So you think that the cops are just trying to protect me?"

Sanders paused. "Until this morning, that's exactly what I thought. And then I met this Kincaid at Einstein's. He showed me a picture. It was a picture of the guy who was with you that day I borrowed your lecture notes."

Sounding anxious, Joiner asked, "What did you tell him?"

"Rob, I told him the truth. I told him that I'd met this guy, Joey, that one time at my apartment."

Joiner's head dropped to her chest. She reached for a tissue in her pocket and stifled a sob.

"Rob, I'm your friend. You need to tell me what's going on. I think this Joey is really Joseph Bradshaw, one of the guys wanted in the armored car robbery. Am I right? I mean, why else would the police have had his picture?"

Joiner turned away, blew her nose, and dabbed at the tears running down her cheeks. "Yeah, he is Joseph Bradshaw, but he's not the bad person the cops are making him out to be."

"God, Rob, listen to what you're saying. People died in that robbery. These guys were a part of Warren Jeffs' polygamist church until they apparently became so extreme that they got booted out and then went and formed their own church."

"It's not like that. You don't understand."

Tracy sighed. They had arrived at her apartment building and she parked the Corolla in her assigned spot. The building had a covered ground level parking terrace with a four story apartment complex built above it.

"C'mon. Let's go upstairs. I'll fix us some coffee and something to eat if you're hungry. You can take a bath, and we'll talk this thing through. We'll get it figured out."

They walked to the elevator, got in, and pushed the third floor button. At the apartment door, Sanders reached for her key. If she hadn't been so busy talking, she might have noticed the scrapes and pry marks on the door jamb. She unlocked the door and they entered.

Three of them were waiting in the apartment—the Allred brothers and Joseph Bradshaw. The moment the women stepped into the living room and saw the intruders, they spun and attempted a hasty retreat to the front door. Randy Allred anticipated that move and blocked their exit.

Bradshaw called the shots. Pointing to Sanders, he directed Randy and Robby Allred. "Take her into the bedroom, tape her mouth, and tie her up. Leave her on the bed."

"Don't do that to her," said Joiner. "She won't say anything. It isn't necessary."

"Yes, it is," said Bradshaw. He nodded at the grinning Allred brothers, who grabbed a wild-eyed Sanders by each arm, and dragged her into the bedroom.

"Don't hurt her," shouted Joiner.

"Shut the fuck up," said Bradshaw, pulling a resisting Joiner into the kitchen away from the bedlam.

"Did you think I'd forgotten about this place?"

Joiner didn't answer.

"Why did you disappear? Are you crazy? Did you think you could just walk away from this?"

"Yes, I did, Joey. And that's what you need to do if you ever want to have any chance of a normal life."

"I have a life and you do, too. My life is in the Reformed Church of the Divine Christ. My father is the prophet. We can be together. I know I can straighten it all out with him. He'll love you, Robin, just like I do; and he'll forgive you, just as I do."

"Are you crazy, Joey. This isn't some fairy tale, and your father isn't Robin Hood. It was one thing when he began stealing from the Jeffs and the FLDS. I could understand it—a payback of sorts for what happened to his family. But it's gone way beyond that now...."

Bradshaw interrupted. "Hold your voice down, Robin, and show a little respect, at least for my father and the church, even if you can't do it for me."

"I will not. People are dead, Joey. The government that your father and his church so detest, isn't going to just let you build your private compound in southern Utah, and walk off happily into the sunset. Look what they did to Warren Jeffs. He made it to the FBI's ten most wanted list, and he didn't kill anybody."

Randy Allred poked his head around the kitchen corner. Eyeing Joiner with open contempt, he said, "Everything all right, Brother Joseph?"

"Yes, we're just talking."

"We need to get out of here."

"I know. You and Brother Robert go down and get the van. Bring it as close as possible to the elevator door. We'll be right down."

He glanced suspiciously at Joiner. "Are you sure you don't need my help?"

"No, just go get the van. We'll be right along."

Allred nodded. Moments later, he and Robby left the apartment.

"I want to see Tracy right now before we leave."

"Okay. But don't touch her or make any attempt to untie her."

When Joiner walked into the bedroom and saw Sanders tied wrists to ankles, with silver duct tape over her mouth, tears streamed down her face. She looked at Sanders and mouthed, "Everything will be all right."

Joseph pulled her by the arm out of the bedroom and walked her to the apartment's front door. "No stunts walking out of here. If you do, you'll force us to restrain you. Clear?"

Joiner glared at him.

"Am I making myself clear, Robin?"

"As a bell," replied Joiner, her voice rising with contempt.

"Good. And by the way, we have your laptop. I'll need those e-mails you and I exchanged."

They left the apartment with Bradshaw's arm tucked snuggly under Joiner's in a vise-like grip.

Chapter Twenty-two

Kate and I parted company after lunch. She dropped me at my car and then headed to her office. Now, more than ever, Kate wanted to get a look at the estate of Arnold Ginsberg. The information provided by Susan Fleming would give her sufficient probable cause to obtain a warrant.

I had two issues on my plate. One was a visit to Walter Bradshaw's lawyer, Gordon Dixon. I had decided to follow a piece of advice from an experienced parole officer—if you want to know about what's going on in the lives of offenders you supervise, visit them in their own homes as opposed to any place else. I decided to test that advice on Gordon Dixon. A visit to his home, say around dinner time, might get me an introduction to wife number one, Joan, and perhaps some additional sister wives. In a worst case scenario, I'd end up getting the front door closed impolitely in my face.

The other thing I needed to do was to pay a second visit to Walter Bradshaw at the prison. I had more questions for the prophet.

Unfortunately, fate intervened and propelled me down an entirely different path, one that would ultimately change the course of the SIB and my own career.

My cell phone rang. The caller was Sergeant Marcy Everest, one of my top investigators. "Sam, where are you? We need to meet ASAP."

I didn't like her tone. It had a note of urgency, usually not a good sign. "I'm in Salt Lake City, Marcy. Can this wait until I return to the office?"

"No, it can't, and I don't want to talk in the office."

This definitely wasn't good, I could feel it. In this business, whenever I dealt with a staff member, and the issue combined urgency with secrecy, something was seriously wrong, and it might involve employees. If it was an employee, I hoped it wasn't one of mine. "Okay. I'm headed toward the prison now. Where would you like to meet?"

"I could meet you at Guadalahonky's in fifteen minutes?" Guadalahonky's was a Mexican restaurant located near the state prison often frequented by department employees.

I arrived ahead of Everest and took a seat in a rear booth, in a place that would provide a modicum of privacy. All things considered, Everest had a bright career in front of her. By any measure, she should have been a lieutenant by now. But with budget cuts, it just hadn't happened. She had been with the department since she was twenty-one, and she'd just had her thirtieth birthday. She was also the office practical joker, which provided a sense of levity to an otherwise stressful environment.

She didn't look happy when she sat down. "You don't look so good, Marcy, are you okay?"

"Not really, I hate doing this. It makes me feel like a snitch."

"Tell me about it."

"Terry's drinking on the job."

I sighed. "How do you know that?"

"I smelled it on him. This was the second time. I wasn't so sure the first time, so I let it go. But today, there was no doubt. Patti smelled it, too. We decided that I should talk to you about it right away. I almost challenged him on the spot but then thought better of it. He can be a little intimidating."

"No, I'm glad you came directly to me. When was the first incident?"

"Maybe a week or so ago."

"Where's Terry now?"

"He was at the office when I left."

"Okay, I'll head in right away. I want you to write this up as an incident report—confidential, of course, for my eyes only."

"Christ, Sam, do I have to put this in writing? How are you going to handle this?"

"Yes, you do."

"But…"

"No, Marcy, no buts. I don't like this any better than you do, but we are going to do the right thing. This isn't like a sales clerk in a retail store who occasionally takes a nip on the job. This is a prison. You bring drugs or alcohol onto prison grounds, you just committed a felony. You know that, I know that, and so does Terry."

"Shit," she said, loud enough that it drew looks from surrounding tables. "We don't know if he's bringing alcohol into the prison. He might be drinking someplace else."

"I hope he's not bringing alcohol into the prison. Either way, I can't have him drinking on the job."

I drove straight to the prison hoping all the while that Marcy was wrong, but knowing that she probably wasn't. Terry Burnham liked his scotch, always had. From time to time, I worried about his drinking. Since the death of his wife a couple of years ago, it seemed like he had his nose in the bottle more often than he should have. Yet I'd never gotten any sense that he might be drinking on the job.

I debated about how best to handle the situation. If Burnham was in the office and I could smell the alcohol, I might be able to handle it without involving Marcy Everest. I admired her for coming forward, not everybody would have. At this moment, she had to be feeling lousy. The pressure in this business to simply look the other way when faced with illegal or unethical behavior from a fellow officer can be enormous.

For me the feelings were personal. Burnham was not only the best and most experienced investigator in the SIB, he was also my friend. Most of the investigators in the SIB were relatively young. Burnham's age and years of experience working in law enforcement outside the prison system had always brought a sense of stability to the office. I had always trusted him to capably run the place in my absence.

By the time I got back, Burnham was gone. "You just missed him," said Patti, looking up from her computer. "He left about ten minutes ago."

Marcy arrived moments after I did. There were just the three of us left in the office. I dropped into Burnham's chair and tried to open his desk. It was locked. I then rooted around in my own desk until I found the small ring of keys I was looking for. One of them was a master, and it would unlock every desk in the SIB. I unlocked Burnham's. The silver flask was hidden in a bottom drawer covered with files. I opened it and took a sniff.

"Shit," I muttered. I was hoping that if Marcy's allegation proved true, that at least he wasn't bringing the stuff on to prison grounds. Obviously, that wasn't the case. The entire episode would have been a lot more manageable if Terry had been doing a three martini lunch someplace and then showing up at work afterward.

Marcy and Patti were both looking over my shoulder glumly when I discovered the flask. "What happens now?" asked Patti.

"I don't have many options. In the morning, I'll have to notify the director of institutional operations here at the prison as well as the executive director's office. Terry will be relieved of his duties pending an investigation by the Salt Lake County Sheriff's Office."

"Oh, geez, do we have to handle it that way?" said Marcy. Her eyes were welling with tears. "Can't you just take care of it quietly. Maybe you can talk to him, get him into treatment, something like that."

"I know it's painful but we can't do it that way. I'm sure we can get him some help, if he's willing. And we might be able to save his job, maybe."

The unknown factor would be the response from the department's new executive director, Benjamin Cates. I wasn't sure what he'd want done. If only my former boss, Norm Sloan, were here. Then maybe....

"Please don't talk about this to anyone else in the office. Marcy, I'd like your report in my hands first thing in the morning. Both of you can expect to be interviewed by somebody from the sheriff's office. I'll try to catch Terry either tonight or at his home in the morning. I'd rather spare him the humiliation of coming into the office only to be turned around and sent home on suspension."

I went into my office and closed the door. I called Marilyn Hastings, a clinical social worker, who contracted with the department to provide employee assistance counseling. I explained what I knew and asked her if Burnham could get in to see her the next day. After juggling something else on her calendar, she agreed to meet him for what she described as an assessment session at ten-thirty the next morning.

"You haven't even placed this guy on suspension, correct?"

"That's right. He has no idea this is coming."

"Wonderful. So we don't know whether he'll even show up tomorrow."

I saw no reason to bullshit her. Hastings had been around the block more than a few times, and I suspected that she'd seen it all.

"He's got a temper. If I had to take a guess at his initial reaction, I'd say defensive and royally pissed off."

"That's pretty common at first," she said.

"I'll do everything I can to convince him to see you, but I wouldn't bet the farm on it if I were you?"

And that's how we left it.

Chapter Twenty-three

Burnham rented a small home in the Sugarhouse area of Salt Lake City. Sugarhouse was a funky part of town, that as late as the early 1950s, had housed the state prison. In recent years, it was going through a renaissance of sorts with a mix of new construction, coupled with the restoration of many older homes. Its proximity to downtown and the University of Utah made it a popular place to live.

Terry was sitting in a leather recliner in front of a big screen television watching a Packers/Bears football game when I tapped on the front door. He had a glass of what I assumed was scotch-and-soda in one hand and the bottle of Johnny Walker in the other. He looked hammered. He waved the bottle at me and motioned for me to come in.

I sat on a leather couch next to him. "Tough day, huh."

"Yeah, sort of. To what do I owe the pleasure of your visit, Sam?" he slurred.

There would be no easy way to say it. "Lately Terry, I've been growing increasingly concerned about your drinking. You seem to be hitting it pretty hard."

"I can handle it. No need for you to worry about it."

"I wish it were that simple."

"What'ya mean?"

"I think you've been drinking on the job."

A note of alarm began to register through bloodshot eyes. "Who says?"

I held up the flask I'd recovered from his desk. "I do, Terry. It pains me to do this, but I came here to inform you that you're suspended from duty effective immediately. There'll be an investigation conducted by the sheriff's department."

For a moment, he was silent, chin down almost on his chest. "So, this is how it ends, huh."

"Not necessarily, but it's going to be up to you." I handed him my business card with the contact information printed on the back for Marilyn Hastings and the employee assistance program.

"What's this?" he growled.

"It's an appointment tomorrow morning for you to see the department's EAP counselor. You need to get some help for the drinking problem. And you need to start right now."

"Fuck the EAP and fuck you," he sneered. "I don't have a drinking problem."

"I think you do, Terry. I'm your friend, not just your boss. I'd like to try to help you get through this, but you've got to take the first step. And the first step is a treatment program."

"And if I don't."

"It's the best chance you've got if you want a shot at saving your job. Get into treatment, Terry, and do it now. This thing's going to get looked at all the way up the line—everybody from the sheriff's office to the DA, and internally, by Director Cates and his staff."

I got up to leave. I felt like I'd worn out my welcome, and frankly, there wasn't much else to say. Burnham was drunk and surly. To stay longer would have invited a knock-down, dragged out argument. He didn't look up or say a word as I left.

The afternoon had been emotionally exhausting. I felt like I needed a drink, maybe two. The drive home gave me time to think. My planned visit to Gordon Dixon's home and a second interview with Walter Bradshaw would have to wait a day.

In the morning, I would have to make a painful call to the sheriff's department, one that would trigger an internal investigation against Terry Burnham. That investigation might lead to criminal charges and bring about the end of his career with the department.

I was going to have to walk a fine line on this one and I knew it. People would be watching, plenty of them. On one hand, if Burnham tried to help himself by immediately seeking treatment for the alcohol problem, I would do everything in my power to salvage his career. On the other hand, I had to lead by example. Most of the investigators in the SIB were young. They were going to be here a lot longer than Terry or me. They had to understand that the rules apply to everyone and that nobody gets a free ride. I would do nothing to obstruct or try to influence the outcome of the investigation. And I had a pretty good idea what that outcome would be.

◇◇◇

Aunt June had decided to make tonight's dinner a celebratory one in honor of the newest member of the Kincaid family. When I walked into the house, I discovered that Bob the Basset Hound had not only arrived on the premises but had already begun to stake out the house as his personal territory. He eyed me suspiciously, gave one half-hearted woof, and then went back to his nap, flopping in front of the fire place.

Aunt June put me right to work. "Mind setting the table while I finish tossing the salad," she said. "I've ordered in pizza. It should be here any minute. We weren't sure what time you'd make it and Sara was starving."

"No problem. How does she like the dog?"

"I tell you, Sam, that little girl was so excited when I picked her up at school this afternoon that there was going to be no waiting until you got home from work before we went to see Bob. This was supposed to be a short home visit, but Sara's been playing with the poor guy all afternoon and he's exhausted. If you're okay with it, I think Bob has found a new home."

"You like him?"

"He's a sweetheart. He'll fit right in, and Sara adores the little guy."

"He doesn't look so little to me. I'll bet that dog hasn't missed a French fry in years."

"He does need to lose a little weight. That'll be your job."

"Great."

"Nicole called—again. I think you'd better give her a call."

I looked at my watch. "I'll give her a call after dinner."

We ate pizza, a Caesar salad, and a loaf of warm French bread. Sara was on such a high that it was difficult to get her to sit still for five minutes and eat. Afterward, she came around the dinner table and hopped into my lap. "Thanks for letting me have Bob, Daddy. He's sooo cute."

She was working me and I knew it. "So you think we ought to keep, Bob?" I asked.

Sara looked at me like I was crazy—a look that said how could I even ask such a question. "Of course, Daddy, he's very happy here."

"Okay, then. It's a done deal. Bob's the newest member of our family," I said. "Don't you think Bob Kincaid sounds a little funny for a dog? Should we give him a new name?"

She paused for a moment. "No. He looks like a Bob, don't you think?"

How could I argue with that? "Yes, I think he does."

I went into my study after dinner and closed the door. It was nearly ten o'clock Atlanta time. Part of me didn't want to return the call. What really was there to say? Nicole and I were now adversaries in a way we'd never been before. Always in the past, acting in Sara's best interest trumped whatever strain existed between us. It felt different now. I didn't expect Nicole to capitulate in her effort to gain custody of Sara, and I certainly didn't plan to. Yet this had been her second attempt to reach me. I decided to make the call.

Nicole answered on the first ring. The call was brief, strained, and semi-cordial. We exchanged awkward niceties before I took the first shot.

"Why the hell did you do this, Nicole? I think we've both tried to act in what we always believed was Sara's best interest—at least until now."

"I am acting in Sara's best interest, always have and always will. I won't have our daughter in the line of fire because of your job. You damn near got her killed a few months ago. I recognize that, and if you were honest with yourself, so would you."

What could I say to that? Nicole was right. A case I was investigating placed not only Sara's life in danger but Aunt June's as well. I tried to imagine what my new Atlanta lawyer would want me to say. Probably nothing, and that's exactly what I did. I answered with another question.

"Why the process server on our front door, Nicole? You didn't have to do it that way. If you had just called, I would have accepted service of the legal papers anywhere."

"Point taken, but in the final analysis, I don't see what difference it makes," she replied.

"The difference is that I had a total stranger stalking my house. It really upset Aunt June, and what if Sara had seen the guy. She would have freaked out."

"Have you told her yet?"

"Not yet. I know I'm going to have to, but I don't want to do that until it's absolutely necessary."

An awkward pause followed before I said, "I guess I was hoping you might change your mind and I'd never have to tell her."

"I'm not going to change my mind, Sam. Why don't you change yours?"

"I don't think so. Why did you bother calling me, Nicole?"

"I have a proposition I'd like you to think about."

"I'm listening."

"What if we retained joint custody of Sara but changed the primary custody to me. I'd be willing to reduce the amount of days I travel. My folks have agreed to stay at my place when I'm gone so that Sara's life wouldn't be disrupted."

"That's nice of them," I said, doing my best to sound sincere.

"Sara can spend summers with you and Aunt June. She's about reached an age where she can travel alone. With my travel benefits, she can visit anytime she wants. She loves to snowboard, so we'd want to schedule some winter trips to Utah."

"And what about the major holidays?"

"Same arrangement we have now. We continue to alternate Christmas, Thanksgiving, and her birthday. By my calculation, she'd be spending between seven and eight months with me and four to five with you. What do you think?"

Before I could answer, my cell phone rang. "Hold on a minute, I've got to answer this." I set the office phone down while I rummaged through the mess on my desk in search of my cell. When I found it, I glanced at the caller identification. The call was coming from Robin Joiner's friend, Tracy Sanders. I answered.

"Detective Kincaid, this is Tracy Sanders," the voice said, choking back sobs. "They were waiting for us. They've taken Robin...."

"Hold on Tracy, slow down and try to calm down. Where are you and what happened?"

I listened.

"Alright, here's what I want you to do. Stay where you are, don't move, and try not to touch anything. I'll have units from Salt Lake P.D. at your place in minutes. I'm coming down from Park City just as fast as I can make it. Sit tight." I disconnected.

"Nicole, I gotta go, emergency. I'll get back to you as soon as I can."

I dialed 911 and had uniforms responding within seconds. I grabbed my gear and headed out the door.

Chapter Twenty-four

I called Kate's home number on my way down the mountain and got no answer. I then tried her cell. Same result. As a last resort, I dialed her office number thinking that she might be working late. I was about to disconnect when Kate's partner, Vince Turner, picked up. Turner informed me that Kate had left the office an hour earlier and had mentioned stopping at the New Yorker for a drink. The New Yorker is an upscale restaurant and private club located in the heart of downtown Salt Lake.

Since she wasn't answering her cell or her home phone, I figured the New Yorker might be a good bet. I pulled into valet parking, flashed my identification at the young attendant, and told her I'd be right back.

When I spotted Kate, I stopped in my tracks. She was seated at the bar with her back to me. She wasn't alone. Seated next to her was deputy district attorney Tom Stoddard, her old boy-friend. They were leaned into each other, shoulder to shoulder, sharing a laugh. At the conclusion of the banter, they looked into each others eyes, lifted glasses, and Stoddard whispered something in her ear before they touched glasses in a toast.

Okay, I'll admit it, I felt threatened. The scene playing out before me involved my girlfriend enjoying an intimate moment with an old lover. I felt like a voyeur watching a scene unfold through the lens of a camera. For a moment, I wasn't sure what to do. I could discreetly withdraw, call the restaurant on my cell and have her paged. Or I could take a deep breath, walk right up and act like nothing was wrong. I decided on the latter approach with only one caveat: not to behave like a jealous, insecure, idiotic, twit. Instead, I decided to play this out with as happy a face as I could muster considering the circumstances.

I walked up behind Kate and tapped her on the shoulder. They both glanced over and the smiles instantly disappeared. The look on their faces ranged between simple surprise and outright guilt—almost like two kids who'd just been caught by their parents screwing in the back seat of the family sedan. "Sorry to interrupt, but we've got a problem. Robin Joiner has just been kidnapped from Tracy Sander's apartment. Uniforms are on scene securing the place and trying to calm her down."

Kate stood and reached for her purse. "When did it go down?"

"Not sure. They left Sanders tied up in the bedroom. From what I could tell it took her a while to work herself free."

"How did it happen?"

"Not sure of that either. She was pretty shook up. She said there were three of them waiting inside the apartment when they arrived."

Stoddard chimed in. "Can she identify anybody?"

"Oh, yeah, she recognized Joseph Bradshaw right away. She wasn't sure about the other two, but I'll bet we're talking about the Allred boys or one of the Allreds and Joey's brother, Albert."

I turned to leave. "Since Tom's here, maybe he ought to come along—wouldn't hurt to have a DA on scene. I'll meet you at the apartment."

"Sure," he said, as I began to walk away. "I'd be glad to help."

Kate said, "Wait, Sam, I'll ride with you."

"No, why don't you drive your own? That way when we're finished, I can head back to Park City."

Almost as an afterthought, I said, "You two okay to drive?"

Kate shot me a look. Stoddard didn't say anything.

Okay, that was a bit caustic. But what's that old saying, 'friends don't let friends drive drunk,' especially not cop friends.

<>< >

By the time we arrived, Sanders had calmed down, and the crime scene was under control. She'd been tied up but was otherwise unhurt. The responding patrol officers hadn't waited. They'd immediately requested a CSI unit. The CSI team was already busy photographing the place, dusting for latent prints, and gathering evidence. And there seemed to be ample physical evidence left in the apartment.

The Bradshaws if nothing else were sloppy. It seemed that they left a calling card every place they made an appearance. Sanders' apartment was no exception. A cursory look around the place suggested that they had made themselves right at home. They'd cleaned out the fridge, helped themselves to milk, soda, chips, cookies, and even beer. The place looked like a junk food eater's nirvana. The duct tape and scissors used to secure Sanders had been tossed on the living room floor. The lab crew would probably find latents plastered on everything they touched.

It occurred to me that at the rate the Bradshaw family was racking up new offenses, once apprehended, they probably wouldn't see the light of day for about a hundred years. And given the copious amount of evidence left haphazardly at every crime scene, prosecutors would be drooling with anticipation at the prospect of trying these cases.

Kate had pulled Sanders off to one side and was talking to her in hushed tones. Stoddard stood nearby, hands in pockets, listening attentively. After several minutes, Kate broke away and strode over to where I was standing.

"What's the plan?" I asked.

"She's pretty shook up and doesn't want to stay here tonight."

"Can't say as I blame her."

"I'm going to get her something to eat and then take her down to headquarters and show her a photo lineup. She was positive about Joey but didn't recognize the other two."

"We've got a pretty good idea who Joey hangs with, and besides, you're gonna find their prints all over this place," I said.

"Will you come along?"

"No, I think I'll pass. You don't need my help for this. I'll check with you in the morning."

As I turned to leave, Kate grabbed me by the arm. Glancing at Stoddard, she said, "We need to talk. It wasn't what you think."

"Don't assume you know what I'm thinking. You're busy and I'm beat. Let's just let it go until tomorrow. We'll have a chance to talk then."

<>◇<>

After I left Sander's apartment, I made another phone call to the home of Betty Joiner. If our information was correct and she was employed as a dealer in one of the Mesquite casinos, she might well be at work. She hadn't returned my earlier call, and I had the distinct feeling that she didn't plan to. Perhaps her relationship with Robin was so badly fractured that the two wanted nothing to do with each other.

The number rang several times before a low, gravelly sounding voice came on the line and said, "I'm not here to take your call, you know what to do." I quickly deduced that Betty Joiner would not be a lady I'd want blowing sweet nothings in my ear on a cold winter night. Her voice bore an uncanny resemblance to George Papalopsis, the Greek auto mechanic in Park City, who serviced my SUV.

I left a blunt message hoping that it might provoke a return call. "Mrs. Joiner, this is Sam Kincaid from the Utah Department of Corrections. I left you a message earlier that you haven't returned. If you're home, would you please pick-up." I paused—nothing.

"It's urgent that you call me as soon as possible. I regret having to tell you that the status of your daughter's case has changed from that of a missing person to the victim of an aggravated kidnapping. Robin was abducted from a friend's apartment sometime late this afternoon. Regardless of the time, please call me the moment you receive this message." I left my cell number and disconnected.

Five minutes later, my cell phone rang. It was Betty Joiner. She was probably home all along and decided that the gravity of the circumstances outweighed whatever baggage existed between mother and daughter. I was approaching Lamb's canyon along I-80 when the call came. I couldn't have been in a worse location for cell phone reception. We exchanged a brief, garbled message, and then the line went dead. I sped to the top of Parley's summit, pulled off to the side of the interstate, and quickly redialed her number.

She answered on the first ring. "Yeah."

I wasn't in the mood to waste time on small talk. "Thanks for getting back to me, Mrs. Joiner. Tell me what you can about your daughter's relationship with Joseph Bradshaw."

She paused. "Is that who kidnapped her?"

"We think so, Joey and some others. Now tell me about their relationship."

"They met when Robin was a freshman attending Dixie State College in St. George. They ended up in a class together and became friends."

"How long ago was that?"

"Maybe five, six years."

"Did the relationship evolve into something more than just friendship?"

"Like an intimate relationship, is that what you mean?"

Jesus! Let me get you a crayon and I'll draw you a picture. "Yes."

"Yeah, it did. I'm not exactly sure when they became serious, but it's been an on-again, off-again relationship for quite a long time."

"Did Robin know that the Bradshaws were members of Warren Jeffs FLDS church, and if so, had she become involved in polygamy?"

"She didn't know, at least not at first. I'm not sure when or how she found out. At some point, he must have told her. And hell no, she was never involved with polygamy. What kind of daughter you think I got?"

I was beginning to wonder.

"In fact," she said, "Robin was doing everything she could to get Joey away from the family and the religion. I told her more than once that I thought she was wasting her time. She wouldn't listen—kids you know."

"I take it you didn't approve of the relationship," I said.

"No shit, Sherlock. How happy would you be if you discovered that your daughter had become involved with one of those child abusing scumbags?"

Point taken. I didn't want to ask the next question but I did. Maybe I didn't want to hear the answer. "As you know, Mrs. Joiner, some members of the Bradshaw family have been involved in committing crimes. Because of her relationship with Joey, do you think it's possible that Robin has participated in any of those offenses?"

"Not on your life, mister." Her voice had dropped another octave. "Like I already told you, Robin was trying to get Joey away from the family. She's a social work graduate student at the university, not some trashy street criminal."

"I'm relieved to hear that," I said, not necessarily believing it, but hoping that I sounded sincere.

I gave Betty Joiner Kate's phone number and promised her that one of us would keep her abreast of developments in the case.

Chapter Twenty-five

When I arrived at the prison early the next morning, I found a note on my desk summoning me to the maximum security housing unit, where the prophet, Walter Bradshaw, had asked to see me. There was also a phone message from my boss, Director Benjamin Cates, requesting that I call him immediately. This call would be about Terry Burnham, of that I was certain.

"Good morning, Sam. Thanks for getting back to me so promptly. I wanted to speak with you for a minute about the incident involving Investigator Burnham."

He had an agenda, that's for sure. I was about to find out what it was.

"I just wanted to be certain that you and I are on the same page in terms of how I want this investigation handled."

"Okay."

"I don't want your office investigating the Burnham case. I prefer to have the Salt Lake County Sheriff's Office handle the matter. I recognize that normal protocol authorizes your staff to carry out the investigation; however, under the present circumstances, that isn't such a good idea."

The 'normal protocol' Cates referred to had to do with department policy. My unit, the SIB, typically conducted investigations involving employee misconduct. In this instance, because the employee in question worked for the SIB, Cates had decided that the case should be handled by an agency outside the department of corrections. Anticipating that, I was one step ahead of him.

"I happen to agree with you, sir," I said. "Early this morning, I contacted the internal affairs unit at the sheriff's office, and they've assigned a detective to conduct the investigation. In fact, she's supposed to be here any minute."

I fumbled through the paperwork on my desk until I found her name. "Yeah, she's a detective sergeant by the name of Melanie Egan. I've never met her before, but they assured me she's top notch."

"Glad you agree with me on this. It isn't that I think your office wouldn't have done a thorough, impartial job. It's really about appearances and the need for public confidence that we won't tolerate this kind of behavior from one of our own."

It sounded to me like Cates had decided Terry Burnham was guilty even before the investigation had begun. Impartiality and public confidence was one thing, but I hoped this wouldn't turn into a lynch mob with the executive director carrying the rope.

‹›‹›‹›

Within thirty minutes of my conversation with Cates, Patti ushered into my office Detective Sergeant Melanie Egan. Egan looked to be in her early thirties, short, plump, with long brown hair pulled back and tied in a pony tail. From her looks and demeanor, all business.

As Patti closed my office door, she said, "Lieutenant McConnell called—wants you to call her as soon as possible." I nodded.

I gave Egan a brief summary of the case beginning with Patti and Marcy Everest's observations of Terry the previous day. I told her about my subsequent search of his desk including the discovery of the flask containing the alcohol.

"Sounds pretty straightforward to me," she said.

"I think so," I replied, a note of sadness and resignation in my voice.

She hadn't missed that. I could tell from the quizzical look she gave me.

"And you're in possession of the physical evidence?"

I nodded, reaching into a desk drawer. I removed the flask, and passed it across to her.

"Thanks," Egan said. "If it's okay with you, I'd like to get your statement on the record and follow that with interviews of your secretary and Investigator Everest."

Again I nodded. Egan produced a small voice-activated tape recorder and placed it on the desk between us. She quickly glanced over her notes and began the interview. After we finished, I offered to let her use the small conference room in our office from which she could conduct the interviews with Patti and Marcy Everest.

After Egan left my office, I closed the door and sat quietly, contemplating where all this was headed. For almost the past twenty-four hours, it had consumed a lot of my time and energy.

I didn't like how this was making me feel. I had to admit that I felt exactly like Marcy Everest did—like a snitch turning on a fellow officer. I would never betray that emotion to anyone else on my staff. I didn't want them to sense my reluctance. I needed them to understand that we had rules and professional ethics for a good reason and that we all had to follow them. Otherwise, the system wouldn't work for anybody.

⟨⟩⟨⟩⟨⟩

The Burnham mess had proven a distraction from the other major mess in my professional life, the Ginsberg murder investigation. I dialed Kate's office and got her on the first ring.

"Sam, we finally got a break. AFIS came back with a print match from the murder weapon."

"Anybody we know?"

"Don't think so," said Kate. "His name is Anthony Barnes. The hit came from a check of military records. It seems that Mr. Barnes was an enlisted serviceman in the U.S. Army. He was on active duty for almost three years, achieved the rank of private first class, and then received a general discharge a little over two years ago from Fort Campbell, Kentucky.

"Know anything about what a general discharge entails?"

"Not a lot. I'm pretty sure that it's a form of honorable discharge, but it does send up a red flag. There's got to be something there that isn't quite right, otherwise the guy would have left the military with an honorable discharge."

"I'll contact the military police at Fort Campbell and see what they can tell me," she said.

"Good place to start, but I think you'll end up contacting the Adjutant General Corp. They'll have the particulars on his discharge."

"You think the military police won't?"

"Probably not. The military police will have a record of any misconduct occurring on or around the base, but I don't think they typically hold discharge information."

"You mean, say, this guy assaulted somebody in a bar and got arrested, that's the kind of information the military police would have."

"Exactly."

"Okay, I'll get right on it. I'll start with the military police and then move on to the Adjutant General Corp if necessary." said Kate.

"Can we put Mr. Barnes in Utah?" I asked.

"Looks like he lives here. I ran him through DMV and he shows a Utah driver's license with an address in Ogden."

"Care to pay him a visit?" I asked.

"Absolutely. I'll be anxious to have him explain how his prints ended up on our murder weapon."

"I'll bet. What have you got for a physical description on Mr. Barnes?"

"Let's see, his driver's license shows that he's six-feet, five-inches, one-hundred ninety-five pounds, brown and brown. Why'd you ask?"

"Oh, just something the medical examiner told me after Ginsberg's autopsy."

"Refresh my memory."

"Dr. Chandler-Soames theory is that we should be looking for a tall perp, at least a couple of inches taller than Ginsberg who she measured at six-feet, two-inches."

"And that was because the tire iron blow to the back of the vic's head was struck at a downward angle," said Kate.

"That's right. So, if the ME's theory is correct, this guy fits the profile."

"When would you like to take a drive to Ogden?"

"Why don't I pick you up in front of your office at noon. We can grab a sandwich, have that discussion we didn't have last night, and then go see Anthony Barnes. In the mean time, I need to pay Walter Bradshaw a visit. He's asked to see me."

"I'll be anxious to hear what he wants to see you about," said Kate. "See you at noon."

Chapter Twenty-six

I met Walter Bradshaw in the same small office in the maximum security housing unit that we'd used previously. He stood as I entered, staring intently with those penetrating, emerald green eyes. He extended a shackled right hand and I took it.

I had to admit that there was something charismatic about him although I wasn't sure what it was. He had a presence. It wasn't difficult for me to understand how he might attract followers and exert leadership over others. Guys like this could be downright dangerous if they carried around too much of the wrong kind of baggage. David Koresh and the Reverend Jim Jones immediately came to mind.

I set a tape recorder on the desk between us. "Walter, I'm not at all sure I should be here. You are represented by counsel. He's not present, and I suspect he doesn't know you asked to see me. Am I correct about that?"

He shook his head. "The machine can't hear you nod," I said. "You've got to give me an audible yea or nay."

"No, Mr. Dixon doesn't know that I asked to see you." Glancing at the recorder, he continued, "And is that thing really necessary?"

"Afraid so. We're going to have to play this one by the book. The tape provides a precise record of our conversation—nothing to interpret, no subtle nuances. It protects us both."

I went over the Miranda warnings with him, unsure of whether an incriminating statement would be admissible even with a waiver of his constitutional rights. When I finished that little tete-a-tete, I asked the obvious question: "Walter, you requested this meeting so I assume you had a reason. What did you want to see me about?"

"I wanted to give you a gift," he said, a slight smile playing at the corners of his mouth.

I frowned. "A gift. What kind of gift? What are you talking about, Walter?"

"You've been trying to solve the murder of Arnold Ginsberg, and from what I can see, you aren't having much success. That's because you've been looking in the wrong place. You believe members of my church committed the crime, and they didn't."

"Okay," I said. "You've got my undivided attention. So what is the 'right place' for us to look?"

He gave me exasperated look like maybe I'd just fallen off the back of a turnip truck. "I'm surprised you can't see it. It's right in front of your nose. I, and my followers, are being framed for the Ginsberg killing by members of the FLDS church on the orders of Warren Jeffs."

"So, you're suggesting that the Ginsberg murder was carried out by members of the FLDS church. Is that what you're saying?"

"Them, or perhaps agents acting on their behalf."

"Agents, what do you mean?"

"The murder could have been carried out by members of the FLDS church, but more likely, it was committed by an agent, someone sympathetic to the cause acting at their beck-and-call."

"You mean a hired gun, someone like Porter Rockwell who defended the LDS faithful during the nineteenth century. Is that what you're saying?"

He nodded.

"It's nice conjecture, Walter, but that's all it is unless you can provide proof."

"What kind of proof do you need?"

"Any kind. An eyewitness would be nice. Do you have any specifics for me—like the names of the people involved? That would be good."

He just looked at me but didn't answer.

I decided to try and keep him talking. "This is all well and good, Walter, but without specifics, it's nothing more than speculation on your part. And frankly, your own motives are a bit suspect, don't you think? Why should anyone believe you?"

"What makes you say that?" his tone sounding slightly defensive.

"It's no secret that many of your early crimes and those committed by your followers were directed against the FLDS church, I guess more specifically, FLDS church property. What made you turn against the members of your own church?"

He paused before answering as if carefully trying to measure his words. "I didn't turn against members of my own church, Mr. Kincaid. Instead, I chose to punish the FLDS church leadership for inflicting unjust suffering upon the faithful. I was directed to do so in a revelation from the Lord."

Sounded like a crock of shit to me.

"Well, that certainly is convenient, the revelation part I mean. I guess you had to come up with some way to justify committing so many thefts, burglaries, hell, even a couple of arsons."

"Believe what you will, Mr. Kincaid, but my people are not responsible for most of the crimes you just mentioned. You have no idea how much anger and resentment, much of it directed at Warren Jeffs, lies just under the surface—even among the FLDS faithful."

"Perhaps I don't. Care to enlighten me?"

"What occurred with the passing of the Prophet Rulon Jeffs was nothing short of a pure power grab by his son, Warren. For the first time in church history, governance passed not to the next most worthy senior man, but from father to son, almost like royalty."

"That's what's made you so angry, angry enough to leave the church, and angry enough to commit crimes against it?" I hoped that my open ended responses, feigned interest in his ramblings, and apparent bewilderment would keep him talking. It did.

"Warren Jeffs destroyed families, and he did so with utter disregard for the consequences and the costs in real human lives. Did you know, Mr. Kincaid, that after his power-grab, Warren permanently banished hundreds of boys and young men from the church, some as young as thirteen? And he did so based on false accusations in some cases, and minor infractions in others?"

"Like what he did to your family?" I said.

For the first time, I saw emotion from this man—tears welling in his eyes. He nodded but didn't say anything. I moved on.

"What makes you think Warren Jeffs is calling the shots? He's locked up in jail in case you missed it."

He grunted. "Nothing, and I mean nothing happens in the FLDS church that Warren doesn't direct," said Bradshaw. "A jail cell can't stop that."

He gave me a slight opening and I took advantage of it. "You mean just like you call all the shots for your church from here inside the prison."

"How would I manage to do that?" he shot back.

I had a decision to make. Should I tell him my theory? I decided to give it a try and see how he reacted. "What if you had a lawyer, one sympathetic to plural marriage, who was willing to be a conduit for information going in and out of the prison?"

He looked at me for a moment without answering, deliberately trying to figure out whether I was running a bluff or actually knew something. "Suppose, just suppose for the sake of discussion your hunch is correct. It is just a hunch, isn't it?"

My turn not to answer.

He paused before going on. "Your supposition, Mr. Kincaid, and that's all it is, is absolutely preposterous. It would be impossible for me to conduct the affairs of the Reformed Church of the Divine Christ from inside a prison cell."

This guy was smart, I had to give him that. And he was fucking with me big time. So I took the bait. "If we take my supposition, as you call it, one step further, that would mean that you, through Gordon Dixon, ordered your followers to kidnap

Robin Joiner. And Robin was forcibly abducted from a friend's apartment last evening. Joey has already been identified as one of the perps, and I suspect, by now, so have the Allred brothers, Albert, or some combination thereof. Care to comment?"

During an interrogation you learn with experience that nonverbal cues are often as revealing as the things suspects say. This was a textbook case. Bradshaw's eyes narrowed to tiny slits, his chin dropped nearly to the desk top, and momentarily, he was absolutely speechless. It was obvious that he knew nothing about last night's kidnapping, which also meant he didn't order it. It wasn't a big stretch to believe that Gordon Dixon was in for a serious butt-chewing the next time there was a lawyer-client meeting.

Bradshaw stammered, "Was anyone hurt?"

"I don't know about Robin, but her girlfriend was left behind bound wrists-to-ankles with duct tape over her mouth."

He considered that for a moment before saying, "I want to see my lawyer."

"I take it this means that our interview is over," I said. "By the way, we know all about Joey's relationship with Robin. Was Robin involved in the armored car hold-up?"

He just stared at me.

Chapter Twenty-seven

On my way to pick up Kate, my cell phone rang. It was Marilyn Hastings from the employee assistance program. "I thought you'd want to know. Terry Burnham showed up right on time for his ten o'clock appointment this morning."

"I'm glad to hear that. How'd it go?"

"It was about what I expected. Aside from being hung over, which didn't help his disposition any, he was guarded, defensive, and in denial about having a drinking problem. That aside, he was just peachy."

"Can you work with him, Marilyn?"

"It's too soon to tell. I'll have to get back to you on that one. The good news is that he agreed to see me again day after tomorrow."

"Will you keep me informed?"

"There are some confidentiality issues, but sure, to the degree that I can."

<><><>

I left my car at police headquarters and rode to Ogden with Kate. I filled her in on the problem with Terry Burnham.

"Damn, I'm sorry to hear that, Sam. I really hoped that he'd found a home inside the SIB, but Terry always struck me as a guy with a lot of baggage."

"What do you mean?"

"The drinking mostly. I've known Terry for almost ten years and he's always had a reputation for hitting the sauce a little too hard, even before his wife died. The drinking seemed to accelerate after her death, although by that time, he had retired from the force."

"I've got him working with Marilyn Hastings. He showed up for his first counseling appointment this morning."

"That's good, I'm glad to hear it, but can I give you a piece of advice?"

"Sure."

"I know your reputation for sticking up for your employees. It's one of those things that your own staff and other cops admire about you..."

"Yeah, yeah, skip the accolades and get on with the advice."

"Promise me you won't go too far out on a limb with this one."

"And you say that because..."

"I've just got a bad feeling about it. I'd hate to see it blow up in your face."

"Are you sure you're telling me everything?" I asked.

"It's just a feeling in my gut. I hope you'll listen."

"I'll consider myself warned."

We took the I-15 north until we turned off on to state highway 89, something locals called the Mountain Road. Our conversation waned and we rode in relative silence the rest of the way to Ogden.

We followed Harrison Boulevard north a couple of miles past the university until we located the home of our suspect, Anthony Barnes. There was a For Sale by Owner sign stuck in the front lawn. Like everything in this neighborhood, the house was old, probably built in the years shortly after World War II. It was an all-brick, flat roofed rambler, with window wells revealing a basement.

We drove slowly past the house, turned around, and parked on the street a couple of doors away. There were no cars parked in front of the residence or in the driveway. The door to the detached single car garage was closed as was the drape covering the home's front window. It looked like nobody was around.

I said, "Were you able to find out anything about this guy? I hate like hell having to walk up to his front door not knowing whether he has an arsenal in their large enough to outfit a marine battalion."

"I called the military police at Fort Campbell. They didn't have any discharge information about him, but they were able to tell me that Mr. Barnes had managed to accumulate a less than distinguished service record."

"Did they give you any specifics?"

"Assault and batteries, mostly. Several bar fights off base and a couple of skirmishes at the NCO club. At the time of his discharge, he'd been banned from using the NCO club. Apparently, when he drinks, this guy loves to fight."

"Wonderful. Maybe that explains the general discharge."

"Maybe."

We walked up the driveway and Kate veered off toward the front door. I remained on the cracked and buckled concrete driveway, walking quickly toward the back of the house. "I'll cover the rear."

Kate nodded.

Nobody answered the front door. I climbed the back steps and peered into the kitchen area, through the formal dining room, and into a dimly lit living room. Nobody was around and everything looked as neat as a pin. We decided to try the neighbors on either side. Kate went one way and I went the other. A few minutes later we were back in the car and able to piece together a bit more information about Anthony Barnes.

"What did you find out?" asked Kate.

"Not a lot. The gentleman next door says that Barnes lives alone, rarely has visitors, and comes and goes at odd times. He apparently drives a late model, black, Honda SUV. What about you?"

"He has a 2003 Honda CRV registered in his name. I already knew that. The couple on the other side told me that the house used to belong to his mother. She died a couple of years ago, and Anthony inherited the place. These folks said that Barnes mentioned that he was having a tough time making the mortgage payment and that he was either going to have to sell the place or rent out rooms. They think he works in a bar someplace in Salt Lake."

"That ought to be easy enough to check," I said. "That might also explain his coming-and-going at odd hours. Bars aren't exactly a nine-to-five kind of gig."

"True enough. Why don't we grab a bite of lunch some place. After we order, I'll call the Utah State Liquor Commission office and see if his name shows up on any liquor licenses. Afterward, we can back-track here to see if he's returned."

"Sounds like a plan, the eating part especially. I'm starving."

"You're always starving."

"Yeah, well, I've got a raging metabolism to go with my raging hormones."

"I don't know about the raging metabolism part, but I can definitely attest to the raging hormones."

"Kind of led with my chin on that one, didn't I?"

She smiled, "Absolutely."

<>‹›‹›

Describing lunch at the Café Mexicana as run-of-the-mill would be kind. I ate enough beans to go with my soggy burrito to require a case of Tums just to make it through the afternoon. Kate's tostada wasn't much better. But that's what happens when you take your restaurant recommendation from a guy using a pay phone outside the convenience store where you just gassed your car.

But maybe the indigestion was less about the lunch and more about the conversation, which included Kate's evening of giddy conviviality with her old boyfriend, Tom Stoddard, at the New Yorker lounge the previous evening. My initial feelings of surprise and jealousy had given way a day later to a more rational and objective view of the incident. After all, appearances could be deceiving—or not.

"Okay," I said. "Cut to the chase. What was that bullshit I saw going on between you and Tom last night? You did tell me it wasn't what I thought."

"Let me tell you what happened. I dropped by his office to have him take a look at the affidavit I'd written for the search warrant application, you know, the one we're going to serve on Greg Samuelson in order to get Ginsberg's estate information. If you recall, it was either get a search warrant or I have to sleep with the guy. Which would you prefer?"

I smiled, "Smart ass."

"Tom suggested we stop for a drink and I didn't see the harm. It was just two old friends catching up. There was nothing going on for you to be upset about."

I wasn't convinced. "If there was nothing to it, you might have told me about it."

"You're right. I should have, and I'm sorry I didn't."

"It looked awful damned cozy to me, like two old lovers reliving the past and perhaps toasting the future."

"It wasn't like that, Sam. Tom might want it to be that way, but I don't. There is, however, something I'd like to talk with you about. It's been on my mind for a while."

Oh, oh, I thought, here it comes. "Sure, go ahead."

"You need to be patient with me, Sam. Sometimes, I think you want our relationship to move along faster than my psyche can handle. I need a little time to adjust."

"If I've been putting pressure on you, Kate, I'm sorry. I didn't intend to."

"I know you didn't. Just remember that six months ago, I was a career cop, dating a deputy DA, with no plans for marriage, much less children. And then you entered my life, and all of a sudden, things are different. For the first time in my life, I can hear the M word without wanting to put on my track shoes and run. And this relationship comes with a ready-made family. Sometimes, it just freaks me out a little."

"I'm glad you told me that. I'll pay more attention to the kinds of things I say and do. I love you, Kate, but it's gotta be right for everybody—you, me, Sara, and Aunt June. If you need some space, there's nothing wrong with that. We can take a step back."

She reached over and squeezed my hand. "I don't want to step back but I do want your understanding. By the way, my folks are planning a trip out here. I've been telling them about you and Sara and Aunt June for months now, and they're eager to meet everyone."

"And are they a little nervous over the ready-made family?"

"A little, I think. Dad doesn't say much, but he never does. Mom, on the other hand, is a little worried. It'll all be fine once they have a chance to meet you."

◇◇◇

After lunch, we drove past the home of Anthony Barnes. It still didn't look like anybody was home. Kate jumped on her cell and called a contact in the enforcement section of the Utah State Liquor Control Commission. She asked whether Barnes' name appeared on any state liquor licenses.

"Guess what, Sam?"

"No idea. What?"

"Anthony Barnes is not listed on any state liquor licenses."

"So the neighbor was wrong, big deal!"

"Ah, but I'm afraid that it is a big deal," said Kate.

"How so?"

"Mr. Barnes, while not a bar owner, is licensed as a bartender. Guess where?"

"You're bustin my chops with this, Kate. Where?"

"The Lucky Gent."

"The gay bar, huh."

"One and the same I'm afraid."

I looked at Kate. "You thinking what I'm thinking."

"Probably," said Kate. "What are you thinking?"

"Until now, we've been operating under the theory that the Ginsberg killing was the work of Bradshaw's religious followers. That made sense when you considered the facts: Ginsberg was about to become a star witness in the armored car robbery; his testimony would have helped convict Walter; and he was murdered just hours before his scheduled court appearance. It seems like such a good fit."

"Not anymore," said Kate. "Now we've got a direct link to Ginsberg's killer in the form of a gay, ex-military man with no known ties to the Bradshaw family or their church. It stinks of the bereaved partner, Rodney Plow, don't you think?"

"Maybe. Your hunch about Rodney may have been right all along. What's still missing is anything connecting Anthony Barnes with Rodney Plow."

"Not for long," said Kate.

<><><>

Robin Joiner had been here once before. Joey had brought her here for a romantic getaway on her last birthday. They had spent the night. She recalled that Joey seemed deliberately vague when she'd asked him who the cabin belonged to. Now she understood why.

The old house, located high in the Wasatch Mountains, served as a hideout for the Bradshaw clan and probably belonged to a polygamist or someone sympathetic to the cause. It was a small log cabin situated a couple of hundred yards off the paved road. It afforded maximum privacy because it was surrounded by a thick canopy of mature evergreens. Unless you knew where to look, the turnoff down the single track dirt road was almost impossible to see. Access during the winter would probably require skis, snowshoes, or a snowmobile. It was a perfect place for anybody on the lam.

Since her arrival, she and Joey hadn't exchanged more than a few words. He tried, but when his clumsy attempts were met with silence, he quickly moved on to other priorities. He was clearly preoccupied, but with what, she wasn't sure.

While she wasn't restrained, they kept a close eye on her. She slept on a single bed in one of two small bedrooms. Joey and Albert slept on mattresses on the floor. She had been allowed outside for two short walks, each time escorted by Joey. She considered making a run for it but thought it unlikely that she would make it as far as the paved road. The potential consequences of a failed attempt scared her. She didn't believe that Joey would hurt her, but she was unsure about the others, particularly the Allred brothers.

Joiner watched and listened. She picked up bits and pieces of conversations. There was an energy among the four men, a sense that something important was about to happen. In an instant she realized that the Faithful were about to engineer the escape of Walter Bradshaw from prison.

Chapter Twenty-eight

It was late in the afternoon by the time Kate and I left the Matheson Courthouse with a signed copy of the search warrant. We drove the few short blocks to the law firm of Smith, Samuelson, and Wood.

Getting our hands on Ginsberg's estate information had suddenly become a priority. If the estate left significant assets to Rodney, it could provide a strong motive for Ginsberg's murder, particularly in light of Plow's adulterous behavior with his personal trainer, Steven Ambrose. Ambrose had become a person of interest in the case, someone we needed to find out more about.

Greg Samuelson met us in the lobby of the law firm. He accepted service of the warrant and flashed Kate his best smile. He was a good looking guy, probably in his early forties, with a full head of dark hair. He wore a designer suit that would probably have cost me a month's salary. I figured that nobody had teeth that white without spending a grand per for expensive veneers.

"Gee, Kate, I'd hoped you would accept my offer of drinks and dinner. Remember what I said—everything's negotiable. You might not have needed this warrant." He paused, waiting for a response.

Kate indulged the silly shit with a flirty grin of her own. "Sorry, Greg, the warrant seemed a lot safer." That comment produced another slick, if patronizing grin. I, on the other hand, recalled Shakespeare's well worn line, "First let's kill all the lawyers."

Samuelson ushered Kate and me into a posh conference room that appeared to serve as a law library. He put one of his assistants to work copying everything in the file. Ten minutes later, he poked his head into the room to inform us that his assistant would join us momentarily with the required documents, and that we were welcome to use the conference room for as long as we liked. He also told us that he was available to answer any questions that we might have about the estate.

The estate documents included a will, a revocable trust, and miscellaneous correspondence between Ginsberg and Samuelson. We both read the file until Kate glanced up and said, "Interesting stuff, huh."

"I should say. It appears that Rodney was set to receive a very nice inheritance package until just a couple of weeks before Ginsberg's murder. Then it changed abruptly."

"I'll make you a bet that the estate changes will conform to Susan Fleming's report to Ginsberg concerning Rodney's infidelity. I'd bet that that changed everything."

"I'll pass on the bet, thank you very much, but I don't think there's any question about one thing: If Rodney had been a good boy, he stood to inherit the Salt Lake City house, a condo in Santa Fe, and a significant amount of cash."

"I don't see anything in the file that indicates whether Arnold and Samuelson discussed the reason for these changes to his estate," said Kate.

"Let's get him back in here while we've got the chance and ask him," I said.

Kate was reading from the trust. "Other than several small donations to groups like the Gay-Straight Alliance and the ACLU, it appears that the chief beneficiary is now Ginsberg's brother in New York."

"I didn't see anything in the file indicating whether Rodney had received the bad news," I said. "That's something else we need to ask Samuelson."

Samuelson joined us in the conference room. "Did your client ever discuss the reason for the recent changes he made to his estate?" asked Kate.

Samuelson paused, apparently trying to remember. "As best I recall, Arnold did not give me any specific reasons for the changes. And unless a client wants to go into that, I typically don't ask. It's none of my business, and the few times I've gone down that road with other clients, I feel like I'm in the wrong business. Some of this stuff needs to be processed with a shrink, not a lawyer. I do seem to remember having the impression that all was not well between my client and Mr. Plow. But Arnold never got specific. In some ways, he was a bit reclusive."

"Have you heard from Mr. Plow regarding the contents of the Will and Trust?" I asked.

"No, I haven't, and that's a little unusual, although I suppose it's possible that my client had the discussion with Mr. Plow prior to his murder. Why go through the humiliation of making an appearance at the law firm if you've already been given the bad news?"

<>
 <> <>

On the way back to the police department, Kate and I discussed what we'd learned.

"Frankly," said Kate, "I'm a little concerned."

"About what?"

"In a nutshell, motive. Had Ginsberg not changed his estate, Rodney would have had ample incentive to want to see him dead, particularly if a new lover had entered the picture."

"And now?"

"That motive's gone, particularly if, as Samuelson suggested, Rodney had been told that he was out of the Will."

"Good point. What you're saying is why kill Ginsberg absent a financial payoff of gargantuan proportions?"

"Exactly."

"People kill for a variety of reasons, Kate. Assuming Plow had been told, maybe anger or a desire for revenge took over. In any event, we don't have to prove motive."

"True, but it's a lot stronger presentation to a jury when you can show it. I've always been uncomfortable with a murder investigation when I can't come up with the why.

"Can you work late with me tonight? I could use the help."

"I think so. Let me give Patti a call to see if I've got any fires burning in the SIB. And then I'll have to call Aunt June. I'm on doggy-dad duty tonight, but maybe I can get a stay of sentence."

Kate was smiling. God, the woman had a great smile. "What's on tap for tonight?"

"I've been assigned to be Bob's personal trainer. We're scheduled for our first two-mile walk this evening."

"You mean Bob the Bassett Hound?"

"None other. The poor, little dummy doesn't know it, but he's now on a diet. Aunt June and Sara have worked out an exercise schedule for him, complete with weekly weight loss goals, with yours truly nominated as drill sergeant."

Now Kate was really laughing.

"Keep it up," I said, "but remember that if you do join the Kincaid family, it could be you exercising Bob the Bassett Hound."

"No thanks. I think that duty is better suited to your personality type."

"Screw you. Speaking of which, if I do stick around tonight, do you think we could go back to your place later and mess around?"

"I think that can be arranged. Let's call it payment for services rendered. And guess what? You won't even need a two-thousand dollar suit or veneered teeth."

Chapter Twenty-nine

I called home and managed to get a one day reprieve from my duties as Bob's personal fitness trainer. Aunt June went along easily. Sara took a little extra convincing.

Kate and I took a few minutes to check messages from our respective offices. For me, it turned out to have been one of those rare days in the Special Investigations Branch where nothing of significance happened. I'd received two calls, one from Terry Burnham and the other from Susan Fleming, the knock-out PI. I had a good idea what Burnham wanted. Fleming, on the other hand, was a different story.

I dialed Burnham's home number and didn't get an answer. The call kicked into his voice messaging system. The fact that he wasn't home, or just not answering, worried me. Maybe he was out some place with his face in a bottle, or perhaps he was sitting home alone in a drunken stupor. Christ, I was worrying about him like he was my child instead of an employee. If time allowed, I decided to ask Kate to stop at Terry's house so that we could check on him.

Fleming's office phone rang several times without answer before it forwarded to another number. A couple of rings later, she picked up.

"Hello, Sam, thanks for getting back to me. I wonder if we might get together. There's something I need to speak with you about."

"Can we do it over the phone?"

There was a pause. "I'd rather not. Could your spare a few minutes tonight?"

"Well, I'm tied up at the moment. I'm not sure how late I'm going to be. Can you tell me what this is all about?"

"Your child custody lawsuit," she replied, without hesitation.

She had my undivided attention. "How did you find out about that?"

"That's what I want to talk to you about."

"Okay, but this will have to be fast because I'm working tonight. How about Squatter's Brew Pub on 300 South, in say, fifteen minutes?"

"That works for me," she said, and disconnected.

I left Kate at her office, promising to return shortly. I arrived at Squatter's ahead of Susan Fleming. The place was noisy and jammed with after-work revelers. I found a couple of seats at the bar and ordered a draft. Minutes later, Fleming walked in and took a seat on the bar stool next to me. Every guy in the joint had turned his head to gape. She ordered a glass of house Pinot Noir.

"Not a beer drinker, huh?"

"Once in a while, but not that often," she replied.

"I don't mean to be short, but I'm really pressed for time. Tell me how you learned about the lawsuit?"

"Sure. I received a call from a lawyer in Atlanta asking me to spy on you. I believe he represents your former spouse. Small world."

I nodded. "And he specifically wanted you to do what?"

She arched her eyebrows. "Well, in these types of cases, it's all about suitability. Which parent will be able to provide the best environment to raise the child? Like it or not, that includes character issues, morals, that sort of thing."

"In other words, this attorney wanted to hire you to look around and see whether you could dig up some dirt in my personal life, like who I might be sharing a bed with, that sort of thing."

"Personal life or career."

"So what did you tell him?"

"I told him I wasn't available and recommended somebody else for the job."

"Why did you do that?"

"You mean turn the job down or recommend somebody else to do it?"

"Both."

Fleming shrugged. "Want a straight answer?"

"That's always the best kind," I said.

"When we met the other day, I thought you were cute. Figured maybe we could go out some time. Spying on you in a child custody case probably wouldn't endear me to you." She was smiling.

I smiled back. "You're right about that. I appreciate your letting me know. If it's not a trade secret, can I ask who you recommended for the job?"

"Larry Holding. He's a former Kearns cop. He went private several years ago after assaulting the girlfriend he was seeing on the QT behind his wife's back. Kearns PD didn't like that very well and canned him."

I took a gulp of my beer. "Sounds like a real charming guy. How do you know him?"

"In this line of work, it's a pretty small world. We have monthly PI luncheons where we network and mostly talk shop. Occasionally, we refer business to one another. So, Mr. Kincaid, are you footloose and fancy free, or spoken for?"

"You don't waste a lot of time, Susan. Truth is, I'm spoken for, but if anything changes, I'll definitely give you a call."

She sighed. "The good ones are always taken, or so it seems. Mind if I ask who the lucky young lady is?"

I started to answer but she interrupted. "Never mind, I think I know."

Now it was my turn to raise my eyebrows.

"It's that female cop you were with the other day, McConnell. Am I right?"

"How'd you know?"

"The way you looked at each other. It was obvious." She handed me a business card with her home phone number written on the back.

We finished our drinks and got up to leave. I picked up the tab. It was the least I could do for the tip Fleming had provided. We promised to stay in touch. As I turned to go, she said, "Sam, just so you'll know, Holding drives a late model, silver, Ford Explorer."

I thanked her again and headed back to Salt Lake PD to meet Kate.

Chapter Thirty

Kate and I sat huddled in the conference room adjacent to her office on the second floor of Salt Lake PD headquarters. She wanted to know all about my meeting with Susan Fleming. I filled her in.

"Are you a little surprised that Nicole would hire a PI to snoop around in your life?"

"Hurts my feelings, actually, particularly to think Nicole might be behind it. It feels more like something her father would think of, and probably be willing to fund. I'd like to think Nicole doesn't even know about it, but that's probably being naïve."

"Think we should do anything about it?"

"What's to do? I think we just go on living our lives. We've got nothing to hide and nothing to be ashamed of."

"Are you going to say anything to Nicole?"

"I doubt it—might as well let 'em think they've got a well guarded secret. I will tell my lawyer, not that there's anything she can do about it."

We turned our attention back to the case at hand. We studied flip charts taped to the walls containing investigative leads, various case theories, and an organization chart of the Reformed Church of the Divine Christ. With the recent revelation of a possible gay connection to the murder of Arnold Ginsberg, the case had taken on increased complexity.

"While we were in Ogden this afternoon, I received a call-back from the Army, a Major Lungren, regarding Barnes and his general discharge," said Kate.

"And...."

"Seems that he got the general discharge as a result of his overall service records, which wasn't very good, and, get this, because he was found in violation of the military's Don't Ask, Don't Tell policy."

"The fact that Barnes is gay should come as no big surprise considering where he's employed. The bigger question now is what does it all mean? What's your take, Kate?"

"At first glance, it all points to Rodney Plow. But, what if our assumption is wrong?"

"Meaning...."

"What if Ginsberg's murder, while connected somehow to the gay community, has nothing to do with Rodney Plow?"

"Possible, I suppose. You're suggesting that Barnes, and an unknown accomplice, killed Ginsberg for some reason that has nothing to do with Rodney."

"Yup. We need to find out whether Barnes and Ginsberg were acquainted. It's certainly possible they knew each other because they both hung around the Lucky Gent. We just don't know. More importantly, how are we going to find out?"

That gave us both pause to stop and think. Finally, I said, "This might be a long shot, but I used to have a gay snitch in the prison population who frequently provided good information about things going on inside. I was always amazed at what other guys would tell him or what he'd overhear. He was one of the best snitches I ever had."

"Is he out?"

"Yeah, he paroled about a year ago."

"You think he'd help us?"

"Don't know. I'm not even sure I can find him. As I recall, he paroled to Salt Lake City. He hasn't returned to prison, I do know that. He talked about applying through the Interstate

Compact so he could move to California, but I don't know that he ever did it. Want me to look into it?"

"You bet. I don't know anybody who can help us on this one. We'd want him to spend some time inside the Lucky Gent, maybe wear a wire. What incentive might he have to help us?"

"I'm not sure. We'd probably have to pay him. If things worked out, maybe we could get him off parole a little sooner."

"Can you get on this right away, Sam?"

"Sure. I'll have to run the whole thing by his PO. Let's hope he doesn't have a no alcohol clause in his contract. If that's the case, bars are a big no-no. In the meantime, nothing prevents us from asking other people, including Rodney, about a possible relationship between Barnes and our murder victim."

"I'm with you on that but I think it would be a mistake for us to focus exclusively on Plow and close our thinking to other possibilities. Sometimes in this business, we're guilty of forming a single, albeit logical theory, that turns out to be dead wrong. And sometimes, innocent people end up in prison because of it."

"Spoken like a true left-wing liberal," I said, smiling at her. "I happen to think you're right, Kate, but, let's not ignore the obvious: Rodney stood to gain a lot of dough if something happened to Ginsberg. There's also the little matter of Steven Ambrose. How do you think he fits into all this?"

"Wish I knew, but at least we've got him on our radar screen. We know where he lives, what he does for a living, and we also know about his infidelity with Rodney. We just need to keep digging."

"I agree although there's no physical evidence linking him to the crime, and infidelity alone sure doesn't make him a killer. Speaking of physical evidence, aren't you waiting for additional forensic test results?"

She grabbed her pen and began scribbling in her planner. "Yeah, the hair and fiber guys haven't gotten back to me yet. From what I hear, they're buried. I'll make a note to call them first thing in the morning."

"Okay," I said. "So what do you want to do now?"

"I think we should pay another visit to Rodney. We'll ask him about his relationship with the deceased, the estate, and see what, if anything, he has to say about Steven Ambrose."

"I may have a better idea. Why don't you go visit Rodney while I pay a visit to Steven Ambrose. If we both go see Plow, ten seconds after we leave his house, he'll be on the phone to tip Ambrose. This way we catch them both off guard and don't lose the advantage of surprise."

"Works for me," said Kate.

"What about Barnes?"

"With Anthony, I think we've got a couple of options. One, we can drag him in for questioning and see if we can break him down; two, we can place him under surveillance, leave him out there for a while—see what he does, who he sees. Who knows, maybe if we give him a little rope, he'll lead us directly to Rodney."

"I like the second option better. If we question him now and fail to break him down, he might decide to bolt. And, absent a confession, the only evidence we've got is the partial print."

"That's true," said Kate. "That'll also give us time to find out if your old snitch can help us."

"And the Bradshaw clan?"

"They're out of the picture for the moment unless something brings them back to center stage for Ginsberg's killing. In the meantime, the family remains high on the department's most-wanted list. Your old friend Hyrum Locke is talking to the FBI. They're discussing the possibility of a task force, and you know what that means?"

"A disorganized cluster-fuck with the FBI calling all the shots," I replied. Hyrum Locke was Chief of Detectives and Kate's boss. He was also an egotistical, self-serving ass.

"Ya think? Let's get to work."

<>‹›‹›

The plan was a go. For lawyer Gordon Dixon, what he was about to do would become a defining moment in an otherwise mundane life, a life filled with a deep and abiding commitment to his family and to his religious beliefs—beliefs grounded in the practice of polygamy. The fact that his legal career was about to come to an abrupt end didn't bother him at all. It had been an undistinguished law practice—a decade plus of representing petty criminals, handling real estate transactions, and writing the occasional will.

He had just finished loading the last of the boxes. Glancing around the soon-to-be-vacated law office, Dixon turned to his wife. "Did you remember to have the phone service turned off?"

"I did, and the other utilities, too. Let's get these boxes loaded into the truck and then we'll be out of here. Are you ready for tomorrow?"

"Everything's set. I'm nervous, but I also feel privileged to have been asked by the Prophet to perform such an important task."

"You're doing God's work. Everything will be fine. I'm excited about the prospect of finally being reunited with my sister wives. It's been a long time."

Joan Dixon, the prophet's younger sister, had been Gordon's first wife and his rock for nearly twelve years. They'd met as undergraduates and married during his first year in law school. It had been a good union. Upon graduation, Gordon had been recruited by then President Rulon Jeffs of the FLDS church, to handle a variety of church legal affairs. All that had changed after Warren Jeffs ascended to the church presidency and the purge began. Scores of young men, some just boys, were banished from the church. The banished included Walter Bradshaw and his two sons, Albert and Joseph. The boys were sent away first, and then Walter.

When they finished loading the truck, Gordon Dixon took one last look around the empty office. "Tomorrow begins a new chapter in our lives," he said, "We'll all be together again soon, either here on earth, or in the Celestial Kingdom."

Chapter Thirty-one

While Kate gathered information about Steven Ambrose, I tapped into department records searching for information on the whereabouts of my former snitch, Sammy Roybal.

I found Roybal at the home of his grandmother, in the Rose Park area of Salt Lake's west side. Despite his California inclinations, he hadn't left Utah. That didn't surprise me. I'd known Sammy for nearly six years during two separate prison commitments. Despite his criminal lifestyle, he always seemed highly devoted to a large, local, extended family. He'd been raised by a mother who'd been widowed since the age of seventeen. His father had been a small time crook with a heroin problem. He died of an overdose before Sammy was born. Sammy and a half-sister had been raised by his mother and a collection of aunts, uncles, and grandparents.

By any measure, Roybal's criminal career was also a petty one, punctuated by brushes with the law for such things as drug possession, theft, check and credit card forgery. It wasn't the seriousness of his criminal record that had earned him two stints at Point of the Mountain, but the length of it. Through sheer persistence, he accumulated a long record of petty crimes beginning at age fifteen. He had also managed to annoy every cop, prosecutor, and judge that worked with him because they saw him so often. He was now twenty-six and recently paroled for a second time. The fact that he'd been out for several months was a good sign since most inmates failed within the first ninety days. If you could keep an ex-con violation-free beyond ninety days, the odds improved that he might make it.

In prison, Sammy found a comfortable niche because he was both smart and gay. He worked as a legal assistant helping other inmates prepare writs and appeals in the law library by day, and ran a thriving prostitution business at night. The inmates hadn't nicknamed him Slammin Sammy for nothing. In the course of performing both jobs, Sammy Roybal heard a lot. He slipped me information on everything from crooked staff to drug trafficking to inmates with escape plans. He was even responsible for preventing a couple of planned gang hits on other inmates in the prison population. I almost hated to see the guy paroled.

When I called, his grandmother answered the phone. I'd managed to catch him just before his departure for an evening on the town. I could only imagine what that might entail.

"Hello, Sam," he purred into the phone. The guy had propositioned me more times than I cared to count.

"Hi, Sammy, got a little job for you if you think you might be interested."

"Anything for you, big boy," he cooed.

"Knock that shit off, would you? You know I don't like it."

"My, my, aren't we a little grouchy tonight. What's the job?"

I explained about the Lucky Gent, Anthony Barnes, and the murder of Arnold Ginsberg. He listened patiently until I finished.

"What's in it for Slammin Sammy, big boy?"

I had always found that Roybal responded well to material things or the cash that could buy them. In prison, we quietly added money to his commissary account, always making it look like the money came in from a family member on the outside. I figured between what Kate could pull from her budget and what I could take from mine, we'd have more than enough cash to interest Sammy. I tossed a number at him.

"And you'll cover all my expenses as well?"

"What expenses, Sammy?"

"Oh, expenses like the food I'll need to order, and of course, my bar bill."

"Okay, okay, we'll cover your expenses, too."

"I'll do it. Anything to help my good friend, Sam Kincaid," he said. "But I won't wear a wire. I won't have that cold goo taped to my hairless chest." He giggled. "It's not the kind of lubricant I like, and besides, it's not in the place I like it."

"Fair enough," I said, trying my best not to sound like a judgmental, homophobic jerk. We exchanged cell phone numbers, and Sammy promised to visit the Lucky Gent later in the evening.

<>‹›<>

Kate had given me a home address for Steven Ambrose. She'd also pulled his vehicle registration information. Ambrose drove a 2006 Jeep Wrangler and lived in a condo in Midvale. Susan Fleming's report gave me addresses for the health club he worked out of as well as an office on South State Street where he booked his massage appointments.

We left Salt Lake police headquarters at the same time in separate cars. We decided to use our cell phones to coordinate the timing of the interviews. We also decided not to question either subject until we found them both.

Kate followed me to Sugarhouse. I wanted to stop at Terry Burnham's house, check things out, congratulate him for his start in alcohol counseling, and encourage him to stay with it. When I called earlier, he hadn't answered. I was relieved to see his car parked in the driveway and the lights on in the house. Now if only he was sober. We parked on the street and approached the front door.

We could see Terry through the front window. He must have heard us approach because he looked up from the television and hollered at us to come in. He was sitting in front of the TV watching an NFL game while drinking a can of diet coke and eating Doritos. The house had been cleaned up. It was a far cry from the mess it had been the night before when I stopped by to tell him that he was suspended from duty.

We exchanged greetings and small talk before Terry asked, "Sam, can you tell me anything about the investigation?" Before I could answer, he continued. "And what about this head-hunter from the sheriff's office IA unit, Egan, I think her name is?"

"Slow down a minute, take a breath, will you?"

"Sorry. Sit down guys. Can I get you anything?"

We both declined. "I don't know her either, Terry. Her name is Melanie Egan. She's a sergeant in the unit with a solid reputation. She transferred into IA from patrol a few months ago."

"Don't know if that's good for me or not," he said. "She called late this afternoon, and I'm scheduled for an interview at ten in the morning."

"Where?"

"Her office. How do you think I should play it?"

"Just be honest with her, Terry. Explain what happened and what you're doing to correct the problem."

"The waiting is killing me. How soon do you think I'll hear something?"

"Just hang in there. I don't know for sure, but I think we'll know something fairly soon. This isn't a particularly complicated case. Once Sergeant Egan interviews you, I think she's finished. It's just a matter of how quickly she puts a report together. In the meantime, don't drink, continue seeing Marilyn Hastings, and do exactly what she says."

We got up to leave. Burnham was suddenly looking sheepish. "Sam, I owe you an apology for last night. I was so far out of line. I know you were trying to help me out. I'm really sorry."

"Don't worry about it. That was the booze talking last night. Just keep working on getting your shit together. That's what you can do for me."

As we walked to our cars, I glanced at Kate. While not unfriendly, she hadn't spoken to Terry beyond hello and goodbye. "What's bothering you, Kate? You almost came across as hostile in their."

"Sorry, I didn't mean to. It's just that I don't have a good feeling about this. The investigation has moved so quickly."

"So?"

"Well, you don't know this Egan, right?"

"True."

"And you don't really know how your new boss is going to be looking at this?"

"True enough, I guess."

"You essentially advised Terry to throw himself on the mercy of the system. What if the system decides not to treat him leniently? Isn't it possible that he could be charged with a felony?"

"Possible, but not very likely. Based on similar cases I've seen over the years, this one doesn't merit a felony filing. A misdemeanor, maybe."

"For your sake, Sam, I hope you're not so close to this that you can't see the forest for the trees. I don't know what you've got up your sleeve, but I hope it doesn't blow up in your face."

How did she guess? Indeed, I did have something up my sleeve. But it wasn't time to play that card, at least not just yet.

Chapter Thirty-two

Kate and I left Burnham's separately. I headed out to see Steven Ambrose while she drove to Ginsberg's home hoping to find Rodney. The medical examiner's office had released Ginsberg's body, and his brother from New York was in town making funeral arrangements. I wondered if Kate would find Rodney at home assisting with the funeral plans or whether he might be out on the town celebrating his new found freedom.

I located Ambrose's Midvale condo. The covered parking spaces had assigned numbers to correspond with individual condo units. Each unit had been assigned one parking stall with a storage closet located at the front. I circled the lot until I found number 142, a match with Ambrose's unit number. There was no sign of his late model Jeep Wrangler. I drove around the rest of the complex to be sure that he hadn't parked the SUV elsewhere. The Jeep wasn't there.

I parked in the visitors section, grabbed a flashlight, and stepped into the cool night air. Dusk had given way to darkness, reminding me that the autumn days were growing shorter. The evening temperatures were also falling fast—a sure sign that Utah's arctic winter was just around the corner.

I found Ambrose's condo. The lights were off and it looked like nobody was home. I knocked on the door. No answer. I returned to Ambrose's assigned parking stall, looked around, and seeing no one, turned the handle on his storage closet door. It was unlocked. I had just turned on my flashlight when the headlights from an approaching vehicle lit up the area around me like a Christmas tree. I stepped into the storage locker, doused the flashlight, and closed the door behind me. Safe enough, I thought. This would give the approaching car a chance to pass and I could then return to my illegal snooping.

The driver of the approaching vehicle had other plans. Instead of passing, it turned head-on into the parking stall where I now found myself trapped like a thief in the night. The idling engine was now just inches from the storage locker and the headlights illuminated the cracks around the door. I held my breath. If this was Steven Ambrose, imagine his shock if he opened the locker door only to find a perfect stranger staring back at him. What the hell could I say? 'Hi, I'm your new neighbor—just checking for termites. If you'll excuse me….' Maybe if he opened the door, I should just whack him with my flashlight and make a run for it.

The driver cut the engine, got out, and started to walk away. Just as I began to breathe again, my cell phone began to chirp. Christ, it must be Kate wondering why I hadn't called. I grabbed it, not sure whether I should smother it, swallow it, or smash it into a million pieces. To stop the noise, I punched the answer button but didn't speak. I didn't dare. Again, I held my breath hoping that whoever got out of the vehicle hadn't heard the bloody phone go off. Seconds passed and I didn't hear the sound of footsteps returning. Cautiously, I opened the door and peeked out. A red Jeep Wrangler occupied the stall. Steven Ambrose must have come home and, thank God, hadn't heard me rummaging inside his storage locker.

I took a fast look around the shed. It contained the usual assortment of stuff people commonly store, nothing to get excited or suspicious about.

I checked my cell. It was Kate who had called. I called her back.

"What the hell are you doing?" she asked, sounding genuinely irritated.

"You don't want to know. I'll tell you later. I feel like Inspector Clousseau in one of those old Pink Panther movies. Ambrose just got home. I'm ready to go in for the interview. What about Rodney?"

"Rodney's home but he was less than enthusiastic about my stopping by—said he hadn't been sleeping much and was going out for a while. Let's go get 'em and we'll catch up afterward." She was gone.

◇◇◇

Ambrose answered the door carrying a partially consumed bottle of Coors Light. I introduced myself, flashed credentials, and explained what I wanted. He invited me inside. We sat in the living room, me on the leather couch, him in a leather recliner. He offered me a beer. I declined.

"What brings you to see me, Detective Kincaid? And if you don't mind my asking, how did you get my name?"

"Well, Steven—may I call you Steven?…"

"Please call me Steve, that's what most people do."

"Okay, Steve. As a part of our investigation into the murder of Arnold Ginsberg, we're talking to anybody who might have information that would help us figure out who committed this horrible crime. As to how we got your name, I'm not exactly sure." *I lied.* "I can tell you that in cases like this, as we talk to people, they invariably supply us with the names of additional people who either knew the victim, or somebody else connected to the case." *That part was true.*

He studied me for a moment, sipping his beer. "Okay, fire away. How can I help?"

"Maybe you can begin, Steve, by telling me how you became acquainted with Arnold Ginsberg?"

"Sure. I'm a personal trainer and I met Arnold through the club. He was a member."

"The club you're referring to, that would be the Fit for Life Club, in Sandy, correct?"

"In Midvale, actually, but yes."

"And Arnold worked out at the club?"

"Sometimes, yes."

"Did Ginsberg employ you as a personal trainer?"

"Uh, no, not exactly. Mr. Ginsberg paid me to serve as a trainer and fitness coach for his partner, a guy named Rodney, oh, what's his last name? Plow, that's it—Rodney Plow."

"Would it be fair then to say you are better acquainted with Rodney Plow than you were with Arnold Ginsberg?"

"Yeah, that's true."

This guy wasn't volunteering much. "Just so that I'm clear, you earn a living as a personal trainer/fitness coach, is that correct? Are you employed doing anything else?"

He stammered. "Well, yes. I'm also a licensed massage therapist."

I feigned surprise. "Oh, and do you work on your massage clients at the Fit for Life Club?"

"On occasion, but I have an office on South State in Sandy."

"Okay. And did you provide massage services to Arnold Ginsberg or Rodney Plow?"

On this one, Ambrose hesitated before answering. "I don't recall ever giving a massage to Arnold, but I do work on Rodney occasionally." He forced a laugh. "Sometimes I work Rodney out so hard that he needs a massage afterward."

"That a pretty regular thing with Rodney, the massage, I mean?"

"No. Only occasionally."

"And do you provide massage services here in your condo?"

"No. I never bring clients back here. I always use the massage studio in Sandy. I don't keep a table here."

"That's funny," I said. "We've got reliable information that you and Rodney get together periodically right here in your condo during the day when Arnold is at work. Now, if you never bring clients over, Steve, what would you be doing here with Rodney?"

All the color drained from his face. For a moment, he didn't know how to respond. He went into denial mode. "I don't know what you're talking about. I've never had Rodney Plow here."

"Cut the bullshit, Steve. Want me to show you the surveillance photos?"

He broke eye contact and took another swig of his beer. "Okay, what if he was here a few times, what does that prove?"

"Only that you're a liar. And if you'll lie about something like this, I have to wonder what else you might be lying about?"

"Such as?"

"No, Steve, I'm asking the questions here. Isn't it true that you and Rodney have had an intimate relationship going on for some time now, all of it, of course, occurring behind Arnold Ginsberg's back?"

He looked at me wondering exactly how much I knew. "We're friends, that's all there is to it. There's nothing wrong with that, so why don't you stop trying to run a guilt trip on me?"

"That's interesting, Steve. Let me refresh your memory about something. Do you remember the woman who 'accidentally' walked in on you and Rodney several weeks ago in your office? That's the time the two of you were locked in a sixty-nine position on the massage table. That woman was a PI, for Christ's sake. She'd been tracking you and Rodney around town for weeks. We've got surveillance notes and photos, not to mention her eye-witness testimony of what was going on that day in your office. Still want to deny the physical relationship?"

He thought for a moment and then shrugged his shoulders. "Okay, so we were involved. What does that prove? I didn't have anything to do with Arnold's murder if that's what you're implying."

I just stared at him for minute. "Stranger things have happened. As I said before, if you're lying about this, who knows what else you're lying about? Now, how long have you and Rodney been an item?"

"Six, maybe seven months."

"How did the two of you get together?"

He looked resigned. "It happened over time. Mutual attraction was part of it. It didn't take very long before I realized that Rodney was tiring of the relationship with Arnold—big age difference for one thing."

"Did Rodney ever mention to you the possibility of killing Arnold or hiring someone else to do it?"

"God, no. We were having an affair, man. That's a long way from murder."

"Maybe so, but not always. Got to ask you this: Did you have anything to do with either planning or carrying out the murder of Arnold Ginsberg?"

"Of course not. I had nothing to do with it, and I don't know who did. Are we about done?"

"Yeah, Steve, I think that about raps it up. Just a couple more questions and then we'll be finished." He raised his eyebrows and shrugged his shoulders in mock frustration.

"Are you gay, Steve, or do you go both ways?"

"I'm bi, not that it's any of your business. I was married once. I've got a seven-year-old son. What does this have to do with anything?"

"Probably nothing. Just one more question. I need to know your whereabouts on the evening Arnold was killed. That would have been last Monday, say between four in the afternoon and eight P.M."

"You think I had something to do with this, don't you?"

"Not necessarily, Steve. This is all pretty routine in a murder case. You're not the first person I've asked, and I can assure you, you won't be the last."

He sighed. "I had checked into the Snowbird Lodge earlier in the afternoon. I spent the night there."

"What time did you check in?"

"I don't recall exactly, but I think it was mid afternoon."

"Were you with somebody?"

"No, I was alone. That's not unusual for me. I use the Snowbird Lodge occasionally as a getaway from the hustle-and-bustle of the valley. I particularly like to hike the area in the fall with all the gorgeous colors."

"Who were you hiking with?"

"Like I said, I was alone. I checked into my room, took a short nap, and then went out for a hike. I got back about dusk."

"What did you do then?"

"I got cleaned up and then went out to dinner in the lodge restaurant."

"What time was that?"

"Oh, I'm not sure. It was dark though."

"You've got to do better than that, Steve. You must have some idea what time you went to dinner."

"Well, I can't be sure, but if I had to guess, I'd say sometime between eight and nine."

"I assume you kept receipts."

"For the hotel room, yes—I'm not so sure about the dinner." He walked over to his dining room table and began rummaging through what looked like a stack of mail. Moments later, he handed me the Snowbird Lodge receipt. "I paid for the dinner with a Visa card, but I don't know where the receipt is."

"That's okay, this helps," I replied.

I stood up to leave. "That will be it for now. Thanks for your help. By the way, mind if I have a look around your condo?"

The look of disgust on his face suggested that I'd just crossed an invisible line. "You got a warrant?"

"No, but if you don't have anything to hide, I just thought...."

"Well, think again. I'd like you to leave now."

◇◇◇

I left Steven Ambrose with the strong suggestion that he not leave town without notifying either me or Kate. I intentionally decided not to ask him about Anthony Barnes or the Lucky Gent. I didn't see the point in telling him that we were already on to Barnes. There would be time for that later. In the meantime, if he was mixed up with Anthony in some way, and my interrogation rattled his cage sufficiently, maybe he'd contact him. The prospect of a connection between Steven Ambrose and Anthony Barnes made my mouth water. I also made a mental note to contact Ambrose's ex-wife and see what, if anything, she might be able to tell me.

Kate and I hooked up on our cells and agreed to meet at her place and drop one of the cars. We were both anxious to compare notes about what we had learned during our respective interviews. We decided that a good place to debrief would be the parking lot of the Lucky Gent.

How was I to know that a short stop at Kate's condo would turn into a two hour delay before we made it to the bar?

Chapter Thirty-three

By the time we left Kate's place, it was after midnight. We drove in relative silence to the Lucky Gent on 300 West in South Salt Lake City. There were still a handful of cars in the lot despite the lateness of the hour. The bar had to be close to last call. We spotted Anthony Barnes' black Honda CRV parked in the rear near the back door. We parked across the street in the parking lot of a plumbing supply business. I dialed Sammy Roybal's cell number but he didn't answer.

"Don't know about you, but I feel pretty good right now."

Kate smiled. "Took the edge off, didn't it? It did for me, too."

"I wish we'd hear something from Sammy," I said. "I neglected to ask him what kind of wheels he'd be driving. He could be inside right now and we wouldn't know it.

"I can tell you one thing. I'm sure as hell not going to walk in there looking for him. If I did, it would be like wearing a flashing neon sign that read, 'Hey, catch the straight cop.' If I know Sammy, we'll hear from him before long."

"What makes you so sure?" asked Kate.

"Cool, hard cash. Sammy'll want a down payment for this evening's work. He's a pay-as-you-go kind of guy."

"Assuming he's inside, I wonder what he's learned?" said Kate.

"Hard to know. I can tell you that Sammy is a prolific talker with a line of bullshit a mile long. If there's anything to learn, Sammy will get it."

We sat for nearly an hour. Customers drifted out of the bar, and the parking lot slowly emptied. The down time gave us a chance to compare notes. I went over what I'd learned in my interview with Steven Ambrose. Kate listened attentively. When I finished, she said, "What do you make of his alibi?"

"On one hand, he was real fuzzy when it came to time lines—couldn't remember when he checked in or what time he went to dinner. On the other hand, I've got a credit card receipt in my pocket for the room."

"It doesn't necessarily mean he used the room. It only proves that he or someone using his credit card checked in."

"True. It occurred to me that if he was involved in the murder, the Snowbird Lodge would be a good choice for an alibi. It's out of town, but close enough that you could check in, drive to Salt Lake City, commit a murder, and haul your ass back with your alibi still in tact. I'll go up their tomorrow. I'll bring along a photograph of him and we'll see if the front desk and restaurant staff can identify him. Maybe I can also pin down some times."

Kate had about the same level of success with Rodney Plow as I had had with Ambrose. After significant prodding, Plow admitted the affair, but chose to cast it as an inconsequential fling that occurred because of Arnold's growing inattentiveness. Rodney had not only denied any involvement in the murder, but he vociferously expressed shock and outrage that Kate had dared ask. Like me, Kate hadn't said anything about Anthony Barnes or the Lucky Gent in her interview with Plow.

"I'm glad we opted not to play the Anthony Barnes and Lucky Gent card with those two," said Kate. "We will have hit the mother lode if either of our interviews spooked these guys into an emergency strategy session with Barnes."

I nodded. "That would be the connection we're after, that's for sure."

Just before closing, Sammy walked out of the Lucky Gent. He was alone. I redialed his cell number, and this time, he answered.

"When you get into your car, look right across the street. We're parked in the plumbing supply lot."

He pulled up next to us, shut the engine off, and rolled down his window. "Think you guys could have parked in a more obvious place—might as well have parked under a spot light."

"Yeah, well, you didn't exactly make us now, did you? Learn anything useful in there tonight?"

"Not much. It's gonna take Sammy a while. I chatted up this guy, Tony, like you asked. He was workin behind the bar. After a few drinks, and me complimenting the shit out of his bar, he mentioned that he was buying the joint. I'll go back tomorrow night and keep working on him. You got some cash for Sammy?"

I looked at Kate. "What'd I tell you?" Kate and I had pooled our available cash. Between us, we'd managed to come up with $90.00. When Sammy reached for the dough, I asked, "Did you get me a receipt?"

He looked at me like I'd just kicked him in the nuts. "Are you crazy, man? You think Sammy's going into a place like that and asking for a receipt?"

I was laughing at him. "Hey, relax, Sammy. I'm just teasing you, man." I reached across and handed him the money. He counted it quickly before looking up with a scowl.

"This all you got? This'll barely pay my bar bill." He was working me now.

"What did you expect? You didn't exactly come back with a boat-load of good information tonight, ya know."

"Hey, man, Sammy's just gettin started. Sammy'll be all over that faggot tomorrow like a wet blanket."

"You do that, and I'll get you more cash tomorrow. In the meantime, don't bust my chops."

He ignored me. "Yeah, well tomorrow, bring Sammy something besides pocket change. I can get this kind of cash out of a coke machine." With that, he drove off.

"That guy's a piece of work," said Kate.

"You're telling me."

A little after two, Barnes came out the front door of the bar, locked it, and walked to his Honda. We followed him a short distance to an all-night Denny's restaurant where he ate a meal by himself while we sipped burnt coffee purchased from a nearby convenience store.

By three, he was back in the Honda, but he wasn't headed home, at least not to Ogden. We followed him again, this time to an old house on ninth east near downtown. He parked on the street and walked to the front door. We weren't close enough to tell if he had a key or just walked in. The house was dark.

"He's staying with somebody down here," I said. "Let's give it a minute and then cruise by the house slowly. I'll get the address."

We drove back to Kate's condo so that I could pickup my car. "Want to stay over? I hate having you drive all the way back to Park City this late."

"Thanks, but I'm feeling the need to spend some time with Sara and Aunt June. I've been working a lot of hours lately. Besides, I think I'm on duty later this morning with Bob the Bassett Hound. He's due for round one of his new weight loss training program. I'll be marching his sorry butt all over Park Meadows come morning."

"I hate to tell you, but it's already morning."

"Don't remind me."

Forty minutes later, I was home. Bob the Bassett Hound must have heard me tiptoe in through the garage. I heard a couple muffled woofs coming from Sara's bedroom. The lazy mutt didn't even come out to see who was in the house. Some watch dog.

Chapter Thirty-four

I woke to a wet tongue caressing my cheek, and I knew instantly that it wasn't Kate's. It was Bob the Bassett Hound probably hoping that a little early morning schmoozing might save him from a vigorous round of exercise with me. Not likely.

Sara was sitting on the bed, witness to the spectacle, giggling her head off. "I'll give you something to giggle about." I grabbed her, held her down on the bed, and gave her a major tickle. While it might be too early to tell, it seemed like Bob was having a positive effect on her. Since his arrival in our home, the problem of getting Sara to bed at night had abated.

I got up to the aroma of fresh coffee and the sound of Aunt June milling about the kitchen. She was in the midst of fixing breakfast.

"Good morning, Sam. I didn't hear you come in last night. I hope that I didn't let Sara into your bedroom to early."

"Not a problem. There's nothing quite like waking up to a big wet one from Bob the Bassett Hound."

Aunt June chuckled. "I hope you don't mind, but Baxter will be here shortly. I invited him to breakfast, and then he and I are off to a couple of garage sales. I warned him that we were getting a late start—early bird catches the worm, you know. If you go to these things late, the best stuff is already gone."

"What's he looking for?"

Before she could answer, Sara interrupted, "When's breakfast? I'm starving."

"Sara, don't interrupt. You're doing that a lot lately. Aunt June and I were talking. Since you're here, you can help me set the table. Breakfast will be ready in a few minutes. We're waiting for Uncle Baxter."

I turned back to Aunt June. "Sorry, you were saying."

"Beats me, I'm not really sure whether Baxter is looking for anything in particular. Frankly, I think he enjoys going out and rummaging through other people's stuff. And then if something strikes his fancy, he goes into negotiating mode. It seems like a waste of time, if you ask me."

I hadn't asked her, and I'll make you a bet that Uncle Baxter hadn't either. By the time Sara and I had finished setting the table, Baxter had arrived. We all sat down to a great breakfast. There's nothing better then Aunt June's pecan waffles, homemade, hot cinnamon applesauce, hickory smoked bacon, and fresh orange juice. After Sara had left the table, the adult conversation turned to the child custody lawsuit.

"Is anything going on, Sam?" Baxter asked. "How are you getting along with Allison Kittridge?"

"She's just fine—seems like a straight shooter. I think she thinks our chances are pretty good, but she made it clear that there are no guarantees. She anticipates that the court is about to set some kind of pretrial conference and that I'll need to fly to Atlanta."

"Have you spoken with Sara about this?" said Baxter.

"Not a word and I don't intend to, unless it becomes absolutely necessary."

"I think that's wise," he replied.

Aunt June chimed in. "Frankly, I'm worried that if we don't tell Sara, she might hear it from Nicole, or from her parents. They call once or twice a week, Nicole more often."

"I've asked Nicole not to say anything, but we can only hope."

I debated about whether I should tell Baxter and Aunt June about what I'd learned from Susan Fleming, but I decided against it. I didn't see the point. The fact that some sleaze-bag PI would probably be snooping around in my private life would only worry

Aunt June and there was nothing that she, or for that matter, I, could do about it anyway.

After breakfast, Sara and I cleaned up while Aunt June and Baxter made a dash for the garage sales. While we loaded the dishwasher, Sara asked about her mom. "Daddy, when do I get to see mom again?"

"Well, honey, we'll have to check on that. Why don't we call your mom today and ask her when she'll be coming to Salt Lake City. You know it's only a few weeks until Thanksgiving. It's your mom's turn to get to have you. Isn't she lucky?"

"Yeah. Can Bob come with me on the plane?"

I hadn't thought of that one. This would probably be a question I'd be hearing for a while. "Honey, I think that's going to be kind of hard to do. The airline won't let Bob on the plane with you. He's too big. Do you know where he'd have to ride?'"

"Where?"

"Down below where they put the luggage. I think that might really scare him, and we don't want that, do we?"

She looked sad. "No. Maybe Bob could ride with the pilot. Mom works for the airline."

"Well, that's true, she does. But I think they have rules that prevent pets from riding with the pilots. The other passengers might get a little nervous if they saw a dog sitting up front with the pilot. But we can see what your mom thinks. How does that sound?"

"Okay. When can we call her?"

"Let's call her right now. I don't know if she's home, but we can always leave her a message. And even if she's not home, she always calls you back."

I found it impossible to keep track of Nicole's flight schedule. We always tried her at home first. If we didn't get an answer, we assumed that she was traveling. We would then try her cell phone.

This time Nicole didn't answer her home or cell numbers, so Sara left a message. We spent the next little while watching television together. I asked her if she wanted to go with Bob and me on his fitness walk. No big surprise. Television won out. I was beginning to worry that television watching was on the increase, while reading and playtime outside was in decline. I didn't like that. I made a note to talk with Aunt June about it later.

I took Bob on a vigorous three mile walk through the neighborhood in Park Meadows. When we got back, he flopped in front of the fireplace like a guy who'd just run the Boston Marathon. We definitely had some work to do in the weight and physical stamina department. That much was clear.

I took Sara and a neighbor friend, Jennifer, to their noon soccer game at a city park. Sara had lots of saves in goal and her team won. I dropped the girls at Jennifer's house afterward and then went to work.

◇◇◇

Gordon Dixon maneuvered the Ford Taurus into the right lane and turned on his blinker to exit the freeway. The massive Utah State Prison compound loomed immediately to the west, visible to anyone traveling in either direction along I-15. The palms of his hands were damp with perspiration and his arm pits were soaked. Smuggling contraband into the state prison was not a matter to be taken lightly. It was a felony offense virtually everywhere. Utah was no exception.

He approached the guard shack at the main gate of the prison. A uniformed officer approached carrying a clip board. Dixon lowered the driver's side window. "Good afternoon, officer," he said with a smile.

"Good afternoon, sir. I'll need to see your driver's license. What brings you to the prison today?"

Dixon handed over his license. "I'm an attorney—here to see my client." The officer looked at the driver's license and then at Dixon. He wished that he'd been able to convince the Bradshaws to implement the plan on a weekday instead of the weekend. Lawyer visits to inmate clients were common on weekdays, less so on weekends.

The officer jotted down Dixon's information and handed the license back. He walked deliberately around the car looking through the windows. When he finished, he returned to the guard shack and raised the gate, motioning Dixon through.

He parked in the visitor's lot under the watchful eye of the guard tower. He took a deep breath and gathered himself. This was the moment of truth. Once he entered the visitor's processing area, there would be no turning back.

He checked his leather briefcase. He had intentionally filled it with a variety of client files including that of Walter Bradshaw. He'd learned from past experience that the fuller the briefcase the less thorough the search. The prison staff was acutely aware of the lawyer-client privilege. Unless they had some specific information to the contrary, they weren't allowed to read the legal correspondence. That didn't mean that they wouldn't open the envelope and inspect the contents before allowing Bradshaw to return to his cell. In all likelihood, they would do that.

Dixon had carefully packaged the drug into a small white envelope, and then carefully taped the envelope to the back of a stapled, twenty page batch of pretrial motions that he'd recently filed with the trial court. He had intentionally taped the drug halfway into the document and up near the staple where there was less chance that it would be noticed. If it was discovered, he would probably be arrested before he ever made it out of the prison.

Dixon got out of his car, locked it, and walked to the visitor's entrance. There was a short line in front of him and he had to wait. Several additional visitors came in and lined up behind him. In his experience lines were a good thing. The longer the line, the more harried the prison staff. The officer, a mostly bald guy who had to be packing an extra fifty pounds on a short, plump frame, spoke first.

"Sir, I'll need your picture identification and the name of the inmate you're here to visit."

Dixon again produced his driver's license and handed it to the officer. "My name is Gordon Dixon and I'm an attorney. I'm here to visit my client, Walter Bradshaw."

The officer hardly glanced at him and didn't say a word. He logged the driver's license information into his computer, handed the license back, and asked Dixon to sign the visitor's log. The visitor's log carried a written warning to anyone entering the prison that smuggling contraband was a felony offense.

Dixon signed in and moved through the line until a female corrections officer, who looked fresh out of the academy, stepped forward and said, "Sir, I'll need that briefcase you're carrying. And then if you'll empty your pockets, take off all jewelry, your belt and shoes, and your sports coat, I'll have you walk slowly through the metal detector."

Doing his best not to betray the apprehension that he was feeling, Dixon walked slowly through the metal detector without setting off the alarm. He glanced at the young corrections officer. The nametag on her uniform shirt read Officer Claudia O'Brien. She had opened his briefcase and emptied the contents on to a folding table. She did a cursory search of the files and then picked up the sealed manila envelope containing the drug.

This was the moment of truth and Dixon decided to take a chance. He gave her his best smile and said, "Officer O'Brien, would it be helpful if I opened the envelope for you? It contains court documents intended for my client."

O'Brien momentarily appeared to consider the offer. She shook and squeezed the envelope to see if anything seemed out of the ordinary. Finally, she said, "Thanks, but I don't think that'll be necessary."

Dixon took a deep breath and choked down the sense of panic he felt clear to his toes. Officer O'Brien reloaded the briefcase and handed it back to him. "If you'll take a seat in the waiting room, somebody will call you as soon as Bradshaw has been brought over from max."

Twenty minutes later, a squat but muscular looking corrections officer stepped into the room and called his name. To Dixon, the officer looked menacing. His head was shaved and he looked like he'd spent half his life in a gym pumping free weights. He was so large through the chest and shoulders that it looked like he was about to pop the buttons off his uniform shirt. Maybe this was the kind of employee you had to have to control a maximum security prison Dixon thought.

The officer led him into the visitor area designated for inmates like Bradshaw who weren't allowed contact visits. That was basically anybody in max or administrative segregation. Bradshaw was already seated when Dixon entered the room. They looked at each other, smiled through the shatterproof glass and reached for the phones.

Dixon had always been cautious during these encounters. It was safer to assume that somebody was listening in despite the legal constraints. He'd reflected this to his client many times. He had rehearsed this conversation with Bradshaw during his last court appearance.

The meeting was brief. Small talk quickly gave way to a discussion of the legal issues confronting Bradshaw as well as impending trial strategy. Bradshaw was scheduled to go to trial in nine weeks. After that, he would have a date with the state parole board.

"Is it your view, Gordon, that all necessary preparations have been made for my trial?" The two men stared at each other.

"Yes, Walter, I think we're about ready." Bradshaw nodded.

It was Dixon's turn to ask the prearranged question. "And how have you been feeling, Walter? Getting enough exercise, are you?"

"No, never enough exercise. I haven't been feeling particularly well today."

"Did you notify the staff?"

"I did. They told me if I wasn't feeling better by tomorrow, they'd put me on sick call."

Glancing down at the manila envelope, Bradshaw said, "What have you brought for me today? It looks like another stack of boring legal documents."

"A variety of things, but mostly copies of various pretrial motions I filed with the court. I finally received the DA's list of trial witnesses. That's in the envelope as well."

"I'll be sure to look them over, and if I have any questions, I'll have them ready for you at our next meeting."

With that, the visit ended. Dixon placed Bradshaw's case file back into his briefcase leaving the manila envelope out. He handed the envelope to a corrections officer who would give it to Bradshaw once it had been appropriately scrutinized. If they were going to find the drug, it would happen here. Normal protocol required that the envelope be opened in Bradshaw's presence and the contents examined.

Dixon turned to leave, knowing that if the drug was discovered now, he would never make it out of the prison. He'd be arrested for smuggling contraband and turned over to the county sheriff. He felt an exhilarating sense of relief when the last steel door clanged shut behind him and he cleared the final prison checkpoint without being detained. Freedom never felt better. This part of the ordeal was over.

Chapter Thirty-five

It was mid-afternoon by the time I left for the Snowbird Ski Resort. As I backed out of the garage, I spotted the silver Ford Explorer parked across the street and down a couple of houses. I could see a guy slumped behind the steering wheel. That would probably be Larry Holding, the PI Susan Fleming had warned me about. As I drove off, he followed at a discreet distance. He trailed along behind me all the way to Snowbird.

Kate had left a voice message on my cell phone asking me to call her. She answered on the first ring. I told her where I was going. "What are you up to?" I asked.

"I just came from a meeting with Arnold Ginsberg's older brother. He's come from New York to claim the body. I also gave him an update on the investigation."

"Is he planning the funeral here in Salt Lake City?"

"No. There's going to be a local memorial service for him at the mortuary on Monday. I guess Rodney applied the full court press on that one."

"Can't really blame him for that," I said. "I'll bet most of Arnold's friends are here in Utah, not New York."

"I'm sure that's true. It also reinforces Rodney as the bereaved partner. Anyway, then the body is going to be flown to Kennedy Airport. There'll be a Jewish service on Wednesday, and then he'll be buried in a family plot in upstate New York next to his parents."

"Always painful to lose a loved one," I said. "I'm not sure what you've got going now, but I'll spring for a late lunch if you want to join me at Snowbird. Interested?"

"Thanks, but at the moment, I'm sitting down the street from the house we followed Barnes to early this morning. I got here shortly before eleven. So far, he hasn't moved. I figured he'd probably be sleeping late since he didn't get in until the wee hours this morning."

I promised to catch up with her as soon as I took care of my business. I wanted to interview the front desk and restaurant staff at the Snowbird Lodge to see whether I could pin down Steven Ambrose's presence on the property, as well as the time he checked in and went to dinner. During our interview, he had been vague about that. I wasn't sure whether his faulty memory was genuine, or whether it was deliberately designed to provide a plausible timeline for his alibi.

The drive up Little Cottonwood Canyon was stunning. On its worst day, it always was. Today was far from its worst day. Blue skies punctuated by puffy white cumulus clouds dotted the skyline while steep canyon walls shrouded the two lane road in a blanket of shade. High and deep in the cracks and crevices of the rocky mountainside, places that almost never saw the sun, I could see traces of the season's early snow, snow that had found a permanent home until sometime next summer. Most of the color was already on the ground, save a few stubborn Aspens, whose autumn leaves of orange and gold clung to their branches in quiet desperation, like a young child clinging to his mother on the first day of school.

I parked in one of the guest check-in stalls at the front of the lodge. I contacted the front desk manager and got lucky right away. Computer records showed that Ambrose, or someone using his identification, checked in at 3:05 P.M. I showed the manager and a female front desk clerk a blown up driver's license photo of Ambrose. It wasn't a particularly good picture, but they both made the identification. Not only did they remember him but they had his Visa credit card receipt and a photo copy of his driver's license taken when he checked in. There was now no doubt that Ambrose had arrived at the lodge around the time he said.

My attempt to pin down the time he ate dinner in the lodge restaurant proved more difficult. He hadn't made a dinner reservation. After leaving me to sit for a few minutes, the food and beverage manager, Albert Mason, returned with a Visa credit card receipt. "Here, I did manage to find this," he said. "I'm afraid that I can't help you out on the time this card was used. If you can wait for about forty minutes, the wait staff will be in. They start work at four. Maybe they'll remember him."

I couldn't make out the signature on the receipt, but the imprint belonged to Steven Ambrose. Absent someone in the restaurant who could identify him from his photograph, I really had no way to determine who had used the card. It might have been Steven or someone sent in his place. The credit card receipt also did nothing to help me establish what time he had come in for dinner. The only way I was going to find that out was to wait until four o'clock when the servers showed up for work.

I found a plastic evidence bag in the glove box of my car along with a pair of tweezers. I explained to Mason that I'd have to take the credit card receipt. The receipt might have Ambrose's prints on it and I didn't want to add mine.

I thanked Mason and wandered into the bar where I ordered a coke and sat down to await the arrival of the restaurant help. I chatted with the bartender and showed him a picture of Ambrose. He had worked the previous night but didn't recall seeing him. A few minutes later, a guy who looked markedly similar to the same character in the silver Ford Explorer plunked his ass on the bar stool next to mine. He ordered a gin and tonic. We made small talk for a few minutes. He introduced himself as Ray.

"I'm sorry, I didn't catch your name," he said.

I smiled. "That's because I didn't give it to you. My name's Clark," I said, extending a hand, "Kent, Clark Kent." We shook hands. We exchanged a glance that suggested we both knew I was jerking him around.

Just then my cell phone chirped. It was Kate. "Excuse me, Ray," I said, and stepped away.

"What's up?"

"Barnes is moving."

"Where are you at?"

"He's southbound on the I-15, and we're about to exit east on I-215."

"Need some help?"

"I'm probably okay for the moment—hope I don't lose him. I'm anxious to see where he's going and what he's up to. Are you still at Snowbird?"

"Yeah, do you need me to break away?"

"Nah, but keep your phone on. I'll let you know where I end up. You can join me when you're finished."

I returned to the bar and ordered another Coke for me and a gin and tonic for 'Ray.' "Excuse me for a minute," I said. "I've really gotta take a piss." I hurried through the lobby and into the parking lot. Holding's Explorer was parked a couple of stalls away from mine. I unfolded my Swiss Army knife and made a small incision in the right rear tire. That would keep 'Ray' busy for a while. I hustled back into the bar and rejoined my new friend.

Shortly after four, I was sitting in the restaurant with a bus boy named Manuel Sanchez. He spoke broken English, and acted like he was afraid that I was about to ask to see his green card. Seated next to him was Billy Thornton, a food server. "Any relation to Billy Bob Thornton?" I quipped. Okay, so it was a shoddy attempt at humor, so what?

Thornton gave me a weak smile, saying, "I think I've heard that one before."

"Pretty lame, huh," I said. He nodded.

I showed them the photo of Steven Ambrose. Thornton remembered him. Sanchez seemed less certain. They bantered back-and-forth, but couldn't agree on what time he'd been in the restaurant. Thornton thought it was around nine. Sanchez thought it was earlier.

As I got up to leave, Sanchez disappeared into the back. Thornton stuck around. "The reason I'm pretty sure that it was sometime around nine o'clock is because it was slow last night. We close at nine-thirty. When it's slow, and you're not making any money, all you want to do is get out of here. The reason I remember him is that I felt irritated that the guy came in by himself so late in the evening. In the scheme of things, it wasn't like his five dollar tip amounted to much. All I wanted to do was go home."

I thanked him and left.

Chapter Thirty-six

As I walked through the lobby, I noticed Larry Holding, a.k.a. Ray, seated on a sofa reading a newspaper. I nodded as I walked past. "Nice meeting you, Ray." He gave me a weak smile and a half-hearted wave. I figured he hadn't yet seen his right rear tire.

Outside the lodge, I dialed Kate's cell number. She didn't answer. That worried me. I figured my best shot at getting reception was right here. Once I began the steep and windy descent through Little Cottonwood Canyon, the likelihood of my having cell phone reception was slim to none. I headed for the Salt Lake valley as quickly as I could.

As I pulled on to the highway, I glanced in my rearview mirror. Holding had backed the Explorer out of its stall and driven a few feet before stopping. The last thing I saw in my mirror was Ray getting out of the truck to check his tires.

As I emerged from the canyon my cell phone rang.

"Where are you, Kate?"

"I'm sitting in the parking lot at Starbucks on 1300 East, just south of Fort Union. How soon can you get here?"

"Ten minutes if I step on it. What have you got?"

"I followed Barnes here. Ambrose showed up ten minutes later. They're inside now, having what appears to be a serious conversation."

A few minutes later, I slipped into the passenger seat of Kate's new 500 Series, BMW. "Damn, you've got good taste in cars."

"Just like my men."

"I couldn't agree more." I'm not fussy. I'll take compliments any time I can get them.

I told her about my encounter with Larry Holding. "You actually slashed one of his tires," she said, sounding incredulous. "And then you just left him up there."

"Slash is kind of a strong word. Let's just say I nicked one of his tires."

I forged on. "What the hell did you think I was going to do? Flatten his tire, apologize, and offer the scumbag a ride home." It was really a rhetorical question, although I thought it was safer if I answered it myself rather than hear more from Kate on the subject. I had to admit that trashing peoples tires didn't seem like appropriate police behavior, but, under the circumstances, it felt like poetic if not vigilante justice.

"So, what's going on here?" I asked.

"I don't know. They've been in there for a while, though."

I noticed a digital camera in her lap. "Are you planning to snap some pictures when they come out?"

"Yeah, but it's better than that. I actually went in and managed to snap a couple of pictures of them together."

I shook my head. "How did you manage that? Did you just walk up and say, smile, you're on candid camera?"

She laughed. "Not exactly. I stood in the hallway by the door to the ladies' can and just fired away."

I actually didn't care how she'd done it. I was just glad that she had. We could use the photos during what I was now sure would be a future interrogation of both subjects.

"Here's what we ought to do," I said. "When they come out, if they go some place together, we both follow, taking turns as the lead car. If they split, and that's what's likely to happen, you follow Ambrose and I'll take Barnes. Ambrose doesn't know you, but he'll sure remember me. We can stay in touch by cell phone and get together afterward."

Kate nodded, "Okay."

I returned to my car and we continued to wait. I called Sammy Roybal's cell but he didn't answer. I left a message reminding him that I needed him at the Lucky Gent later in the evening to continue schmoozing with Barnes.

A few minutes later, Barnes and Ambrose walked out of Starbucks together. They took off in opposite directions. Ambrose headed south on 1300 East while Barnes headed north. If my guess was correct, Barnes was probably headed to work at the Lucky Gent. I followed him until he turned into the bar parking lot fifteen minutes later.

I called Kate. She had followed Ambrose to his office on South State. I joined her there.

"Anything going on?"

"I followed him out here and figured he had a massage appointment. I was about to bag it and call you. And then guess who rolled in?"

"How about Rodney Plow?"

"You got it."

"What do you make of that?"

"Well, it could be a coincidence, I suppose."

"I thought you didn't believe in coincidences."

"I don't. How's this for a case theory. What if Rodney planned Ginsberg's killing and got his lover, Ambrose, to do it."

"And how does Anthony Barnes fit in?" I ask.

"Not sure. Maybe Rodney knew Barnes from the Lucky Gent and recruited him to assist Ambrose. Or maybe it was Ambrose who brought Barnes into the conspiracy."

"Good theory. Now if we can only prove it. So far we haven't been able to establish a solid motive for Rodney to kill his partner. It's possible that Barnes and Ambrose are the killers, and Rodney isn't involved."

"Don't forget the infidelity."

"I know, Kate, but there's got to be more to it than that. Think what a good defense attorney will tell a jury: You don't have to commit murder to get out of a relationship. For all we know, Ambrose may have arranged the murder because he's in love with Rodney. Maybe Rodney wouldn't leave Arnold."

"Possible, I suppose," said Kate. "Ambrose decides to kill Ginsberg to get him out of the way and recruits Barnes to help him."

Kate's phone rang. She glanced at her caller identification. "Oh, damn. This is one of our lab guys. He left a message for me earlier and I forgot to call him back."

She answered and immediately went into apology mode. "Sorry, Earl, it's been kind of busy out here. Can you hang on for a few minutes? We'll be right in."

Kate disconnected and glanced at me. "I think we just got a forensics break. Let's get downtown right away. I don't see much value in sitting out here any longer."

I didn't either. I followed Kate downtown to police head-quarters.

Chapter Thirty-seven

We headed straight for the crime lab. Kate introduced me to Earl Stafford. Stafford was a forensics specialist who looked like he'd been around for about a hundred years. I'd never met him before. He had a few wisps of hair across the top of his head and a pencil thin mustache. He looked at us with small specs perched on the end of his nose. His area of expertise was hairs and fibers.

"What have you got for us, Earl?"

"Well, Lieutenant, when we examined the victim's navy sports coat, we discovered a single strand of hair."

"Hmm," said Kate. "And…."

"I can tell you that it's human hair, not animal. When I put it under high magnification and compared it to the samples the ME took from the victim, I was able to eliminate him. The color and diameter are different."

"What part of the body did the hair come from?"

"It's head hair."

"Have we got the root?"

Stafford smiled. "It wasn't cut. We've got the follicle."

That was important because sometimes a single strand of hair with the root attached can provide enough DNA for testing. The problem was we needed comparison samples from a suspect in order to test. While comparison can show similarities between hair samples, it couldn't prove a definite link to a particular suspect. DNA could.

We thanked Stafford and turned to leave. "Oh, by the way," he said, "When I examined the hair under different light, I could tell that it had been dyed. It looks to be a gold color."

Kate and I looked at each other. Steven Ambrose's hair had been bleached with streaks of gold.

◇◇◇

We stopped downtown for dinner at PF Chang's. I was starving. Kate, claiming not to be very hungry, ordered an egg roll and an iced tea. I ordered Hunan beef with fried rice and a side order of pot stickers. I'd been with Kate long enough now to know that she would eat her egg roll and then go to work on my Hunan beef like she hadn't seen a hot meal in a year. I'd learned to compensate by ordering extra food. I had been trying for months to convince her that this habit of claiming not to be hungry, and then attacking my plate like locusts at a backyard barbeque, must be a symptom of an eating disorder. She assured me that it wasn't, instead merely a girl thing. I wasn't so sure.

While we waited for food, I called Sammy Roybal's cell phone number again. He hadn't returned my original call, and he wasn't answering this one. I left him another message.

"I think I liked dealing with Sammy better when he was an inmate. At least I always knew where I could find the little prick," I said, genuinely irritated.

"It must be easier working with an inmate snitch than one on the outside."

"In some ways it is, and in other ways, it's not. Passing snitch information is easier and less complicated outside the prison than it is inside. I worry more about the safety of inmate snitches than those outside in the community. If we make a mistake inside, the snitch can easily end up with a shank in his neck."

We devoured dinner while trying to figure out what to do next. "Thank God for forensics," said Kate. "I think we should go to work on an affidavit for a court order to obtain DNA and hair samples from Steven Ambrose. We've got more than enough."

"I think you're right. If we take the affair between Plow and Ambrose, and then factor in Steven's meeting earlier today with a suspect whose prints are on one of the murder weapons. That should do it."

"And let's not forget Ambrose's alibi," said Kate. "It's convenient for him in one sense, but hardly airtight. It's clear that he had ample opportunity to check into the Snowbird Lodge, return to Salt Lake, commit the murder, and make it back to Snowbird in time for a late night dinner in the restaurant."

As we kicked around our options, I suggested a different plan. I had thought of a way that would increase the pressure on Rodney Plow and possibly provide the missing link to Anthony Barnes. It might also give us a way to circumvent having to get a court order for the hair and DNA samples.

After a hurried dinner, I followed Kate back to Ambrose's office not expecting to find either of them still there. But they were—both cars parked exactly as we left them a couple of hours earlier.

The plan called for us to separate them. I would go to work on Plow while Kate used her charms to cajole Ambrose into voluntarily providing hair samples, saving us the time and hassle of getting the court order.

We stepped quietly to the office door. The lights were on and we could hear muffled voices inside. Kate gently turned the door knob. It was locked. She glanced at me, shrugged her shoulders and rapped on the door. "Mr. Ambrose, this is Lt. McConnell, Salt Lake P.D. Homicide. Could you open up, please? I need to talk to you."

There was a short pause. We could hear the hushed sound of whispered conversation. They were probably trying to figure out how to play an obviously awkward situation. After a moment, the door opened a crack and Ambrose peeked out.

"Can't this wait until morning, Detective McConnell? I'm here with a client."

"Sorry, but it can't. And we also need to speak with Mr. Plow." She motioned toward the parking lot. "I believe that's his car parked next to yours."

With a look of resignation, Ambrose opened the door and motioned us in. I could tell that he wasn't happy to see me again, especially so soon. I ignored him and addressed Plow.

"Mr. Plow, I think we may have a break in the investigation. Would you mind stepping outside with me for a moment so that we'll have some privacy?"

I didn't wait for his answer. Instead, I guided him by the elbow right out the front door. Kate promptly closed it behind me. She would go to work on Ambrose. Plow looked decidedly uncomfortable. That could be because he felt embarrassed that we'd caught him in another tryst with his lover before Ginsberg was even cold in the ground. Or, his discomfort might be the result of his own involvement in the conspiracy to murder his old partner. I was about to put some pressure on him and see how he reacted.

"Rodney, have you ever heard of a gentleman by the name of Anthony Barnes?"

He looked like he was about to throw up. "No," he stammered. "Should I...."

"Not necessarily. Do you ever spend time in a gay bar called the Lucky Gent?"

"Not very often, but I know that it's a popular hangout for members of the gay community. Why do you ask?"

For the moment, I ignored his question and asked another. "What about Arnold? Did he frequent the Lucky Gent?"

"I'm sure that he's been in the place, but I can tell you that Arnold didn't hang out in bars, gay or straight, much at all. He was kind of a homebody. It was a struggle getting him out of the house at all unless it had something to do with his work. What's this all about anyway, and who is this Anthony Barnes?"

His anxiety meter appeared high. It was time to bait the trap. "Anthony Barnes works as a bartender at the Lucky Gent. He's an ex-military guy with a nasty temper, who left the service under something of a cloud." Pretty accurate so far, I thought.

"What's that have to do with Arnold's murder?" he said.

It was time to be deliberately evasive. "For the time being, I'm afraid that I'm not at liberty to disclose that. But I will tell you that we now have evidence linking Barnes to the murder."

He pressed, "What kind of evidence?"

"As I said, I'm not able to discuss that at the moment. But I can tell you that we'll have something definitive for you very shortly."

He pressed some more. "That's not good enough. I demand to know....I have a right to know how the investigation stands."

I apologized but held my ground. "Look, I can't be more specific right now, but I will tell you that what we've developed is very solid and very incriminating evidence. Just give us another day or two."

"Well, at least tell me whether you've questioned this Barnes."

"We haven't questioned him yet, but we're about to. We've been waiting for a bit more information to come in, and I think we're about there."

"If you have this very incriminating evidence, why haven't you arrested this Barnes? What if he takes off?"

"He won't, Rodney. Why should he? Remember, he doesn't even know that we're on to him. There's no reason for him to run. If we believed there was any chance that he'd rabbit, we'd pick him up. But I can assure you that Anthony Barnes' world is about to come crashing down around him."

We had been having this discussion while walking slowly through the parking lot outside Ambrose's office. It was dark and it was getting cold. I decided to leave him with one parting shot. "We'd better get back inside," I said. "There's one more thing that I need to tell you and I'm sure that it will come as a shock."

The look on his face was one of, oh, shit, what now? "Yes...."

"We don't mean to pry into your personal life, who you choose to see, that sort of thing. But you should know that we now consider Steven Ambrose to be a person of interest in the murder of Arnold Ginsberg."

Plow feigned a look of great surprise before saying, "What do you mean? You think Steven is somehow involved in Arnold's death?"

"All I can tell you is that Kate is in there with him right now asking that he voluntarily provide hair and DNA samples."

"What if he refuses?" asked Plow.

"Then we'll be back tomorrow with a court order requiring him to provide the samples."

"You think he could be involved with this Barnes fellow?"

On this one I lied. "We aren't sure yet. Look Rodney, all I'm telling you is that it might be a good idea to put some distance between yourself and Ambrose. And I wouldn't discuss the case with him under any circumstances until we get this sorted out."

Plow's demeanor changed on a dime from shock at the news that Ambrose might be involved in the killing to one of tears and sorrow. His voice cracked when he spoke. "To think that my meaningless little fling with Steven might have triggered Arnold's murder is almost more than I can endure."

The guy could turn it on and off like a faucet. His dripping, emotional performance could have earned him a gig on a daily soap. I steered him back to the office just as the door opened and Kate emerged. I could see Ambrose standing in the background looking like a mortar round had just gone off in his ear. We said our goodbyes and left.

Chapter Thirty-eight

Robin Joiner knew that something was about to happen and she had a pretty good idea what it was. She just didn't understand how they were going to pull it off. Two new faces had arrived at the remote cabin, faces she didn't know. The man didn't speak to her, but the woman hugged her and introduced herself as Sister Joan. They were about the same age and had arrived at the cabin together. She heard Albert Bradshaw address the man as Brother Gordon.

Weapons were being cleaned and loaded. Joiner counted four handguns, two short-barreled shotguns, and two rifles that appeared to be some type of assault weapons. She observed gloves, ski masks, rolls of duct tape, and what looked like several pairs of plastic handcuffs.

The man called Gordon unfolded a large schematic and placed it on the small dining room table. The four men gathered around him, and for several minutes, they quietly discussed what Joiner believed was a plan to engineer the escape of Walter Bradshaw from prison. But how were they going to do it? Surely, they couldn't be planning a frontal assault on the state prison. That would be suicide.

While the men planned, Sister Joan busied herself in the kitchen heating soup, making sandwiches, and filling plastic cups with drinks. When the meeting ended, Albert blessed the food and then everybody ate. Joey filled a paper plate with chips and sandwiches and brought them to Joiner on the couch. He set the plate down and returned moments later with soft drinks.

"You better have something to eat," he said pointing to the plate. He forced a smile. "Around this place, you never know when you might get another chance."

"I'm not hungry." She stared at him until he broke eye contact. She whispered. "Look, Joey, I don't know what horrible thing you have planned, but I beg you not to do it. If you love me, if our relationship means anything to you, don't do this. Let's just leave. We can run away and start over......"

"Stop it, Robin. My place is here and so is yours. We're only going to be gone a short time. Sister Joan will remain here with you. I want your word that you will behave yourself and do exactly what she says. Do I have your word?"

Joiner just stared at him. "Okay then, you give me no choice. You'll have to be tied up until we return."

"You don't have to tie me up. I won't try to get away and I'll do whatever Sister Joan tells me to do."

He looked at her trying to assess whether or not he could believe her. Before he said anything, Albert appeared. "It's time to go." He dropped plastic cuffs into Joey's lap. "Here, tie her up."

Joey hopped off the couch and stepped over to Albert. A hushed exchange that Robin could not hear ensued between the brothers. They were arguing, of that she was sure. And she was certain that she knew what they were arguing about. In the end, she was cuffed in front, probably an uncomfortable compromise for both brothers. They gathered in the living room of the small cabin, five men and one woman, standing in a circle holding hands. Albert led them in a short prayer. Before leaving, the men loaded weapons and supplies into a waiting van and a passenger car.

◇◇◇

Walter Bradshaw picked at his dinner. He was anxious. What he was about to do would jeopardize his life. He understood that. It was also his ticket to freedom. He understood that as well.

One thing he felt absolutely certain about was that the merciful Lord Jesus would protect him.

So far things had gone according to plan. At the conclusion of his visit with Brother Gordon, Dixon had handed the manila envelope containing the legal documents and the drug to a uniformed corrections officer. Bradshaw shuffled out of the visitor's room taking the baby steps required of a prisoner trying to walk while shackled at the waist and ankles.

He watched as the first officer handed the envelope to a supervisor. Bradshaw waited, trying to look unconcerned, as the sergeant opened the package, removed the documents, and peered into the empty envelope. The officer flipped quickly through the pages giving them a visual check and then held the document by its stapled corner shaking it back and forth to see if anything dropped to the floor. When nothing did, he put it back in the envelope and handed it to Bradshaw.

Bradshaw glanced at his watch. It was almost eight o'clock. It was time to ingest the drug and wait for the onset of symptoms before calling for help. He took a few minutes to say his evening prayers asking God to forgive his sins and to help him in his hour of need. He took the legal documents and examined them carefully until he found the tiny makeshift envelope containing the drug. He sprinkled the powder on to a stale white roll, ate it, and then sat down on his bed to wait.

◇◇◇

Kate and I took up positions on opposite sides of Ambrose's office. When Plow and Ambrose decided to move, we intended to follow. If they moved separately, Kate would follow one and I'd take the other. If they left together, we'd tag team them wherever they went.

While we waited, I checked my cell phone for messages. Good news. Sammy the Snitch had finally returned my call. I dialed him back. He was just leaving his home headed for the Lucky Gent. Aside from being a good listener, I had a specific request for him. We wanted Barnes' phone records. We had his home number and Kate had already gone to work getting those records. His cell phone was something else. We assumed that he had one, but we weren't sure.

"Sammy, see if you can come up with an excuse to use Barnes' cell phone. I'm sure he's got one, and we need to know who his service provider is. Think you can do that?"

"No sweat. Sammy can get that information easy. I'll get back to you in a little while. You gonna pay Sammy tonight?"

I could never quite get used to Sammy talking about himself in the third person but he'd always done it. "Yeah, Sammy, I'm going to pay you tonight. Call me later when you have something."

Fifteen minutes later, Plow and Ambrose left the office. To our disappointment, they drove their own vehicles, and neither made an attempt to contact Anthony Barnes, at least not in person. Instead, they drove to their respective homes. Kate and I hooked up a few minutes later outside the Lucky Gent. Perhaps we hadn't spooked them, or at least not sufficiently to send Plow scurrying to see Barnes. And it occurred to me that maybe our theory was wrong—maybe there was no grand murder conspiracy with Rodney calling the shots.

Chapter Thirty-nine

Registered nurse Ruth Benally was enjoying a quiet Saturday night shift reading a romance novel in the state prison's infirmary when the emergency call came. She grabbed a canvas bag containing medical supplies and instruments and rushed to the maximum security unit leaving an inmate trustee and a nurse's aid to oversee the infirmary. When she arrived, Benally was quickly ushered into the cell of Walter Bradshaw. A gurney was outside the small cell, definitely not a good sign, she thought.

Bradshaw was conscious and able to communicate with her. "Mr. Bradshaw, tell me what you're feeling?"

"Pressure in my chest, tongue and lips feel numb," he mumbled. He looked pale and his skin felt cool and clammy. She noticed that his speech sounded slurred. She took his temperature. It was normal. She took his pulse. It was weak. Benally grabbed her stethoscope and listened to him breathe. Bradshaw's heartbeat was irregular and his breathing was slow and shallow. The symptoms suggested a person going into cardiac arrest.

She turned to the shift supervisor. "Get me an ambulance right away. If they can't respond quickly, you'd better call the university and have them dispatch the life flight chopper."

"He's that serious," whispered the sergeant, looking over Benally's shoulder.

"Afraid so," Benally said, turning back to her patient.

"Look at me, Mr. Bradshaw. Can you hear me?"

He nodded.

"I'm going to give you an aspirin. I want you to let it dissolve on your tongue. Do you understand?"

Again Bradshaw nodded.

A minute later the duty sergeant leaned in and said, "ETA on the ambulance is five minutes."

"The sooner the better," she said. "I'm going to start him on oxygen and then let's lift him on the gurney."

Bradshaw was strapped to the gurney and whisked out of maximum security to an awaiting ambulance. Following required procedures, the duty sergeant placed one corrections officer inside the ambulance and dispatched two additional officers to follow in a separate vehicle.

In what later was determined to be a clear violation of department policies, the Silver Shield ambulance failed to wait for the accompanying security detail and sped away from the prison in a dash to the University of Utah Medical Center.

◇◇◇

Amanda Bradshaw, Albert Bradshaw's first wife, sat in the family's old Ford Escort on the frontage road near the entrance to the state prison. At eight forty-five she saw the ambulance enter the prison grounds. Five minutes later, the ambulance blasted past her in a kaleidoscope of flashing red, blue, and amber colors. Within seconds, it disappeared into the darkness only to reappear as it crossed a freeway overpass before entering the interstate.

Amanda made one short call to Albert on the soon-to-be disposed of cell phone. "The bird just left the nest. No posse in pursuit." Albert smiled as he disconnected reveling in the good news.

Running code three, it took the ambulance nearly twenty-five minutes to make it to the hospital. As the driver approached the emergency room entrance, he saw two hospital employees waiting curbside. What he didn't see were the four gunmen wearing ski masks and armed with short-barreled shotguns and automatic weapons hiding in the shadows near the hospital entrance.

As the ambulance rolled to a stop, the driver slammed the gearshift into park, jumped out, and ran to the rear to help unload the passenger. As for veteran corrections officer Frank Nance, he never had a chance to react. No sooner had he uncoiled his tall lean frame from the back of the ambulance than he found himself staring at four heavily armed men.

"What the hell," he said.

"Hands up and nobody move. Do what you're told and everybody goes home," one of the gunmen shouted.

Nance glanced around. Where the hell was the rest of the security team? He started to reach for his radio.

"Don't do it," yelled a different gunman. Nance froze. The last thing he saw was a silver van pulling up next to the ambulance and one of the gunmen wheeling Bradshaw toward it.

In a matter of seconds, Nance and four medical personnel found themselves stuffed unceremoniously in the back of the idling ambulance with duct tape wrapped around their ankles and across their mouths. Their wrists were handcuffed behind their backs using plastic cuffs.

The stolen Voyager sped from the hospital grounds. Albert Bradshaw nodded at the others, "So far, so good." By his calculation, the entire exchange hadn't taken much more than one minute.

Everything had gone according to plan. They had been lucky. Nobody showed up unexpectedly to interfere with the rescue. If their luck held a little longer, they would make it to the rendezvous site, dump the Voyager, and separate driving two different vehicles.

The Allred brothers, while not the brightest bulbs in the box, had turned out to be first-rate car thieves. They always kept the family in fresh vehicles enabling them to remain mobile and avoid capture.

Gordon Dixon drove the Voyager. Joey was seated up front next to Gordon. Albert glanced nervously over Dixon's shoulder and then checked his watch. "We're behind schedule getting to the rendezvous site, Gordon. Move it."

Dixon started to protest. "But I don't want to get stopped...."

Albert interrupted. "Let me worry about that. Step on it, now."

Albert's tone left no margin for negotiation. After turning on to Foothills Drive Dixon punched the accelerator. He watched the needle slowly increase until he was doing almost fifty, weaving in an out of traffic, hoping he wouldn't pass a cop.

Albert glanced at the speedometer. "That's fast enough, Gordon."

The Allred brothers were busy tending to Walter. They had reattached him to a portable oxygen tank. The prophet seemed to be in and out of it—momentarily lucid and the next incoherent. When they'd researched the drug on the internet, the only treatment they had found was oxygen and another drug they had been unable to procure. Time, oxygen, and a healthy dose of prayer would bring his father around. Albert felt certain of it.

◇◇◇

Corrections officers Jess Colby and Anthony Bennett arrived at the hospital about five minutes behind the ambulance. "Christ, I hate this hospital duty," grumbled Colby.

"Not me," said Bennett. "I like the diversion. Anything that gets me out of the unit for a while. It's a change of scenery." Officer Tony Bennett had been the butt of a lot of good-natured kidding over the years about his name. Years ago, one of his fellow officers had dubbed him Tony the Troubadour Bennett, Troub for short. He'd been called Troub ever since.

"Let's park behind the ambulance, Troub," said Colby. "We can move the car as soon as we've established security."

They parked behind the idling ambulance and walked into the emergency room. Nothing seemed out of the ordinary. What they failed to hear was the EMT kicking at the back of the ambulance door. When they couldn't find Nance immediately, Colby tried to reach him on the radio. No reply. The two men looked at each other. "The ambulance," said Colby.

They opened the rear door of the ambulance with weapons drawn. They found five individuals trussed up like Thanksgiving turkeys and no sign of Walter Bradshaw.

"Shit," muttered Colby.

The alarm went out immediately. The state public safety dispatch center notified their counterparts at Salt Lake City PD. In a matter of minutes, police units from the highway patrol, the sheriff's department, and Salt Lake City PD converged on the University Medical Center. The FBI was also notified. A temporary command post was established on the hospital grounds to coordinate the search.

As soon as the command post was established, several police units descended on the house Bradshaw's first wife, Janine, and daughter-in-law, Amanda, rented. The sparsely furnished old house was empty except for some ratty old furniture that looked like it had probably come from a thrift store.

◇◇◇

Gordon Dixon slowed the Voyager and turned into a large parking lot at Red Butte Gardens. He gunned the van across the lot and parked next to the stolen Ford F-150 truck and the older Nissan Sentra. The pickup had a shell over the bed and would serve as a means of transporting the prophet. Janine Bradshaw was waiting in the truck and would act as the driver. Walter was quickly lifted from the Voyager and placed in the back of the truck.

Randy and Robby Allred stripped off the bib overalls and placed them in the trunk of the Sentra along with the ski masks they'd worn during the rescue. After hurried good-byes, they left. The plan called for the Allred brothers to return to the Arizona Strip and prepare other church followers to join the prophet. The others squeezed into the back of the truck. This arrangement gave them the best opportunity to avoid detection. The cops would be looking for the Voyager and not for a pickup truck. They also wouldn't expect a female driver.

If everything went according to plan, they would return to the remote cabin high in the Wasatch Mountains within the hour.

Chapter Forty

We heard the call go out over Kate's portable hand-held police radio from their surveillance location outside the Lucky Gent.

"Holy shit," said Sam, reaching quickly for his cell. "This is where I need Burnham." I scrolled through my directory until I found Marcy Everest's home phone number. I dialed, and on the second ring, she answered. I explained what had just happened, and directed her to the state prison.

"Make sure that Bradshaw's cell is secured and that nobody gets in without authorization. Oh, and by the way, stay on the lookout for the feds. They might show up."

"You want us to let them in?"

"Sure, but only after we've taken that cell apart. If they show, call me right away."

"Okay. What's going to be the best way to reach you?"

"I'm on a stakeout in Salt Lake City. Call me on my cell if you need help." I disconnected.

"Anybody else you need to notify?" asked Kate.

"Not really. This one will go right up the chain of command until it reaches our new executive director, Benjamin Cates. I wouldn't be surprised if he hasn't already been notified. He's about to experience his first major crisis as a state corrections boss. And the press will be looking under every rock to see who they can slap the blame on."

"Do you need to go to the prison?"

"I don't think so. Prisoner transportation is not an SIB responsibility. The security staff at the prison knows how to handle this. The sheriffs department will respond, and Marcy will be there to assist. She'll call me if there's a problem."

"What do you think happened?" asked Kate.

"It's hard to know, but it must have started with some kind of medical emergency. Whatever it was, the prison medical staff must have concluded that it was life threatening. We don't transport inmates to the university hospital for a headache or a bloody nose, I can tell you that."

"But how would the Bradshaws have found out about it? They must have been waiting at the hospital."

"Jesus, you're making me nervous. It does smell like a setup, doesn't it?"

"I think so. I hope for your sake that they didn't have inside help."

"Don't even go there. If this were to turn into another corrections scandal, I might just as well shoot myself right now."

For the next hour-and-a-half, we monitored the radio traffic from our location outside the Lucky Gent. With the passage of time, it became clear that the Bradshaw gang had disappeared into the cold autumn night, either by slipping through the cordon of police vehicles searching the area or by finding a convenient rock to hide under.

A few minutes past midnight, my cell phone chirped. "Hi, Marcy, what's up?"

"You were right. We ended up with visitors. Besides the crime scene unit from the sheriff's office, two dicks from Salt Lake City PD showed up with a couple of FBI agents in tow."

"Did they behave themselves?"

"They weren't a problem. They asked a few procedural questions but mostly stood around watching."

"Anything turn up in the cell search?"

"As a matter of fact, yeah. The lab boys found traces of a white powder they can't seem to identify. They don't think that it's any of the conventional stuff—not PCP, meth, H, or coke."

"Well, what do they think it is?"

"They didn't know but think it might be something exotic."

"Exotic. What the hell does that mean?"

"I'm not sure, maybe something unusual. They hustled the sample off to the state crime lab for analysis. They said they'd let us know as soon as they have something."

"Great. Who provided medical treatment for Bradshaw at the prison?"

"The duty RN was a woman named Benally. She responded to max at the request of the shift commander."

"How did she describe his medical condition?" I asked.

"When we interviewed her, she said Bradshaw was exhibiting classic heart attack symptoms. She said the only real choice they had was whether to send him to the hospital by ambulance or call in a life flight chopper."

"Who made that decision?"

"Benally did, with the approval of the shift commander."

"They followed department policy to the letter," I said.

"Have you spoken to other inmates in Bradshaw's housing unit?"

"We interviewed several inmates housed near him and came up empty. Bradshaw kept his own counsel. Inmates didn't talk to him much, and he didn't talk to them."

"I'd like to know how he got his hands on that drug, whatever it was. Have you pulled his visitor's log? Who's been in to see him recently?"

"I already pulled it—got it right here in front of me. Let's see, his last family visitor was his wife and that was four days ago. Now his lawyer, a guy named Gordon Dixon, came in to see him earlier today."

"Gordon Dixon, huh, now that's interesting."

"How so?" said Marcy.

"Fellow polygamist, married to Walter's younger sister. I can't prove it, but I wouldn't put it past Dixon to bring something into the prison that he shouldn't."

Marcy frowned. "That makes sense. Given the lawyer-client privilege, it would certainly be easier for an attorney to smuggle in contraband than just about anybody else."

"If the drug turns out to be something exotic, the chance of Bradshaw getting it from another inmate is pretty remote. That would mean it was brought into the prison from outside. Gordon Dixon seems like a good bet."

I thanked Marcy for the update and disconnected.

"Cut to the chase, Sam. How did this thing go down?"

"I'm afraid you and I are probably thinking the same thing that the entire episode smells like a setup. What if Dixon managed to smuggle the drug into prison and passed it to his client? Knowing the drug would apparently cause heart problems Bradshaw takes it at a predetermined time and ends up with a ticket to the hospital. It's common knowledge that serious medical emergencies end up at the University of Utah Medical Center. The Bradshaw clan is waiting when the ambulance arrives and hijacks the patient, simple as that."

"What about inside help from someone employed at the prison?"

"Anything's possible, I suppose, but at the moment, we don't have a shred of evidence linking an employee to any of this. But rest assured, we'll do what we always do and thoroughly check it out. We'll sit down with everybody working the day Dixon came to visit his client, and I'm going to tell Marcy to take a careful look at nurse Benally."

"All good steps, I think, but there's still one thing that doesn't quite track," said Kate. "For this to make sense, you'd have to believe that Bradshaw intentionally took a drug knowing that it would induce a heart attack that might kill him. Who would do that? And how did the family plan to provide medical treatment?"

"I don't know, sympathetic physician, maybe?"

"Possible, I guess, but I think it's a stretch."

"Hell, I don't know, Kate. Maybe in the end it will turn out to be as simple as desperate men doing desperate things. Maybe they figured this was the only reasonable shot they had of snatching him. They sure weren't going to break him out of prison, and they probably figured the odds of grabbing him going to or from court weren't so hot either."

The conversation waned until we saw Sammy Roybal emerge from the Lucky Gent. He hopped into his car and drove past us, motioning us to follow. He pulled into a convenience store several blocks from the bar. He got out and so did we. We followed him into the store where Kate and I doctored up two cups of used motor oil masquerading as coffee, while Sammy filled his own mug with what looked like about a half-gallon of the stuff. He also picked up several Twinkies and Hostess cupcakes which we bought. The guy clearly wasn't getting his dietary information from Weight Watchers or Jenny Craig.

Kate cringed when he hopped into the back seat of her new Beamer with Twinkie-covered fingers and a less than sure grip on the coffee mug. There go the leather seats I thought.

I said, "Tell me you got something good for us tonight, Sammy."

He grinned. Between bites of a cream-filled cupcake, about half of which disappeared into his lap, he mumbled, "Sammy never disappoints a friend."

"Yeah, ever try using a napkin?" snapped Kate. I gave her a look. So much for establishing rapport with our snitch.

Between a mouthful of cupcake and coffee running down his chin, he managed, "Lt. Kate having her period?"

Kate started to say something but thought better of it.

I didn't relish the idea of refereeing a fight between Kate and Sammy, especially over the leather upholstery in her car. "What have you got for us, Sammy," I said, trying to steer the conversation back on track.

"Sammy's got his new best friend, Tony, eating out of his hand. He's very interested in a line of jewelry Sammy just happens to have."

"Nothing stolen, I presume," said Kate.

Sammy ignored her. "Sammy and Tony are getting along great until he gets this phone call. After that, he acts funny, like something's bothering him."

"What time was the call?" I asked.

"Uh, one hour ago, maybe a little longer," he said.

"Were you able to overhear any of the conversation?"

"No. The music in the bar was too loud, and he don't stand still. The longer he talks, the more upset he gets."

"That's not going to help us much," said Kate.

"Sammy grinned at her. "Would it be helpful if Sammy could give you the phone number that called my new friend, Tony?"

"Yeah, it would," I said. "What is it?"

The grin got bigger. "How much money you got for Sammy tonight?"

"Stop fucking with us and just give me the number," I said.

He gave us his best hurt look and said, "Maybe Lt. Kate isn't the only one having her period."

I gave him a cold stare that I knew he understood.

"Okay, okay." He held open his left hand. Kate hit the interior light and we both stared at the number scrolled on his palm.

Kate squinted as she tried to read it. "That's Rodney's cell phone number. How did you manage to get it?"

"My new friend, Tony; he's interested in buying some of Sammy's jewelry. Sammy borrowed his cell phone to call the individual holding the jewelry."

"Who'd you call?" I asked.

"I called my cousin, Juan. When Tony wasn't looking, Sammy checked his received calls and that number was the last one. You also wanted his service provider. It's Verizon."

"Good work, Sammy," I said. "What else did you find out?"

He reached into his leather bomber jacket pocket and pulled out a small piece of paper which he handed to me. "This massage guy you asked Sammy about. Sammy asked Tony where I should go for a hunky massage. He writes this guy Steve's name and number down on the slip of paper and tells Sammy to call him for an appointment."

"Did Tony say anything else to you about Steve?" asked Kate.

"No, but Sammy can find out a lot more. Would you like Sammy to call Hunky Boy Steve for a massage?"

Sammy's look of lusty anticipation turned to a scowl when I politely declined his offer. "Not right now, Sammy, but I'll let you know if we need you to do that for us."

We paid Sammy more than the information was worth and then sent him on his way. Barnes' call from Plow had probably been a warning that we considered him a suspect in Ginsberg's murder.

The noose was tightening on Plow, Ambrose, and now Anthony Barnes. If we could feel it, surely, they could, too.

Chapter Forty-one

Robin Joiner knew that if she ever was going to have a chance to escape, this was it. She was alone in the cabin with Joan Dixon. The bad news was that the cabin sat in a thick stand of pine trees rendering it invisible from the paved road. The good news was that the highway wasn't more than two hundred yards away. If she could make it to the paved road, it wouldn't be difficult to attract the attention of a passing motorist.

Although they had placed plastic handcuffs on her wrists and taken her shoes, the cuffs had been placed in front, not behind her back. That gave her a decided edge if she could only find a way out of the cabin.

Albert had ordered her not to leave the leather couch unless given permission by Sister Joan. Dixon, though not overly friendly, wasn't acting hostile either. If she could convince Sister Joan to treat her as a member of the family, someone who could be trusted, instead of a prisoner, an opportunity to escape might present itself.

Dixon was seated in a leather recliner directly across from her. She was reading a book and appeared to be the picture of calm stoicism in the face of what had to be a high-stress situation.

"What are you reading, Sister Joan?"

"A biography of Joseph Smith," she replied, without so much as a glance in Joiner's direction.

"I don't see how you can do it," said Joiner.

"Do what, Sister?" said Dixon, looking up from the page.

"Be so relaxed with so much going on. I'm really worried about Joey. I love him so much, and I know he's in danger. You must be worried about Gordon."

"Brother Joseph and Brother Gordon will be just fine. You, Sister Robin, need to have more faith in our Lord and Savior, Jesus Christ," she nodded, self-righteously.

This is working well thought Joiner.

Robin briefly considered trying to overpower Dixon. She was seated less than ten feet away, but she'd seen Albert pass her a small handgun before leaving. They had stood in the kitchen engaged in whispered conversation periodically glancing at her as she sat on the couch. The gun was nowhere in site, but Joiner was convinced that Dixon had it within easy reach.

Shortly after ten, an opportunity presented itself. Dixon's cell phone rang. When she answered, Joiner could immediately tell that Joan couldn't understand what the caller was saying. "I can't hear you. You're breaking up," she said. There was a pause, and then Dixon said, "You're still breaking up. Hold on a minute while I change locations." She got out of her chair and walked out the front door to the covered front porch.

Robin bolted to the back bedroom pausing only to close the bathroom door. Perhaps it would buy her a few more precious seconds. Her hands were shaking. She fumbled momentarily with the lock on the window until it gave. Using all her strength, she managed to lift it just high enough to squeeze her slender frame through the opening. She went out head first and landed on a soft bed of pine needles.

The cabin was nestled against a sheer rock cliff that went straight up, affording no way out. If she was going to make good her escape, she would have to sneak around to the front corner of the cabin and then make a dash for freedom only feet from where Dixon was talking on her cell. She wasn't worried about Dixon's ability to outrun her even with the plastic handcuffs on. It was the handgun that scared her. Would Sister Joan use the gun in an attempt to prevent an escape? She wasn't sure.

As Joiner crept quietly through the darkness, she stepped on a sharp pine cone that penetrated her foot. She stopped momentarily choking back the pain and then continued until she reached the front of the house. The tall evergreens were silhouetted by the lights inside the cabin. Otherwise, it was pitch black.

Sister Joan paced back and forth on the porch. Abruptly, the call ended and Dixon stood motionless, not five feet from where Joiner now stood with her back braced against the cedar plank siding. Joiner was afraid to breathe for fear the sound might break the silence of the perfectly still night and give her away. After what seemed like an eternity, Dixon turned and walked back to the front door.

Joiner heard the rusty screen door creak as Dixon opened it, and that's when she ran. She didn't look back, but heard Dixon shout her name as she sprinted for the highway. The darkness swallowed her almost instantly. The narrow dirt road dropped away from the cabin into a shallow depression, across a dry creek bed, and then gradually climbed until it came out next to the highway. Joiner ignored the pain she felt in her feet as she ran across assorted pine needles, pine cones, and rocks. Near the bottom of the depression, she felt her ankle roll and sprawled headlong on to the dirt road. Pain shot through her right ankle and her hands suffered a serious bout of road rash. Immediately, she pushed back to her feet and continued to run. Within seconds she crested the hill and emerged next to the highway.

Robin heard the unmistakable sound of a truck engine starting behind her. Dixon would come looking for her. She also had to consider the possibility that the Bradshaws could be returning to the cabin at any time. Her best bet was to flag down any vehicle headed back into Salt Lake City. She ran down the highway about a hundred yards and hid in a stand of evergreens next to the road. From this vantage point, she observed Dixon driving slowly back and forth before returning to the cabin. Joiner left the trees and resumed her trek down Little Cottonwood Canyon.

Joan Dixon dreaded the phone call she was about to make. She had lost Robin Joiner by failing to remain diligent. Her nephews would be furious with her, particularly Albert. Joey would be more sympathetic, but that was his nature—a gentle boy by any measure. Albert, who was well known for his temper, would be quick to judge her as incompetent for failing at this important task.

Dixon's husband, Gordon, had always had a difficult relationship with Albert. Albert seemed threatened by Gordon's education as well as the trust and influence the prophet placed in him. Albert resented that relationship and seized every opportunity to try to denigrate Gordon in the eyes of his father.

Dixon dialed the number and Albert answered. "Albert, I've lost Robin Joiner. She climbed out a bedroom window while I was on the phone."

There was a long, uncomfortable pause. "What do you want me to do?" Dixon finally asked.

"How long has she been gone?"

"About ten minutes."

"Get out of there immediately. Did Mandy make it back?"

"She just got here."

"We'll meet at the secondary location as quickly as you can make it." He disconnected.

Biting back the anger, Albert turned to Joey. "Your loyal girlfriend just got away from Sister Joan. She's on the run. I told you to tie her up, but you wouldn't listen. This jeopardizes everything. There's no telling what she might do now."

The stolen pickup abruptly turned around and headed to the alternate meeting location near Park City. Albert called the Allred brothers and informed them of the change.

◇◇◇

It took about fifteen minutes before Joiner successfully flagged down a couple in a Subaru Forrester returning to Salt Lake City from a party at the home of friends. When they emerged from the mouth of Little Cottonwood Canyon, Joiner used their phone and dialed a number she had committed to memory. It was Sam Kincaid's cell number.

Chapter Forty-two

The area was crawling with police. When they left the parking lot at Red Butte Garden, Randy and Robby Allred drove the stolen Nissan Sentra to a twenty-four hour Village Inn restaurant in downtown Salt Lake City. They had decided to get off the street for a little while and lay low. They took a booth off to one side and toward the back, one that afforded a clear view of anyone entering or leaving the restaurant.

The Allred brothers were a lot alike. Robby, the eldest, was just thirteen months older than Randy. The physical resemblance was striking. Many people mistook them for twins. The brothers enjoyed the same sports, the same foods, and even had the same taste in girls—the Scandinavian type, blond hair, blue eyes, fair complexion. Not that they had much experience with women. They didn't.

One notable difference between the brothers was temperament and judgment. Randy was quick to anger and often acted on impulse with little regard for the consequences. On this night, that character flaw would prove fatal.

Both boys had led difficult and troubled lives. They were the eldest sons of a blindly obedient polygamist father with three wives. They had two full siblings and seven half-siblings. At ages sixteen and fifteen, respectively, both boys were summoned to a hastily assembled meeting with Warren Jeffs, Prophet of the Fundamentalist Church of Jesus Christ of Latter-day Saints, at the church compound in Hilldale, Utah. Their father, Joseph

Allred, sat quietly with head bowed while Jeffs declared both boys apostates, and ordered them expelled from church property. To be declared apostates meant that you were damned to Hell and deprived of any contact or support from family members. Randy's offense was a less than stellar attendance record at required church functions; for Robby, it was a combination of poor grades in school and several unexcused class absences.

Robby and Randy joined the ranks of hundreds of adolescent boys expelled from their FLDS homes, often for little or no reason. After a period of homelessness, they were rescued by Walter Bradshaw and became dedicated members of the Reformed Church of the Divine Christ. They adapted easily to the criminal lifestyle and took great pride in carrying out crimes against the FLDS church.

Robby and Randy each ordered sausage, scrambled eggs, hash browns, and a side of hotcakes with hot cocoa to wash it all down. While they waited, they spoke optimistically of a future free of government sponsored persecution where they'd be free to practice their religious beliefs without interference.

During a brief lull in the conversation, Robby's cell phone chirped. "Hello." He paused, listening to the caller. He glanced at his cheap Timex watch. "What time? And she got away? Okay." He flipped the phone closed and replaced it on his belt.

"What happened?" asked Randy.

"Joiner escaped from Sister Joan. The cabin's been compromised."

"Sister Joan couldn't find her?"

Robby shook his head. "I knew it wasn't a good idea to leave her alone with Sister Joan."

Randy shrugged. "She was never one of us anyway. Joey should have kept her away from the family."

"It's too late to worry about that now," replied Robby. "They're going to stay at the secondary location and move the departure date ahead by one day."

The restaurant was almost empty. When the bars closed in another couple of hours, the place would probably become busy.

They ate in relative silence, talking in hushed tones about the route they would use for their drive back to the Arizona Strip. They had spent nearly an hour-and-a-half in the restaurant, and were about ready to leave, when three uniformed Salt Lake City cops walked in. One was a sergeant. The other two appeared to be patrol officers. The sergeant gave them a long look before sitting down. They must have been part of the large contingent of police who had been searching the area in vain trying to find them.

"Don't turn around. There are three cops at a table behind us," whispered Robby.

"Damn, I knew we shouldn't have stopped," said Randy.

"Relax, bro. Nobody's made us yet. We look a lot different than we did a few months ago." The brothers had grown their hair out, dyed it, and were now sporting short beards.

"Just the same, I'd rather not parade myself past half the police force," said Randy. "How are we gonna get out of here, anyway?"

"I've got an idea. Just sit tight for a couple of minutes. It'll look suspicious if we get up and try to leave now."

"Okay, what's your idea?" asked Randy, nervously.

"I'll go to the restroom. I'll stay in there exactly five minutes. That should give you time to pay the bill and get to the car. I'll follow along right behind you. That way we walk out separately and, hopefully, they don't pay any attention."

Randy didn't like it, but he couldn't think of a better way. "Okay, take off and I'll see you outside. And Robby, I love you, bro."

Robby glanced quizzically at his younger brother as he slid out of the booth. "Love you too, bro." He walked the short distance to the restroom fastidiously avoiding eye contact with the cops.

Randy glanced at his watch. His armpits were soaked. He needed to take a deep breath, gather himself, and stroll past the cops like a guy without a care in the world. As he walked past, he glanced down at one of the cops, a sergeant, who was staring at him. Robby nodded at the officer, and then continued to the cash register. The register was located near the front door. He could feel the eyes of the cop boring into his back.

Sergeant Todd Blackhurst scanned the restaurant customers as he and his two subordinates were seated. It was force of habit mostly. The fourteen year veteran never entered a public place in uniform without a careful look around. His eyes stopped on two men seated near the back. One of the men was facing him. He had only a side profile of the other. The officers had spent the past two hours assisting in the hunt for members of the Bradshaw gang who had just engineered the escape of Walter Bradshaw from the University of Utah Hospital. They had been terrorizing Salt Lake County for months, and pictures of the fugitives had been plastered everywhere.

While the two young men seated across the restaurant weren't dead ringers for anybody in the gang, there was something vaguely familiar about them. The age, height, and general body build of the men was about right, but not the hair or beards. The hair was longer and darker than anything he'd seen in the wanted flyers, and all the gang members were clean shaven. These two looked a lot scruffier. Yet the thing that bothered Blackhurst the most was how much the men looked alike—brothers perhaps. The Bradshaw gang included two set of brothers, all in their mid-to-late twenties.

To the two young patrol officers, he said, "Take a look at the two characters sitting to your right near the back of the restaurant. Do they look familiar?"

Both officers glanced over their right shoulders taking in the strangers. "I don't think so," said one. The other officer nodded in agreement.

It was probably nothing thought Blackhurst. He went back to the menu.

A few minutes later, Blackhurst noticed one of the men slide out of the booth and disappear into the men's restroom. Almost immediately, the other one got up and headed to the cash register, passing in front of the officers. Blackhurst stared, and the man stared back, nodding as he walked past. All his cop instincts told him something about these two didn't feel right. He decided to check it out.

<>‹›‹>

Kate and I had left Sammy Roybal and were on our way back to resume our surveillance at the Lucky Gent. We decided to see what Anthony Barnes might be up to once he left the bar.

My cell phone chirped. I didn't recognize the caller. "Hello, Kincaid."

The voice on the other end of the line sounded calm and controlled. "Detective Kincaid, my name is Ross Benson. My wife, June, and I just picked up a young lady who was walking down the highway in Little Cottonwood Canyon. She asked us to call you—says her name is Robin Joiner. She says a gang of hoodlums kidnapped her and have been holding her in a cabin up the canyon. She managed to get away and flagged us down as we were driving out of the canyon."

"Where are you, Mr. Benson?"

"We're in the parking lot at the 7-Eleven Store on Wasatch Boulevard, near the mouth of the canyon."

"Sit tight. We'll be there in about ten minutes. We're going to call the sheriff's office and there may be a uniformed deputy to you even before we arrive. In the meantime, please don't let that young lady out of your sight. I'm going to hang-up, but I'll call you right back." I disconnected.

Kate was already blasting down State Street headed for I-215. I dialed 911.

"Salt Lake County Sheriff's Office, what's your emergency?" said the dispatcher.

I explained who I was as well as the pertinent details regarding the whereabouts of Robin Joiner. I asked them to notify Salt Lake City PD detectives, and urged the sheriff's office to summon their SWAT team. I had one other request.

"Seal Little Cottonwood Canyon immediately—no vehicles allowed up the canyon until further notice. Everything coming down the canyon needs to be stopped and searched."

I called Ross Benson back and asked to speak to Joiner.

There was a short pause. "Hello."

"Hello, Robin. How are you?"

"Scared."

"Are you injured?"

"The bottoms of my feet are bruised and bleeding. They took my shoes, and when I finally got the chance to run, I had to do it in my socks."

"Sorry to hear that. We'll get you medical attention right away. Other than your feet, are you okay?"

She hesitated. "Yeah, but I was wondering..." Her voice trailed off. "How much trouble am I in, Mr. Kincaid?"

"I'm not sure, Robin. We've definitely got some issues that need to be sorted out, and you're the only one who can help us do that. We're going to do everything we can to help you, but you need to help us and yourself. Will you do that?"

Another pause. "I'll only talk to you and your partner, Kate what's-her-name. Michael, from my study group, says I can trust you. Can I?"

"Just cooperate and tell us the truth, and we'll do everything we can to help you. Fair enough?"

"Yeah."

"Who was at the cabin when you got away?"

"There was only one person, Joan Dixon. The others left together a couple of hours earlier."

"Can you lead us to the cabin?"

"No problem. I'd actually been there once before with Joey. I know where it is."

"Good, we'll be there in just a minute."

Within fifteen minutes of our arrival, the mouth of Little Cottonwood Canyon took on the aura of a police convention. I counted nearly thirty officers representing the FBI, the highway patrol, the sheriff's office, and Salt Lake City PD. That didn't include Kate and me, or the sheriff's department SWAT team that was mobilizing at a nearby precinct station. The command post that had been established near the University of Utah hospital was moved to a parking lot at the entrance to the canyon. The road up the canyon was closed indefinitely.

In spite of an overwhelming police presence and the intimidation tactics employed by an overbearing supervisor from the FBI, Robin Joiner held her ground. She agreed to be interviewed, but only if Kate and I did it. I wasn't sure what prompted her to trust us, but the tough girl veneer had given way to genuine angst. I couldn't help but feel sympathy for her. I wasn't sure, but maybe I felt that way because I'm a father with a daughter of my own.

The SWAT team arrived, and a hastily planned meeting was organized to determine how the cabin would be taken. Joiner then led a small army of police up the canyon. She asked if either Kate or I could tag along. I went along as chaperone. Once the SWAT team was in place and the order given, officers were inside in seconds. The place was empty. The lights were on and it looked like Joan Dixon had left in a hurry. A crime scene investigation team from the sheriff's office swarmed the cabin. Physical evidence could prove useful, but what they really needed were people. And so far, the elusive Bradshaw clan had managed to remain one step ahead of the authorities.

Back at the command post at the base of the canyon, Kate and I stood by in frustration while the powers-that-be wasted time haggling over who would get the credit for Joiner's capture, and how to spin the story to the army of assembled media who had traipsed from the first command post at the university to this one. Reluctantly, they had agreed that Kate and I would conduct Joiner's interrogation, but they couldn't agree on where the interrogation should take place, or who should observe it. If we weren't careful, we'd have a convention at the interrogation.

Chapter Forty-three

Sergeant Todd Blackhurst watched as Randy Allred paid the bill and headed out the restaurant's front door. Despite the hard stare, the young man refused to make eye contact, something that only heightened Blackhurst's suspicion. "I wanna check these two guys out," he said to the patrol officers. "Hansen, you come with me. Baker, the other one's in the can. Escort him outside when he comes out of the head. We'll be in the parking lot."

Randy Allred had started to relax. He paid the restaurant bill and stepped into the cold night. He had just reached the stolen Nissan when he heard the voice behind him.

"Excuse me, sir," said Blackhurst. "This your car?"

Allred turned to face the approaching officers. "Yeah. What's the problem officer?"

"No problem, really. We're searching the area for a couple of wanted fugitives. Frankly, you and your partner look a little like them. It's probably nothing, but I'll need to see some identification and check the registration on the car."

"Don't you need a warrant to do this?" said Allred, putting as much self righteous indignation into his voice as possible.

"Not really, son. Now I'll need to see that identification."

Rookie Patrolman Trevor Hansen, weeks out of the police academy, followed Blackhurst into the parking lot, convinced that this shakedown was an exercise in futility. To his way of thinking, these guys didn't look remotely like members of the

Bradshaw gang. Maybe Blackhurst was using this as an excuse for a little in-service training. He figured he'd better play along.

While Blackhurst conversed with the subject, Hansen grabbed his radio and called in the plate number on the subject's car. Almost immediately the registration came back to a Mildred Tanner in South Jordan, and the plates belonged on a 2003 Ford Taurus. This guy didn't look like any Mildred he'd ever met, and the car was a Nissan Sentra, not a Ford Taurus. While Blackhurst conversed with the subject, Hansen unholstered his nine millimeter Smith and Wesson, and held it next to his leg.

Randy Allred removed the wallet from his back pocket and reached inside for his identification. His hands were shaking, and he wondered whether the cop could see well enough in the dark to notice. He handed Blackhurst a temporary Utah driver's license bearing the name Michael Waddoups. He hoped the cop wouldn't notice that the license was expired. He also gave Blackhurst his phony Utah State identification card with his picture on it bearing the same name.

Allred walked past the cop to the passenger side of the Sentra and said, "I'll have to open the glove box for the registration and insurance cards." He was trying to put the Nissan between himself and the two cops. The sergeant wasn't having it. He followed Allred around to the passenger side.

Then two things happened simultaneously: Robby Allred emerged from the restaurant with Officer Baker trailing behind. Patrolman Hansen chose that moment to tell Blackhurst about the discrepancy with the license plate. For an instant, the officers took their eyes off Randy Allred and looked at each other. Randy seized the opportunity and pulled the nine millimeter Glock from the waistband of his pants. The last thing Randy heard was the sound of his brother's, scream, "Nooo, Randy."

Allred raised the gun and fired. The first round struck Blackhurst high in the chest propelling him backward. His Kevlar vest saved his life. Randy fired two additional shots intended for Hansen. Both shots missed. Hansen, crouched in a combat position, squeezed off three rounds in rapid succession.

Two of them struck Randy, one near the heart and another in the throat. From a prone position, Blackhurst fired twice, missing on the first shot, but striking Allred in his left thigh with the second. Patrolman Baker wrestled a struggling Robby Allred to the asphalt parking lot and held him face down until Hansen came over and helped apply the cuffs. Robby was sobbing uncontrollably, struggling to reach his fallen brother.

It was over in a matter of seconds. Eight shots had been exchanged in the melee. Allred lay dead in a large pool of his own blood. Restaurant employees called 911 about the same time Blackhurst called it in. A restaurant customer who witnessed the shooting later described the incident as reminiscent of a western movie scene featuring an old fashioned gunfight.

<>

Joan Dixon and Amanda Bradshaw made it out of Little Cottonwood Canyon minutes before the road was closed. They left Dixon's SUV at the cabin figuring there was less likelihood the authorities would be looking for Amanda's nondescript Ford Escort. They drove east out of Salt Lake City in relative silence, each absorbed in her own thoughts, until they saw the signs for Park City. They were anxious to be reunited with their loved ones. They got off of I-80 at Kimball Junction and met the others at a McDonald's restaurant next to the freeway.

The women went inside and purchased food and soft drinks while the men remained in the vehicles. Walter Bradshaw was in and out of it—having brief moments of lucidity followed by periods of delirium. After a hurried meal, Gordon and Joan Dixon, accompanied by Joey Bradshaw, agreed to take the Ford Escort and drive on ahead of the others to the small, rural town of Heber City. There they would rent rooms in two old motels nestled along the town's main drag and await the arrival of the prophet.

Under normal circumstances, the sight of a man climbing out of the back-end of a canopy-covered pickup truck, and then watching as a middle aged female took his place, wouldn't have struck Summit County Deputy Sheriff Dave Cunningham as suspicious. However, on this night, an all points bulletin had gone out asking all law enforcement personnel to be on the lookout for members of the Bradshaw gang who had somehow managed to engineer the escape of the gang leader, Walter Bradshaw. He thought these subjects bore a striking resemblance to the physical descriptions that had come out in the APB.

Cunningham was sitting in his patrol car across the street from the Kimball Junction McDonald's finishing several reports as the scenario unfolded before him. He watched a mid-twenties-looking male devour a burger as he stood next to the truck. Moments later he was joined by a young female who had just come out of the restaurant. They spoke briefly and then climbed into the cab of the truck. The female drove while the male rode shotgun.

Cunningham pulled his patrol car behind the Ford F-150 as it returned to I-80. He ran a registration check. The plates belonged on a 2004 Toyota Tundra, not a Ford F-150.

Amanda Bradshaw spotted the patrol car almost immediately. "Oh my God, Albert, there's a cop car behind us." Albert glanced into the passenger side mirror just as the emergency lights came on. "Step on it," he said.

Cunningham radioed for backup and turned on his overhead flashers. The pickup accelerated quickly reaching speeds of ninety miles an hour as it approached the exit to State Highway 40. Cunningham blasted his siren in the faint hope that the driver hadn't seen his flashers. The truck continued to gather speed.

As the truck hurtled toward the freeway exit, Amanda Bradshaw hollered, "What should I do? What should I do?" She had started to exit the interstate when Albert said, "Don't get off. Stay on." Amanda jerked the steering wheel left, trying to get back on the freeway, overcorrected, and sent the pickup catapulting off the roadway, down an embankment, rolling three times before it landed on its top.

Deputy Cunningham watched in horror. He saw the vehicle roll several times before it landed on its top in a cloud of dust. He jumped on the radio. "SC101, I've got a high speed rollover on the eastbound I-80 off-ramp to southbound Highway 40. I'll need multiple ambulances, the fire department, and state patrol assistance."

"Okay," said the dispatcher. "Stand by."

Cunningham pulled over on the freeway shoulder and hurriedly ran to the overturned truck. He quickly determined that nobody in the truck cab had been wearing seat belts. The driver's chest appeared crushed by the steering column, the glassy eyes of the dead woman staring back at him. The male passenger had been ejected through the front windshield and Cunningham found his contorted torso some forty feet from the truck. There was no sound or sign of movement coming from the truck bed, either. Cunningham tried to open the canopy door, but it wouldn't budge. "Can anybody hear me in there?" he shouted. No reply.

He could smell gasoline and realized that anybody trapped inside the truck was in imminent danger from a possible fire. A passing trucker stopped his eighteen-wheeler and produced a crow bar which he and Cunningham used to pry open the canopy door. Inside, they discovered the unconscious and badly broken bodies of Walter and Janine Bradshaw.

Cunningham surmised that they'd probably been tossed around the inside of the pickup like rag dolls. He was faced with a difficult decision, one that needed to be made immediately. If he didn't remove the two individuals from the truck, he risked losing them in the event of a fire. If he did remove them, he risked killing them because of the strong likelihood of serious internal injuries. In the end, Cunningham, assisted by the trucker, lifted the bodies of Janine and Walter Bradshaw from the truck wreckage and carried them a short distance to safety. He detected a weak pulse from Walter, but nothing from Janine.

The Dixons and Joey Bradshaw drove until they reached Heber City. They rented rooms in two old motels nestled along the main drag and settled in to wait. Their concern grew when they repeatedly used the disposable cell phone and were unable to reach the other vehicle. It was Gordon and Joan Dixon who first heard the news about the Allred brothers. Minutes later, they heard the news of the high speed chase and the subsequent apprehension of the prophet. They called Joey into the motel room and gave him the news. After prayers, they held each other and cried. There was little else to do.

<><><>

From the command post at the base of Little Cottonwood Canyon, we heard the frantic radio call, 'Shots fired, officer down....' A contingent of FBI agents and Salt Lake Police detectives jumped into two cars and raced to the scene of the Allred shooting. Robin Joiner had been placed in the back seat of an FBI car and didn't hear the radio traffic. We decided not to tell her until after our interview. The grand compromise was that Kate and I would interview Joiner at FBI headquarters with an entourage of brass listening and watching from an adjoining room.

We scripted the interview while driving Kate's Beamer to the FBI office. Joiner had complained about being hungry, so on our way in we stopped at a Wendy's and picked up a burger, fries, and a strawberry shake. We fed her, had paramedics attend to her feet. After that, I advised her of her Miranda warnings and we turned on the tape.

We began at the beginning, asking Joiner several innocuous questions about her childhood, her teen years, and how she became acquainted with Joseph Bradshaw. She insisted that she had been trying to draw Joey away from the family for nearly two years. Joey, in turn, was trying to convince her to become his wife and join the family.

"He asked you to marry him. Is that it?" I asked.

"Yes, several times."

"What did you tell him?"

"I told him I'd marry him if he left the family. He refused. He thought if he persisted long enough, I'd relent."

"Did you understand that marrying Joey meant entering into a plural marriage?"

"We never spoke directly about it, but I know how it works. I know what they believe. They believe that a man must take at least three wives to reach the celestial kingdom. I would have ended up a first wife, and eventually, Joey would have taken additional wives. Those women would have become my sister wives. It was an arrangement I was unwilling to accept."

When we got around to discussing the armored car robbery, I tip-toed into what I knew would be sensitive territory.

"Tell us how you came to be at the Super Target store on the morning of the robbery?"

She took a deep breath before answering. "I wasn't supposed to be there at all, Amanda was."

"What do you mean?"

"Amanda was supposed to be a lookout during the robbery. On the morning of the holdup, Amanda got sick—painful menstrual cramps combined with a hellish migraine. She couldn't even get out of bed. Joey called and asked me to meet him."

"Did you know what they were planning?"

She frowned. "Not until I met Joey that morning. I tried to talk him out of it, but he wouldn't listen. I even offered to run away with him if he would leave immediately, but he refused."

"So you agreed to take Amanda's place and serve as lookout during the robbery?"

She hesitated. "Yes."

"Why did you agree to do that?"

The dam burst and tears began to flow. Kate pushed a box of Kleenex in front of her. "I'm not really sure," she sniffled, dabbing at her eyes. "Joey promised that nobody would get hurt. I guess I believed him."

"Do you think Joey intentionally lied to you, used you, maybe?" asked Kate.

"Used me, maybe. I've had a lot of time lately to think about things. In retrospect, I realize that I believed most of what Joey told me. It's been difficult to accept the fact that I was never as important to him as the love and loyalty he felt toward his family, particularly his father."

"The police report says that after the robbery, you came forward on your own. Why did you do that?"

"When I saw the carnage, I knew the right thing to do was turn myself in. That's what I intended to do. But then I got scared. By then, I'd come forward and was giving a statement to one of the officers. I decided to play along as a witness."

"Tell me something, Robin," I said. "How did you ever expect to have a normal life with Joey? He and the family members are wanted fugitives. The authorities will hunt them until they're caught."

"I told Joey that, but he always said we'd start a new life in a safe place."

Kate perked up. "A safe place. What did he mean by that?"

"I don't know. He never got specific, but I assumed he was talking about going someplace where nobody would know him, a place where we could start over and build a life together."

"And you think that's what they're going to do now?"

She paused. "Don't you?"

Kate and I looked at each other. "They're getting ready to leave the country," said Kate. "That's why the wives went missing and the house they rented left vacant." I nodded.

"And you have no idea where they are now?" I said.

"I have absolutely no idea, and that's the truth."

"So what you're telling us, Robin, is that your involvement as a lookout in the armored car robbery was a spontaneous thing, not something you planned?"

"That's right. I went directly from my meeting with Joey to the Super Target store. Joey gave me a cell phone that I could use to call him if I needed to."

"What did you do with that phone?" Kate asked.

"I threw it away—tossed it in a dumpster at a gas station later that day."

I looked at my notes. I was about out of questions. "Were you involved in the commission of any other crimes committed by the Bradshaws?"

She blew her nose. "No," she whispered.

"You might be asked to take a polygraph examination regarding the veracity of the information you just provided. Would you be willing to do that?"

Without hesitation, she answered, "Yes, I'd be willing to take a lie detector test. I'm telling you the truth. Can I ask you a question?"

"Fire away," I replied.

"What's going to happen to me now?"

There was only one thing to do and that was to tell her the truth. "Robin, you're going to be booked into the Salt Lake County Detention Center, and sometime in the next day or two, you'll be brought in front of a judge for a bail hearing."

"So I'll have to stay in jail until then?"

I nodded. The tears began to flow again. I explained that she'd be represented by a public defender at the bail hearing. That bit of information provided little solace to her.

"Would you like me to call your mother for you?"

She nodded.

What I didn't tell her was that she'd probably end up charged with at least one count of being an accessory-before-the-fact in the robbery case. And considering two people died in the ensuing gunfight, and another had been seriously wounded, Joiner could probably expect to do some time. She'd been drawn into a bad situation by some particularly bad men, and now there was no easy way out.

When the interview was over, Salt Lake City PD detectives booked Joiner into the Salt Lake County Jail. That's when Kate and I learned about the high speed chase near Park City, and the apparent apprehension of the prophet and some of his entourage. Details were sketchy, but from what we could tell, some members of the gang were dead while others were still at large.

Chapter Forty-four

By the time we left the FBI building, it was three-thirty in the morning. We were both exhausted. She drove me back to the Lucky Gent where I'd left my car. She invited me to stay at her place but I declined. Since the murder of Arnold Ginsberg, I'd been working long hours. I was anxious to reconnect with Sara, Aunt June, and Bob the Bassett Hound. Sleeping in my own bed didn't sound too bad either. We agreed to get a few hours of shut-eye and then meet later in the morning. We still had plenty of work to do on the Ginsberg murder, plus I needed to stay abreast of activities in the SIB including the internal investigation involving Terry Burnham.

When I got home, I found a note on the kitchen counter from Aunt June warning me that I would find, not one guest in my bed, but two. It wasn't hard to figure out who that would be. Sure enough, I found Sara asleep in one corner and Bob the Bassett Hound on MY side of the bed with his head propped on MY pillow. From the look of things, the lazy lout was enjoying his new digs. I was so damned tired that I simply pushed him over and laid down on the dog drool he'd left on my pillow.

I slept for several hours until I heard Aunt June. Sara and the dog were still conked out. I got up and looked outside. It was going to be one of those crystal clear, blue sky days in Park City, brisk in the morning, but comfortably warm throughout the afternoon. The best of the autumn colors were already on the ground. I showered, dressed, and joined Aunt June in the kitchen.

I made us coffee and built a fire in the great room fireplace while she served piping hot coffee cake, fresh from the oven. I figured if I drank about a gallon of coffee, I might wake up. It worked for about thirty minutes and then I was on the nod again.

"What's going on today? Do you have to go to work?" asked June.

"I probably should but I'm gonna try not to. I'll need to give Kate a call and see if she's got something we really need to do. I'd like to stick around the house and spend some time with Sara. I've been promising her that I'd take her to the city park and fly that new kite she's so excited about. I've also got a mountain of aspen leaves in the back yard just waiting to be raked.

"What about you?"

"Baxter's invited me out to dinner tonight, but I told him that I'd rather have him come to the house and I'll fix us something. Why don't you invite Kate to join us?"

"That's a great idea. I'll bet she'd like that. I'll call her. But why don't we all go out to dinner? That way you won't have to cook. It'll be my treat. What do you say?"

"A very tempting offer, nephew, one that I'm sure Baxter will like."

I waited for another hour before I called Kate. I wanted to give her sufficient sleep-in time. I managed to convince her that this particular Sunday should be a day of R and R. The woman's a workaholic and it's often difficult to get her to slow down. That's never been a problem for me because, basically, I'm lazy. Whenever I can find a convenient excuse not to work, I usually take it.

I spent all day catching up on household chores and doing things with Sara and Kate. In early afternoon, I packed a picnic lunch and took them to the city park. Kate read a book and snoozed on a blanket while I ran around like a mad man trying to get Sara's kite in the air on a day without so much as a hint of a breeze. Afterward, Kate took Sara on a Christmas shopping trip to the Park City factory stores.

Baxter Shaw met us at the house in the early evening and I took the four of them to dinner at Café Terigo on Park City's

Main Street. It had been a Park City favorite because it turned out consistently good food. After dinner, we returned to the house where Baxter and I settled down with a brandy and watched NFL football. The ladies were in another part of the house doing I'm not sure what.

Baxter headed home when the game ended a little past ten. The poor guy was a dedicated and frustrated Atlanta fan—not much to cheer about lately with the Falcons. Kate spent the night. I'd given her the guest bathroom for her toothbrush, makeup, and female things. She had moved some of her clothes into the walk-in closet in the master bedroom. We slept fitfully and were up shortly before six the next morning. We had coffee and some of Aunt June's leftover coffee cake while strategizing a plan for the day.

<>◇<>

The plane came out of the southwest sky in the early dawn. It crossed the Wasatch Mountains on a path that took it over Mount Tippanogus and the Sundance Ski Resort before entering Heber Valley. The twin engine Cessna circled the sleepy town of Heber City once before landing to the west.

The pilot refueled and then taxied over to the small passenger terminal. Three people boarded the aircraft. Within fifteen minutes, it was airborne again following the same flight path it had taken when it arrived. The Cessna made one short refueling stop in Flagstaff, Arizona, before resuming its journey. The pilot charted a course due south, flying to the west of metropolitan Phoenix and continuing south into Mexico. Four-and-a-half-hours after leaving Heber City, the plane descended through the cloud cover revealing a hazy November day, with the water from the Sea of Cortez shimmering in the midday sun. The plane landed at Guaymas International Airport.

The Dixons and Joey Bradshaw deplaned and passed nervously through customs. They each carried new identity papers which included forged passports. They arranged ground transportation which took them to the isolated ten acre compound in the Sonoran Desert northeast of Guaymas. Gordon Dixon had purchased the property months before, having it deeded to a bogus American shell corporation allegedly in the import/export business.

Here, the surviving family members would begin a new life, a life free from the religious persecution suffered at the hands of state and federal governments to the north. For now, their task was simple: to assimilate into the local culture while maintaining as low a profile as possible. Over time, others would join the enclave, but for now, it would be just the three of them.

<><><>

Kate left for her office ahead of me. I got Sara up at seven, fixed her breakfast, and gave her a ride to school. On the way, she reminded me that I'd promised to help her on a school project, attend her soccer game later in the afternoon at four, and still find time to take Bob for a brisk walk. I tried to tell her how busy I was at work, but on the sympathy meter, that earned me a big, fat zero. So we compromised. I told her the soccer game was iffy at best, but that I would try to make it home in time to help her with her school project. In return, she agreed to take Bob for his evening stroll.

I was in my office at the state prison by eight-thirty. I found a voice mail message from Captain T.J. Dutton of the Salt Lake County Sheriff's Office. Dutton was the commander of the Internal Affairs Division. He asked me to call him ASAP. He didn't say why he was calling, but it didn't take a rocket scientist to figure that it must have something to do with the Burnham internal investigation.

I had just picked up the phone to call him when Patti walked in carrying a steaming cup of coffee. She set it down on my desk and said, "Figured you could use this. Director Cates called this morning promptly at eight. He wants you in his office at noon for what he described as a working lunch. Shall I call him back to confirm?"

"Yeah, you better. Did he say what he wanted to see me about?"

"He didn't, but his tone suggested your attendance wasn't optional."

I nodded.

I caught T.J. Dutton on his way to a budget meeting. "Morning, Sam. I wanted to give you a heads up on something, but it's important you understand we never had this conversation. Agreed?"

"No Problem."

"Sergeant Egan was summoned to a meeting Saturday afternoon with your new boss and his administrative law judge, Rachel Rivers-Blakely."

"And."

"They had Egan go over her findings regarding the Burnham investigation. It's pretty clear cut, really. What I think you need to know is that they intend to make an example of him. Cates made it clear he wants felony charges filed against Terry immediately. And he specifically directed Egan not to present the findings of the investigation to you. She tried to explain to him that that's not how we do things around here, but he insisted."

"I don't get it," I said. "This incident might warrant a misdemeanor charge but certainly not a felony. It's not like we had an employee smuggling drugs into the prison and passing them on to inmates."

Dutton sighed. "Egan told him that, but he didn't want to hear it. Don't forget that many of us know Terry Burnham. I think what you've got is an employee with a drinking problem who needs to go through treatment. But Cates appears to have a different agenda."

"Where does the investigation stand now?" I asked.

"Basically, we're through. Egan's impression is that Cates intends to dispatch Rivers-Blakely to the DA's office first thing this morning, and push for the issuance of a felony information charging Terry with one count of smuggling contraband into the prison."

"Shit. Thanks for the heads-up, T.J., I owe you one. I'll talk to you later."

I'd figured that today's meeting would probably be about Bradshaw's escape from custody. Now I knew different. I also had a pretty good idea what I intended to do about it.

Chapter Forty-five

I was about to leave the office and pay a visit to the Salt Lake County District Attorney's office when Patti called. "Sam, it's Jack Early on line two." Early was an evidence technician employed at the Utah State Crime Laboratory who specialized in drug testing. He'd been in the business a long time.

"Morning, Jack. I'll bet you're calling to tell me what that 'exotic' substance was that came out of Bradshaw's cell the other night?"

"How'd you guess?"

"Why else would you be calling me?"

"Good point. It took us a little extra time and effort, and I gotta tell you, I've never seen this substance in Utah before."

"The suspense is killing me. What is it?"

"It's a drug called Tetrodotoxin, or TTX for short. Some people refer to it as Zombie Powder."

"Never heard of it."

"It's actually a toxin found in the ovaries and liver of Puffer fish, more commonly known as the Blow fish. Blow fish are found in the South Pacific and Indian oceans. The fish is considered a delicacy in Japan. A small number of people each year actually die from eating Blow fish because they're also ingesting TTX. I guess if the chef preparing the fish doesn't know what he's doing, the results can be fatal for the consumer."

"I'll mention that to my girlfriend the next time she asks me to go to a sushi bar. Where's this stuff come from?"

Early snorted a laugh. "That's the interesting part. I can tell you where it doesn't come from, and that's anyplace around here. Apparently, TTX is still used in some voodoo religious rituals and can be found in Haiti. It's also believed to be available in the Algiers section of New Orleans."

"Interesting. How does a person ingest the drug?"

"It absorbs through the skin or the gastrointestinal tract. It can be added to food or simply sprinkled on the skin. Symptoms begin to show in as little as a few minutes to as long as four hours."

"Is there an antidote?"

"No known antidote. When people die from TTX poisoning, it's because of respiratory failure."

"So if somebody has an adverse reaction to TTX, how are they treated?"

"Good question. Oxygen would be used for sure. As far as other drugs are concerned, I'm not sure. I suspect you could treat somebody having an adverse reaction with drugs that support blood pressure. That only makes sense."

"How does the drug react in the body? I mean it doesn't sound like it would give users a raging high?"

"You're right about that, Sam. TTX is basically a neurotoxin that affects a person's neurological system. Its symptoms can include reductions in heart rate and blood pressure, paralysis, speech difficulty, irregular heartbeat, and slow, shallow respirations."

"Christ, the symptoms sound like they mimic somebody suffering a heart attack."

"Exactly."

I said, "The Bradshaws must have known all of this. They smuggled the drug into the prison and passed it to Walter. At an agreed upon time, he took it, knowing that it would trigger a reaction that would earn him a trip to the hospital."

"And might kill him," said Early.

"Yeah, that too. No wonder our prison medical personnel were confused."

"Are there any legitimate medical uses for the drug?"

"In my research, I read that it's used in certain types of neurological research; in diluted form, I guess it's also used as a painkiller for people suffering from rheumatism and arthritis."

"That explains a lot of things, Jack. Have you notified the sheriff's office?"

"Already did that. Everybody who needs to know does."

I thanked him and disconnected.

<>◇<>

By midmorning, I was in downtown Salt Lake City circling the Justice Center in search of a parking place. All of the Reserved for Police Vehicles spots were taken, and at this point, I was ready to feed a meter if I could find one. The drive in from the prison had given me time to plot strategy. I figured my best bet was to make my pitch on Burnham's behalf prior to my noon meeting with Cates. If I spoke with him first, he might give me a direct order to keep my mouth shut and stay out of the case. I didn't want to risk that. What's that old saying? "Sometimes it's easier to seek forgiveness than ask permission." This felt like one of those times.

There was a couple of ways I could play this. I could pay a visit to the deputy DA in charge of reviewing cases brought in by the police. Assuming Cates had dispatched Rivers-Blakely here ahead of me, that's probably where she went. But I knew if an investigation might result in criminal charges against an officer, the DA himself reviewed it before final decisions were made. So that's where I went.

District Attorney Richard Hatch didn't look pleased to see me. "Hello, Sam. You missed Rachel Rivers-Blakely by about an hour. Have a seat." He remained seated behind his desk while I sat in a high-back leather chair directly in front of him. He studied me thoughtfully for a moment before speaking.

"I assume you're here to see me about the Terry Burnham matter." I nodded.

"Does Ben Cates know you're here?" I shook my head.

"Thought so. I think you're about to put me in an awkward situation but it certainly won't be the first time. I suppose I don't have to tell you that you're not in a particularly good place yourself." I listened but didn't say anything.

"Here's something for you to think about. You could get up right now and walk out that door, and as far as I'm concerned, this meeting never took place." He waited and so did I.

He shrugged. "I didn't think so. State your case."

Hatch listened patiently as I walked him through the incident with Burnham. He'd been a deputy district attorney in Salt Lake County for years before running for the top job and getting it. He'd known Terry for years, and I figured that couldn't hurt. It was also to my advantage that the case against Burnham hadn't come to the attention of the media, so Hatch wouldn't have that issue to contend with. When I finished, he took a deep breath intently studying the neatly manicured fingers of his right hand.

"That would appear to be an accurate factual summary of the case," he said. "And it's nice to know the facts are not in dispute. Your take on the matter coincides nicely with Sergeant Egan's report, which I've read, and with what Rivers-Blakely had to say."

"That's good," I replied.

"Yes, it is, but of course, that's not the problem. The problem is Ben Cates wants this guy taken out at sunrise and shot. You, on the other hand, are here seeking leniency for an employee. I may not be able to help you, but for what it's worth, I admire your sense of loyalty to a member of your staff."

"Why can't you help me, Richard? You're the decision-maker here."

"I wish I could assure you that my decision, whatever that may be, is free of political considerations. Unfortunately, that isn't the case."

"Why not?"

He hesitated before answering. "I'm sure you've heard the expression that it's never a wise idea to fall on your own sword. If

I were to do what you'd like me to do, I risk alienating a power-ful player in the Utah criminal justice system, and one that has the ear of both the governor and the legislature."

"That would be Benjamin Cates."

He nodded. "Now if I were to do what your boss would like to see done, I ingratiate myself with him and I can file away an IOU to be used later. I also get the added benefit of going public with the case and come away looking like a tough, but fair minded DA in the eyes of the general public. That's the serendipity."

I shook my head. "Why can't we make decisions in this system predicated on doing the right thing instead of that which is politically expedient?" It seemed like a rhetorical question, even to me, and Hatch didn't bother answering it.

Finally, he said, "You speak of doing the right thing. Politics aside, tell me what you believe the appropriate course of action should be in this case."

"I don't think Terry should walk away unscathed from this incident, and he's not going to. Regardless of what you decide to do, Terry's going to be disciplined by the department."

"What action do you anticipate the department will take?"

"After the appropriate due process, at the very least, he'll be reprimanded and suspended from duty without pay for a period of time. And he might well lose his job. I'd like to see your office file a misdemeanor charge, and offer him a deferred prosecution. Give him a year to keep his nose clean and see if he completes alcohol treatment. If he does, drop the case and keep it off his record. And if that's not enough, fine him and require him to perform community service while he's in treatment."

"And you think this is an appropriate course of action because...?"

"Richard, you've been around a long time and so have I. Terry Burnham is hardly the first alcoholic cop to come down the pike and he won't be the last. There's certainly ample precedent for giving these troubled officers a second chance. We send them through an employee assistance program and try to rehabilitate them. We don't just flush them down the toilet, particularly on a first offense. And let's not forget Terry's had a distinguished police career for almost thirty years without a blemish on his record."

"Well stated, Sam, but I'm afraid I'm going to need a little time before making a decision. And I'm not making you any promises. Are we clear about that?"

"Sure. I understand." I thanked him and got up to leave. When I got to the door, he stopped me.

"Sam, this may not turn out the way you would have liked, but I want you to know I respect the fact that you came here at some professional risk to yourself to support a member of your staff. And if Ben Cates finds out about our little chat, I want you to know that he didn't hear about it from me."

I nodded, thanked him again, and left.

Chapter Forty-six

I still had a few minutes before my noon meeting with Director Cates so I stopped by to see Kate. I found her doing what I needed to be doing, typing reports on the Ginsberg investigation.

She glanced up from her computer screen. "Ready to get back to work?"

"Yeah, but it's going to have to be this afternoon." I told her about the noon meeting with Cates, the call from T.J. Dutton of the sheriff's office, and my subsequent visit with Richard Hatch.

"I've always had good rapport with Hatch," she said. "He's a straight shooter. What do you think he'll do?"

"I wish I knew. I don't think the odds are any better than fifty-fifty. I agree with you. I like Hatch, but I don't think he's inclined to bleed for me, much less Burnham."

"I don't like where you're at on this one. If Cates finds out about your visit with Hatch, he's going to be seriously pissed. And I'm afraid you're going to get caught right in the middle."

"You might be right. I don't think Hatch will wait long to make a decision. It should all shake out in the next day or two."

"What's going on with the Bradshaws?"

"Amanda and Albert were pronounced dead at the scene of the rollover. So was Janine. Massive head and internal injuries. Walter managed to hang on for a while, but he died early this morning on the operating table."

"That's a helleva body count—five dead, Robby, I assume, is hanging on, and three fugitives still on the run."

"That's it. So far there's nothing on Gordon and Joan Dixon or Joey Bradshaw. It's like they disappeared into thin air. I'd bet they're either long gone or hiding under a rock someplace waiting for things to cool down. The task force has scattered its personnel all along the Wasatch front. They're watching bus terminals, airports, and train stations."

I told Kate about the call from Jack Early and what I'd learned about the drug, TTX. She listened attentively before commenting. "Just goes to show how well planned this little escapade really was. It should clear up any suspicion you might have had regarding the prison medical staff."

"It does."

"Has Robby Allred had anything to say?"

"Not a word."

"And Robin Joiner?"

"Robin was interviewed again last night at the jail by a contingent from the FBI, the sheriff's office, and my department. From what I can tell, they didn't learn anything new. I would guess she'll have her initial court appearance sometime today."

"Any chance they'll release her on her own recognizance?"

"I can't imagine. I'm sure the DA will request high bail. They want to keep her around, and they'll argue that she's a flight risk. And she probably is."

"Were you able to reach her mother?"

"I did, and as far as I know, she's on her way here from Nevada."

I headed out the door promising Kate I'd call her as soon as I got out of the meeting with Director Cates. Precisely at noon, I was ushered into his office. I joined several senior staff, mostly prison employees. I still didn't know why we were meeting, but I was relieved I wasn't doing a one-on-one with Cates regarding Burnham's internal investigation.

The meeting focused largely on two issues: Cates wanted a status report on the hunt for the Dixons and Joey Bradshaw.

The news wasn't encouraging. I chimed in with the information Kate had shared with me.

His other agenda item made the senior prison managers uncomfortable. Cates demanded an explanation for the breach in department procedures regarding the security detail that should have accompanied the ambulance transporting Bradshaw to the hospital. By the end of the meeting, it was clear that several prison employees would end up on the receiving end of some as yet to be determined disciplinary action.

As the meeting broke up, Cates turned to me, "Sam, I need to see you for a minute." After everybody was gone, he said, "I wanted to be sure you were up to speed on the status of the IA investigation against Mr. Burnham." He spit out the words, "Mr. Burnham," with as much disdain as his voice would allow.

"Please do," I said.

"I met over the weekend with representatives from the sheriff's office. Their investigation is now complete. Sergeant Egan provided us with copies of her reports. I have forwarded them to Rachel Rivers-Blakely."

I feigned surprise. "Has the case been referred to the district attorney's office for review?"

He hesitated momentarily before answering. "Not yet," he lied.

"Would you like me to take care of that?"

"Thanks, but we'll handle it."

"I'd like to have copies of Egan's reports," I said.

"Not a problem. I'll have Rachel send them to you." He scribbled a note in his planner.

He asked for an update on the Ginsberg investigation and I gave it to him. He was trying his best to act interested in what I was saying, but he clearly wasn't. Mentally, he had moved on to other, more pressing concerns.

In the end, I realized we had just played our own game of Don't Ask, Don't Tell. I didn't tell him about the call I'd received from T.J. Dutton of the sheriff's department or my subsequent visit with Richard Hatch at the DA's office. He probably assumed

I was out of the loop. In turn, he had neglected to mention dispatching Rivers-Blakely to the DA's office in a covert attempt to get charges filed against Burnham before informing me.

I wasn't naïve or at least I didn't think so. I knew this situation was highly combustible, and that if it blew up, it would likely blow up in my face. And that's exactly what was about to happen.

Chapter Forty-seven

Kate looked giddy by the time I got back to her office after my meeting with Cates. "You look happy," I said. "What's up?"

"Two things. I won the office betting pool on the NFL games yesterday." She announced that loud enough to be heard all over the office. Heads came up. One detective who I didn't recognize said, "Blind luck. She couldn't do it again in a million years." Another nodded in agreement and quipped, "She wouldn't know a football from a ping-pong ball." Everybody laughed including Kate.

"Gloating are we. Well, good for you. What's the other bit of good news?"

"We got the DNA results on Ambrose and it was a match." She let that sink in for a minute before adding, "What do you think?"

"I think you must have influence in that DNA lab. I've never seen test results come back so quickly. Who are you sleeping with over there, anyway?"

She smiled as she slugged me in the arm. "I do get around."

"Seriously, I think it's time to kick ass and take names. I'm getting bored to tears with all this damn surveillance," I said.

"Me, too," said Kate. "But let's talk about it for a minute. I think we've got more than enough evidence to bring charges against Anthony Barnes and Steven Ambrose, but what about Plow?"

I shrugged. "Well, that's easy enough. We haven't got shit on Rodney other than his phone call to Barnes' cell. That after denying he even knew Barnes. We might be able to prove motive considering the ongoing sexual relationship between Ambrose and Rodney, but that's about it."

Kate shook her head. "I don't think we've even got that. The affair might go to prove motive on Ambrose's part, but not Rodney, unless we can connect him in some other way. He's already acknowledged the affair but described it as little more than a fling that didn't mean much. That's what he'd say in court, too."

"You're probably right. If we bust the other two, there's a good chance we'd get a confession from one or both. Maybe the DA cuts somebody a deal for testimony against Rodney."

"Possible, but I still think we need something more if we're going to hang a conspiracy rap on him. Let's stay with our surveillance of Barnes for just a little longer. If something doesn't break in the next day or so, we try something else."

"And that would be?"

"We get warrants for Barnes and Ambrose. We bring them in and turn their homes inside out. And then we squeeze their testicles until we get them talking."

"I like it, but I'll leave the squeezing of the testicles to you."

Kate nodded.

I asked, "What about the house on Ninth South that Barnes has been staying at. Have you had time to figure out who lives there?"

"I have. The utilities and property taxes are paid by an elderly woman named Rosemary Tafoya. It turns out that she's Anthony's aunt. Tafoya's clean by the way—no criminal history."

"Let's go talk to her. What have we got to lose? Anthony's already spooked. He's going to be looking over his shoulder from now on anyway. A conversation with his aunt might even be beneficial."

Kate considered that for a moment. "Okay. Let's do it."

Barnes' SUV wasn't around when we arrived at Rosemary Tafoya's residence. We found her in the backyard raking leaves from the aspen trees scattered about the property. This annual autumn ritual was a harbinger of the Rocky Mountain winter soon to follow.

Tafoya was a matronly looking woman, a little on the plump side, wearing no makeup, and with snow white hair wrapped in a blue and white bandana. She invited us inside and offered tea and fresh-baked zucchini bread. Kate declined. Not having had lunch, I jumped on the offer. She disappeared into the kitchen only to reappear minutes later carrying a silver serving tray with sliced zucchini bread on it, and two cups of black tea in delicate, bone china cups. A very nice presentation I thought.

Once settled, she said, "I almost dread asking what brings you to see me."

"Why is that?" asked Kate.

"I fear that it probably has something to do with my nephew, Tony. He's my late sister's boy. He's the only family I've got left. And he's a troubled young man with a checkered past."

"Unfortunately, Ms. Tafoya, it is about Anthony. You describe his life as troubled. Could you explain?"

She sighed. "Please call me Rosy, that's what everybody does."

"Sure, Rosy."

"Tony has had long standing problems in his life with depression. And it's proven nearly impossible to keep him on his meds. He just won't take them on a consistent basis. Add to that his sexual identity problems and it's made for a troubled life."

"What kind of sexual identity problems?" I asked.

"He'd very much like to be a straight male, get married, have children—all the things normal people do. But he's not. He's attracted primarily to men. I don't know whether he's gay or bisexual. He's had girlfriends from time-to-time but never anything stable or long-term. He doesn't seem capable of forming the attachments."

Kate asked, "And what kind of problems has this produced in his life?"

"Well, aside from relationship problems, he got kicked out of the military for reasons I'm uncertain about. I suspect he couldn't adjust to military life. He's had some drug and alcohol problems which led to some scrapes with the law. He doesn't have much by way of job skills. He works as a bartender in a gay night club."

"That would be the Lucky Gent?"

"Yes. Now it's my turn to ask a question," she said. "This isn't a social call. What is it you think Tony's gotten himself involved in?"

Kate and I glanced at each other. "I'm sorry to have to tell you this," Kate said, "but I'm afraid that Anthony is a suspect in a murder case."

"Oh, dear God, no," Tafoya said, putting her face in her hands. When she regained her composure, Kate went on.

"Does Anthony live here with you?"

"Not really. He inherited my sister's house in Ogden, but it's such a long drive back-and-forth to the bar that he sometimes stays over with me. I'm alone, and frankly, it's nice to have the company."

"He's got the Ogden house up for sale," said Kate.

"Tony's got the house up for sale," Tafoya said, a look of surprise on her face. "He hasn't mentioned that to me, but why would he? I know he's been trying to save money."

"What for?" I asked.

"Says he's gonna buy the Lucky Gent."

"Does he have a bedroom that he uses when he stays over?"

"Yes. I've got a bedroom and bath in the basement that I let him use."

"Does he pay you rent?" I asked.

That question seemed to catch her off-guard. "Why, no, why do you ask that?"

"Because we'd like your permission to search it, and if he was paying rent, you might not be able to give us consent—expectation of privacy and all that stuff."

"I see. Yes, you have my permission to search anyplace you need to search. Is it all right if I observe?"

"No problem," said Kate. "We really appreciate your cooperation and insights into Anthony's life."

Tafoya led us into the basement and showed us the bedroom and bathroom used by her nephew. Kate searched the bedroom while I looked around in the bathroom. We both came up empty. Barnes kept a few clothes in the closet and a shaving kit in the bathroom. Other than the personal items, there was nothing.

Rosy Tafoya walked us to our car. She had been more than cooperative and we thanked her for it. I had one last question. "Over the past several days, has Anthony acted or behaved at all differently?"

She paused for a moment. Finally, she said, "No, not really. You have to remember that because of Tony's depression, his moods can change from moment to moment. And sometimes, they do. He can be up and down like a yo-yo."

We thanked her again and got into our car. Before we could back out of the driveway, Tafoya approached my side and motioned me to unroll my window.

"I just remembered something that happened today when Tony left. It seemed a little out of the ordinary, but I guess I just dismissed it."

"What was it?"

"I was raking leaves when I saw him come out of the garage carrying a pick and shovel."

"What did he do with em'?"

"He put them in the back of his SUV and then took off."

"Do you have any idea what he wanted with a pick and shovel?"

"None, whatsoever. He didn't talk to me about it. I just assumed he needed them for work."

"Do you know where he went?"

"I think he went to work. The Lucky Gent doesn't open until five, but he often goes in during the afternoon."

We thanked her again and took off for the Lucky Gent.

Chapter Forty-Eight

Anthony Barnes sat in a booth in the deserted confines of the Lucky Gent nursing his fourth Budweiser. A lone janitor and the hum of the overhead ceiling fans were the only sounds disturbing the quiet. From five in the evening until closing, the Lucky Gent buzzed with the raucous sound of the jukebox and the incessant chatter of bar patrons. Barnes needed the quiet time, especially on a day like today when he needed to think.

Things had suddenly become complicated and now he was in jeopardy. It was time to act, to take control of his destiny. Barnes removed the 22 caliber Colt revolver from the waistband of his pants, opened the cylinder, and checked the loads. It was a good gun when there was work to do up close; it was easily concealed and relatively quiet when discharged. He finished the beer and grabbed a fresh six pack from the cooler before heading to his SUV. He had work to do.

‹›‹›‹›

"What the hell do you think the pick and shovel thing is all about?" Kate asked.

"It's hard to say, but I've got a pretty good idea what it's not. You can bet that he doesn't have a gardening project going on at the Lucky Gent."

"Maybe he needs the tools at his Ogden house."

"Maybe."

As we approached the Lucky Gent, Anthony Barnes pulled out of the parking lot and shot past us going in the opposite direction. "Christ, do you think he saw us?" I said.

"Hard to tell," said Kate, as she hung a U-ball and punched the accelerator on the Dodge. We closed ground quickly on Barnes but tried to keep several cars between us to avoid detection. He meandered through town and eventually headed up Emigration Canyon.

"What do you think he's up to?" Kate said.

"I wish I knew, but I've got a bad feeling that he's up to no good."

We continued to climb until we reached an elevation that put us above the multi-million dollar homes that dotted the hillsides and the businesses that occupied the canyon floor. At this elevation, the canyon resembled remote wilderness. We stayed well back giving Barnes plenty of room. Eventually, his brake lights came on and he turned on to a narrow dirt road and disappeared into a grove of aspen trees. We didn't dare follow with the car, so I took Kate's hand-held radio, jumped out, and followed on foot. Kate took up a stationary position a little further up the road and waited for my call.

I'd hiked parts of Emigration Canyon in the past but I'd never been in this area before. I crept down the winding road with as much stealth as I could manage considering I was dressed in slick-soled Nordstrom's penny-loafers—hardly ideal for back-country hiking. The road dropped gradually until it abruptly came to a dead-end about two hundred yards from the highway. The Explorer was parked at the end of the road. Barnes was nowhere in sight.

I had only one good option. I could see a rocky outcrop above the road where I could stay out of sight and wait for Barnes to return. I nearly killed myself climbing up there in my penny-loafers. I had no idea where he'd gone, and to do anything else seemed foolhardy. I radioed Kate and then settled down to wait. I sat for over an hour before Barnes emerged from what looked like an old game trail. He was drinking a beer and carrying the pick and shovel that his aunt, Rosy Tafoya, had told us about. He put the tools away, tossed the beer can, and climbed into the Explorer. The dirt road was so narrow that he had to back out to the highway.

I used the radio and alerted Kate. We agreed that she would follow Barnes while I went in search of the dig site. I figured that he couldn't have hiked in too far. I followed the game trail a short distance taking frequent detours off the trail into places that looked flat enough to allow digging. I spotted a tall mound of what looked like freshly turned dirt.

I approached tentatively, unsure of what I might find. What I saw shocked me. I muttered to myself, "Holy shit," as I reached for the hand-held radio. Kate asked me to switch to a secure channel before transmitting, one that couldn't be monitored by the press or the general public.

"What have you got, Sam?"

"You know those garden tools we were wondering about? Well, he put them to good use. He's dug a grave up here. The only thing missing is an occupant. My guess is that he's already killed somebody and needs to bury the body, or he's about to kill somebody. Are you still with him?"

"Yeah, I followed him down the canyon about two miles. He stopped at a little joint on the south side of the highway called This is the Place Bar & Grill. He got out of the Explorer and was talking on his cell for awhile, and then went inside."

"What do you think he's up to?"

"My guess is that he's waiting for somebody."

She was probably right. And I could take a pretty good guess at who that somebody might be. "We're going to need backup up here right away," I said. "I'm not sure what's going on, but I've got a feeling that things are about to get dicey. I'd keep the uniforms away. I suspect these guys will spook easily."

"I'm a step ahead of you," she said. "I'll have Vince and his new partner here momentarily. Then I'll come and get you." The Vince she was referring to was Vince Turner, her former partner. Turner had recently been assigned a new partner who he was breaking into the homicide division.

I walked back to the paved road and waited. Kate arrived momentarily. It was starting to get cold and dark. I figured we had less than an hour of daylight. I didn't fancy the idea of spooking around Emigration Canyon when I couldn't see my hand in front of my face. But at least I had an idea about how we might manage the situation.

"You still mount shotguns in the trunks of these cars?"

"Sure do." Kate popped the trunk lid and I retrieved the shotgun.

"Why don't I take the shotgun and return to where Barnes parked the Explorer. I'd say that it's about thirty yards from there to the gravesite. I'll take a position of concealment and wait. You guys follow Barnes no matter where he goes. If he doesn't come back here, you forget about me and stick with him. We can't afford to lose him. If necessary, I can use the hand-held to call dispatch and have somebody pick me up."

"Okay," said Kate. "I'll call you on the radio the minute he moves. And if he does return here, we'll come in on foot behind him."

"Don't spook him. Give him enough room." I grabbed a light jacket I'd left in the car and started back down the dirt road.

"Hey," said Kate. "I gotta future planned with you. Watch yourself out there. And don't cut loose with that shotgun on us."

"Hell, I might be able to start a whole new trend in body piercing."

She smiled and drove away.

I walked down the road to the dead end. A little ways further, I found a new hiding place near the gravesite. If they returned, I would have a ring-side seat for the evening's entertainment. If there was any gun play, it would happen at close range. I waited for about a half hour before the radio cracked.

"Sam, Plow and Ambrose just picked up Anthony. They're in Rodney's car and they're headed your way."

Chapter Forty-nine

It was nearly dark when I heard the sound of an approaching car. The autumn sun had long since disappeared from this ravine. I was cold, yet my hands were sweating as I gripped the 12-gauge shotgun. I jacked a round into the chamber. Strange, that at a time like this, I'd remember a line from an old John Belushi movie where he said, "It's so quiet up here you can hear a mouse get a hard on." That's how this place felt. I remained hidden as I heard the car slowly roll to a stop. I heard car doors slam and the faint sound of voices.

⟨⟩⟨⟩⟨⟩

"I don't know why the hell we had to come way out here in the middle of bumfuck," said Ambrose.

"Relax, Stevie," said Plow. "We can't afford to be seen together in public, you know that. This place gives us lots of privacy."

"Let's get it over with so we can get the hell out of here," said Barnes.

"Get what over with?" said Ambrose, a note of alarm in his voice.

"I've been thinking, Stevie," said Plow. "And it occurs to me that your usefulness has come to an abrupt end. You're, how can I say it gently, no longer relevant."

"What do you mean? What about us," pled Ambrose.

"There isn't any us, Stevie. In fact, there never was. Only in your mind, I'm afraid. I believe Tony has a little spot over in the trees he'd like to show you." Barnes pointed the twenty-two at Ambrose and motioned for him to start walking down the narrow game trail. Barnes followed, and Plow brought up the rear. By the time they reached the gravesite, I could distinctly hear Ambrose crying and pleading with Rodney to spare his life.

"Stop groveling, Stevie," said Plow. "For once in your life, show a little class for Christ's sake."

I stuck my head up just high enough to see what was going on. I could see Barnes pointing a small handgun at Ambrose. Rodney was standing next to Barnes but slightly behind him. There was no way I would allow this exchange to end with Barnes summarily executing Steven Ambrose.

"Ya' know, boys," said Plow, "there's an old maxim—can't remember who said it, but that's not really important. It says three people can keep a secret as long as two of them are dead."

Suddenly, Plow pulled his own handgun and fired twice, striking Barnes in the upper torso. Barnes staggered back a step or two and then fell. Ambrose cried out like a dog that had just had his tail slammed in a car door.

I jumped up leveling the shotgun, and yelled, "Drop it, Rodney."

He turned to face me.

"Don't even think about it. I'll plaster you all over this canyon."

He thought about it for an instant. Then he dropped the gun.

"Down on the ground, face down," I yelled. "Do it now." He did.

I grabbed the hand-held radio. "Shots fired, suspect down. Roll the paramedics, code three."

Within seconds, Kate and the others arrived. Ambrose and Plow were cuffed, separated, and placed in the back of two police cars. Barnes was moaning and seemed to drift in and out of consciousness. He was seriously wounded. Turner called for a life flight chopper while I went to work on Barnes. I thought he might be in shock. I elevated his feet and did the best I could to stop the bleeding. He was subsequently air-lifted to the University of Utah Hospital and rushed into surgery.

My hands were sticky with his blood. They were shaking badly and I couldn't make them stop. Kate walked over and placed her hands over mine, saying, "Whoa, Sam, calm down. Everything's okay now. It's over."

Of course, it wasn't over. In a matter of minutes, the area was turned into a major crime scene complete with detectives, evidence technicians, photographers, and enough department brass from the sheriff's office and Salt Lake City PD to hold a police convention. The only thing missing were the convention hookers. The press swarmed the place. Everybody wanted pictures of the grave. The story would lead on every evening TV news broadcast.

During the next several hours, Steven Ambrose was forced to confront the sober reality that had it not been for the presence of Kate and me, he would have been killed and buried in an unmarked grave in the middle of nowhere. Barnes and Plow had calculated his demise in about as cold and calculated a fashion as humanly possible.

What Anthony Barnes never expected was the double-cross by Rodney. He'd badly misjudged how far Plow was willing to go to hide the murder of Arnold Ginsberg to protect himself. Had things gone according to Rodney's plan, Barnes would have joined Ambrose in the grave.

Both men were booked at Salt Lake City PD and would undergo the same experience later at the jail. Plow immediately invoked his right to remain silent and demanded a lawyer. That wasn't the case with Ambrose.

Prior to the Ambrose interrogation, Kate and I met with Deputy District Attorney Megan Doherty to plot the interrogation. As the on-call deputy prosecutor, Doherty had to respond day or night to these kinds of incidents. I'd never met her, but Kate had worked with her on prior occasions.

After conferring, we met Ambrose in the interrogation room. Doherty began. "Hello, Mr. Ambrose. My name is

Megan Doherty. I'm a deputy prosecutor with the Salt Lake County Attorney's Office. I believe you know Lt. McConnell and Detective Kincaid. If you don't, you probably should. From what I understand, they saved your life tonight."

Ambrose nodded.

"Let me explain what's going to happen next. I'm going to make you an offer, and I'm only going to make it once. If you turn it down, it won't be offered again. Do you understand?"

Again he nodded.

"My office intends to charge Rodney Plow with one count of conspiracy to commit first degree murder in the death of Arnold Ginsberg. We also plan to charge you and Anthony Barnes, if he lives, with one count of conspiracy to commit first degree murder and a second count each of murder in the first degree. In the state of Utah, each of these offenses is punishable by death or life in prison. We plan to pursue the ultimate penalty against all three of you.

"Are you following me, Mr. Ambrose?"

"Yes."

"I'm confident with the physical evidence we already have, which includes your DNA on the victim's clothing as well as what Mr. Kincaid saw tonight, that we'll get those death sentences.

"Are you interested in making a deal, Mr. Ambrose?"

"Maybe. What exactly are you proposing?"

"In exchange for your full cooperation in the investigation, including your testimony against Plow and Barnes, if he lives, we will allow you to enter a nolo contendere or a guilty plea to one count of second degree murder."

"What does that mean?" he asked.

"Second degree murder carries a prison sentence of five years minimum and up to life. In your case, that means the death penalty is off the table. You will have to serve the five year minimum, probably more. Exactly how much more will depend on how you conduct yourself in prison and what you can tell the state parole board."

"Probably a lot more than five years," I thought to myself.

He sighed. "Will you guarantee this offer in writing?"

"At the appropriate time, yes, we will. I want to emphasize that this offer is contingent upon your complete cooperation with Lt. McConnell and Mr. Kincaid. You must answer all their questions fully and honestly or we'll walk away from the deal. Do you understand?"

"Yeah."

"Okay, Mr. Ambrose. We're gonna leave the room and give you some time to think over the offer. We'll return shortly."

As we stood, Ambrose said, "You don't need to leave. I accept your offer, but I want it in writing."

Doherty shook her head. "I can arrange that while you talk with the detectives. Fair enough?"

He nodded.

"Okay," said Doherty. "I'll step out of the room and go prepare the offer. I'll leave you to talk with the detectives."

Kate walked Ambrose through the Miranda warnings and then had him sign a waiver form. He gave us permission to record the interview. Kate began. "Let's start at the beginning, Steven. Tell us how you became acquainted with Rodney Plow and Arnold Ginsberg."

I met Rodney at the health club maybe a year, year-and-a-half-ago. He and Arnold belonged to the club although Arnold rarely came in. I worked there as a personal trainer. I also operate a massage business."

"When did your relationship with Rodney become physical?"

He thought for a moment. "I don't exactly remember, but it must have been eight, nine months ago."

"Rodney came to your massage studio. Is that correct?"

"Yes."

"Did you ever give a massage to Arnold?"

"No, I didn't. I would have. He just never came in."

"And when did you and Rodney first begin discussing the idea of killing Arnold?"

"It's not exactly the kind of thing you jot down, but I'd say it was between three and four months ago."

"Whose idea was it?"

"His, not mine. I'm not that kind of person."

"And what did you think when Rodney first proposed the idea?"

"I told him I thought it was a crazy idea and that I didn't want any part of it."

"How did he respond to that?"

"At first he just laughed and told me to forget about it—that he was just kidding. But he never let it go. He'd always bring it up, over and over, until I realized one day, that the idea of killing Ginsberg didn't freak me out any longer."

"What was in it for you, Steven?" I asked.

"That's the really funny part in light of what's happened. Rod told me he loved me and that with Arnold out of the way, we'd be able to have a life together. He also said that with the money he stood to inherit, plus the insurance, we'd be set financially. We talked about moving to Hawaii or maybe Costa Rica. Some place warm."

"And you were in love with him?"

"Absolutely, I still am."

"You mentioned insurance money. Tell us what you know about that?"

"At first, I didn't know anything. Then one night after we'd been partying hard and had gotten high, Rod told me there was a $500,000 term life insurance policy on Arnold."

"And I suppose he was the beneficiary of that policy?" I said.

"What Rod said was that he'd taken out the policy himself, and forged Arnold's signature on the application. I guess it was one of the those companies where you fill out an application and mail in your payment without ever having to take a physical."

"Do you know the name of the insurance company?"

"He told me once, but I don't remember."

"Tell us how Barnes became part of the murder plot?"

"I'm not really clear about that, but Rod introduced him to me. I just assumed they knew each other from the Lucky Gent. Rod hung out at the place."

"When did that happen?"

"When did what happen? I don't understand your question."

"Sorry. When did Rod first introduce you to Barnes?"

Ambrose scratched his forehead. "About two months ago, I think."

Kate said, "Why do you think Rodney brought Barnes into the plot?"

"Rod knew I was scared, and I guess he figured that I'd never be able to do it by myself. He told me more than once that Barnes was a tough, ex-military guy who had the stomach for it. He also thought there was no way anybody would ever connect him to Barnes."

"By 'it,' you mean that Barnes was a guy who had the stomach to carry out a murder-for-hire?"

Ambrose winced. "Yes," he said.

"Who actually planned the murder?"

"Rod and Anthony. By the time we sat down to discuss things, they already knew what they were going to do. Rod wanted the killing to look like Arnold had been executed—a lot easier to blame it on that crazy polygamist cult, the Bradshaws."

"What do you mean, blame it on the Bradshaws?"

"After they pulled the armored car robbery, the one that Arnold witnessed, Rod saw a great opportunity. He figured that if we killed Arnold right before the scheduled court hearing for Walter Bradshaw, the cops would blame it on the Bradshaws. The timing of the murder also gave Rod a chance to work out his own alibi."

"Speaking of alibis, we assume your stay at the Snowbird Lodge was done to establish an alibi for yourself. Is that true?"

"Yeah, I thought if Rod was going to all the trouble of making sure he had an alibi, I should probably have one, too. The Snowbird thing was all I could think of."

"What about the choice of murder weapons? Tell us about that."

"Not much to tell, really. Guns are noisy. Anthony wanted to use a knife. I couldn't handle that, so for me, we settled on the tire iron."

"When you say, 'we,' does that include Rodney?"

"Yeah, Rod was in it right down to choosing the murder weapons."

We were about out of questions, at least for this interview, when Vince Turner walked in. He handed Kate a note and whispered something in her ear. She turned off the recording equipment and turned to Ambrose.

"Steven, you might be interested in this. It seems that Rodney is indeed, a Rodney. He's just not a Plow. We just received a hit on Rodney's fingerprints from the FBI's Automated Fingerprint Identification System. It seems Rodney's real last name is Shields, not Plow. His California State prison identification number is 16745911. He's got a fairly lengthy criminal record for check and credit card forgeries, theft, and a couple of fraud counts. One of the fraud cases earned him a sixteen month stint in the California State prison at Chino."

I shook my head. "Well, I'll be damned."

Chapter Fifty

I drove home, slept a few hours, and was up in time to take Sara out to breakfast and then drop her at school. I was buried up to my neck in reports that needed to be written. I'd told Kate that I'd sit down first thing this morning and get them done. I promised I'd drop them at her office around lunchtime.

At eleven o'clock, Burnham phoned. He was exuberant. He'd just received a message from his attorney telling him that the DA's office had called with a plea deal. It seems that District Attorney Richard Hatch had decided to follow my recommendation. Terry had been offered a deferred prosecution for one year on a misdemeanor charge. If he kept out of trouble, completed alcohol counseling, and paid a significant fine, the case would be dismissed after a year. It was the best deal he could have gotten under the circumstances and one that might allow him to salvage his career with the department.

I met Kate for a late lunch at the Market Street Grill in downtown Salt Lake City. I gave her my reports and told her the good news about Terry. "Has Cates been informed about the deal?" asked Kate.

"I don't know. I haven't heard anything. You think he's going to be pissed, don't' you?"

"Don't you?" said Kate.

"Probably."

"Frankly, I'm a little surprised Hatch made the decision he did," she said.

"Me, too. I'm damn glad he did it, though. It restores my confidence in the system when I see a bureaucrat make the right decision once in a while instead of one based solely on political expediency."

Just then my cell phone rang. It was Benjamin Cates' secretary. I had been summoned to a meeting with the boss. "I think he knows now," I said.

Kate looked concerned. "Call me as soon as you're finished. I'll be anxious to find out how it went. And Sam, be sure to wear your Kevlar vest when you go in."

"Very funny." I kissed her on the cheek and headed out the door.

◇◇◇

When I was ushered into the conference room adjoining Cates' office, a somber looking group had been assembled. Besides Cates, the party included the department's administrative law judge, Rachel Rivers-Blakely, and Tommy Connors, the new Director of Institutional Operations at the prison. They looked at me like I was a death row inmate who had been fed his last meal and was ready to take that final walk down *The Green Mile*. Cates pointed to a chair directly across from him. Connors and Rivers-Blakely also sat across the table on either side of Cates.

"Something very disturbing happened this morning, Mr. Kincaid, and I'm wondering whether you'll be able to shed some light on it."

"I'll be glad to try," I said.

"I received a call this morning from Richard Hatch. I was disappointed to learn that he had decided to ignore our request that Terry Burnham be prosecuted to the fullest extent possible, and instead, offered him some Mickey Mouse plea deal that sends exactly the wrong message to every employee in this department."

"Sorry to hear that," I lied.

"I'll bet you are." He gave me his best stare, and I have to admit, it was intimidating.

"Have you had a hand in this, Mr. Kincaid, either directly or indirectly?"

So much for Don't Ask, Don't Tell. It was a good, straight-forward question, and it deserved a good, straight-forward answer.

"As a matter of fact, I did. I paid a visit to Richard Hatch myself."

"And when did you do that?" Cates asked.

"Yesterday morning."

"Before or after your visit with me?"

I wanted to answer, *just before you lied to me about whether you'd referred the case to the DA's office,* but I thought better of it. "Before," I said.

"I thought so. I did my best to keep you out of this for all the obvious reasons. You have a clear conflict of interest when it comes to disciplinary matters involving one of your own sub-ordinates. And what's worse is that this particular subordinate is also a personal friend. Isn't that correct?"

"He's a friend, that's true."

Cates took a deep breath and leaned back in his chair, care-fully regarding me before he spoke next. "Do you really believe, Sam, that your conduct in this matter was aboveboard and appropriate?"

"I don't know about the aboveboard part, but, yes, I think it was appropriate."

"How so?"

"I've been at this job for a long time, Director Cates. I've seen just about every form of employee misconduct that can occur within the prison setting, from illicit sex, to drug dealing, all the way to murder. And I believe that the punishment should fit the crime. And in this case, it simply didn't. I don't know whether you want to hear it, but I'd be happy to elaborate on why."

"I don't," he said, curtly. "I've always considered it inappro-priate for law enforcement personnel to engage in the sordid business of plea bargaining. That's not our job. Distasteful as it is, the practice is best left to the prosecutor. In every department

I've ever run, I've required written policies and procedures that forbid my officers from engaging in plea bargaining discussions with the prosecutor's office."

"It's not a part of our P&P," I said, "and it never has been."

"That's about to change," he said. "What I want you to understand, Mr. Kincaid, is that I believe your conduct in this matter is reprehensible. Further, I consider it disloyal to me personally and a serious breach of ethical conduct on your part. Therefore, I'm suspending you from duty for two weeks without pay beginning next Monday. I'm also ordering that a letter of reprimand be placed in your personnel file. You'll be receiving all of this in writing from Rachel at the conclusion of our meeting today, including your administrative appeals rights. Do you have any questions?"

"I think you've made it about as clear as you can."

He sat back and paused. I could tell he wasn't quite finished with me. "Tell me something, Kincaid, how long have you been with the department?"

"I've been in eighteen years, two months."

"I have an opening in our training division," he said. "While you're serving your suspension, I'm going to be giving serious consideration to your future in the department. What I want you to understand is that when you return to work, it might be in a different assignment. Will you be okay with that?"

Was this a trick question? "I guess I'll have to be."

"Yes, I guess you will. That'll be all, Mr. Kincaid. Have a nice day."

⟨⟩⟨⟩⟨⟩

I made two stops before going home for the day. The first was to the district attorney's office and the other was to see Kate. I stopped at the DA's office first. I thanked Richard Hatch for expending the political capital that it would undoubtedly cost him with Benjamin Cates regarding the Burnham affair.

Next, I headed to the district court clerk's office and found out which court had been assigned the case against Robin Joiner.

That turned out to be Judge Judith Brown, or Judge Judy, as we affectionately called her. I figured since I'd already stuck my nose into the Burnham mess, and gotten roundly spanked for the favor, I might as well meddle in one more plea negotiation before Cates' new policy went into effect.

Joiner had just been charged with being an accessory-before-the-fact in the robbery and murder case against the Bradshaw clan. Her role, as a look-out, required some accountability. I understood that. But she was also a young woman who'd experienced a troubled past and who had a promising future as a clinical social worker until she made a very bad decision. I made my pitch to Flo Lattrell, the deputy prosecutor assigned to the case. She was noncommittal but promised she would consider everything I said. That was the best I could do under the circumstances. I would ask Kate to make a similar pitch to Lattrell on Joiner's behalf.

I stopped at Kate's office and spent the next hour giving her a blow-by-blow description of my meeting with Cates. She listened patiently before delivering a verbal tirade against him that would have made a hooker blush, and then heaping copious amounts of empathetic understanding on me. Talking it through was a cathartic experience and I felt better afterward for doing it.

I drove home wondering how to break the news to my staff the next day although maybe I wouldn't have to. These things often had a way of filtering through the department well before any official announcement was made. I wasn't sure if my separation from the SIB was going to be permanent, but it felt like it might be.

There's an upside in life to everything that happens to us. In my case, I was about to have a two-week vacation, albeit an unpaid one, that would allow me to focus my energy on family for a change instead of the job. That was a good thing.

Chapter Fifty-one

Two weeks later

Thanksgiving had come and gone and the Christmas season was in full swing. My two-week suspension was all but over, and I was almost regretting it. It took a few days for me to decompress, but with that accomplished, getting off the treadmill had actually begun to feel good. I had a life again, and I liked it. For two weeks, I had been able to take my daughter to and from school everyday, attend her parent-teacher conference, and watch her rehearse and then perform in the elementary school Thanksgiving play. Sara's soccer season ended dismally on a cold Saturday afternoon in a regional tournament played in a mixed rain-and-snow storm. Sara's team lost four to one.

Kate's parents, Keith and Susan McConnell, had come to town and spent the Thanksgiving week at her place in the Avenues. I had sensed some unease at first, but who could blame them? Kate was their only child, and they had to be wondering who this new guy was with the ready-made family. Kate and I took them out to dinner twice during the week, and Aunt June and Uncle Baxter proved consummate hosts by inviting everybody to the house for a home cooked dinner the night before they left. If first impressions counted for much, I thought we were off to a good start. Kate and I seemed committed to each other, but we had decided to take things slow and easy.

Between Kate and Marcy Everest from the SIB, I was kept up to speed on events related to the recent cases. Nobody had heard anything about the Dixons or Joey Bradshaw. They had simply vanished. Teams of FBI agents combed the Arizona strip, mining the local populace for any information that might provide a lead into their whereabouts. Hilldale, Utah, and Colorado City, Arizona, are tightly knit communities steeped deeply in the culture of polygamy, and so far, nobody was saying anything.

I don't know whether Kate's and my recommendation to the prosecutor helped, but Robin Joiner was allowed to plead guilty to one misdemeanor count with no jail time other than the five days she served immediately after her surrender. She was fined, ordered to perform community service, and placed on probation for a year. I felt good about that and so did Kate. I believed that Robin would take her graduate degree in social work, turn her life around, and become a productive member of society.

Robby Allred had remained loyal and tight-lipped. He had refused to talk and the smart money said he never would. He'd been denied bail because of the flight risk he posed and the heinous nature of the crimes he'd been charged with. From all appearances, it looked like he was headed to trial on state murder and aggravated robbery charges in the armored car heist. Rumor had it that the U.S. Attorneys office was considering filing several additional counts in federal district court. If he managed to avoid a death sentence, it seemed unlikely that he would ever enjoy life outside a prison cell.

As for Terry Burnham, to borrow a well worn cliché, the jury was still out. He remained on paid leave pending the resolution of departmental charges that had been brought against him at the behest of corrections boss, Benjamin Cates. As far as I could tell, Cates still intended to make Burnham a poster boy for what happens to department employees who break the rules. Burnham was showing no sign of a willingness to surrender his job without a fight. As a member of the corrections officer's union, he would be represented by union counsel at his forthcoming disciplinary hearing. All things shake out in time. This would too.

◇◇◇

It was December 12th and I was standing in the Delta terminal at Salt Lake International Airport preparing to board a flight to Atlanta. It was a cold, blustery day and there was a light snow-fall outside. The mountains had been getting it good, much to the delight of the ski resort operators. A good, early snow pack guaranteed a deluge of out-of-state tourists to fill the hotels, res-taurants, and ski slopes during the busy Christmas holidays.

I had heard nothing from Benjamin Cates during my two-week suspension. I didn't know whether I would be returning to the SIB or reassigned to another department. I think I shocked a few people by putting in for two weeks of vacation to run back-to-back with my suspension. I wasn't scheduled to return until after Christmas.

But on this day, my job status wasn't my highest priority. I was on my way to Atlanta to attend a pretrial conference in our child custody case. So far, my ex, Nicole, hadn't blinked, and neither had I. I don't know how it's going to turn out, but they say all things in life happen for a good reason, and for today, that'll have to be good enough.

To receive a free catalog of Poisoned Pen Press titles, please contact us in one of the following ways:

Phone: 1-800-421-3976
Facsimile: 1-480-949-1707
Email: info@poisonedpenpress.com
Website: www.poisonedpenpress.com

Poisoned Pen Press
6962 E. First Ave. Ste. 103
Scottsdale, AZ 85251